THE
RUNNING
WOLF

THE
RUNNING
WOLF

RESSLER

To Cheryl,

THE
RUNNING
WOLF

HELEN STEADMAN

Very best wishes,
Helen S

The Running Wolf

Copyright © 2020 by Helen Steadman

Printed by Impress Books, November 2020

Cover design by Heike Schüssler

ISBN 13: 9781911293538

www.impress-books.co.uk

Praise for *Widdershins*

'This meticulously researched account of a bigoted man's inhumanity to women in the seventeenth century will make the modern reader grateful to have been born in an enlightened age.' Mari Griffith, *The Witch of Eye*

'*Widdershins* is a dark and wonderful novel, rich in historical details, herbal lore, traditions and superstitions. Steadman's clear-eyed storytelling and colourful period voice give life to a vibrant cast of characters drawn against the backdrop of tragic historical events. A compelling and memorable tale!' Louisa Morgan, *A Secret History of Witches*

'Helen Steadman knows her subject inside out and gives great insight into a period of history that we should feel ashamed of. Two very different narrators bring us careering towards the horrifying denouement that you almost want to shield your eyes from.' Fin C. Gray, *Duplicity*

'Infused as it is with aromas of rosemary, fennel and lavender, even the healers' herbs do not mask the reek of the injustice that sits at the heart of *Widdershins*. Powerful and shocking.' Wyl Menmuir, *The Many*

'Steadman's carefully interwoven narrative conjures a world of herbal lore, folk practice and belief and convincingly portrays the psychological and ideological forces that form a perpetrator, and the social structures that sustain him.' Helen Lynch, *Tea for the Rent Boy*

'Her writing reminds me of Hannah Kent's bestselling novel, *Burial Rites*. Helen's writing has a similar persuasive and empathetic force, weaving together historical fact with modern concerns about the treatment of women.' Helen Marshall, *The Migration*

Praise for *Sunwise*

'In *Sunwise*, Helen Steadman's fast-moving and spellbinding sequel to her astonishing debut novel *Widdershins*, the attention to detail and historical accuracy displayed are informative and immaculate, the plot engaging, thrilling and endearing... I was immediately immersed in the world of rural 17th Century northeast England. I can only put this down to the beauty of Steadman's writing and the precision of her plotting; I won't betray any of the plot twists and developments to you here, but *Sunwise* is by turns heartbreaking, hilarious, thrilling, spilling, and endearing. Whatever you do, dear reader, don't miss this one.' Ted Curtis, *The Darkening Light*

'This follows on closely from *Widdershins* – not the initial plan of the writer, but the characters came and grabbed her, and you could sense it happening. Sometimes charming, sometimes disturbing, and very firmly set in its time and place – don't expect an easy ride, though!' Lexie Conyngham, *Murray of Letho, Hippolyta Napier, and Orkneyinga Murders*

In this riveting sequel to *Widdershins*, the story is narrated in two voices belonging to Jane and John, the alleged witch and her witch hunter, both radically opposite in tone and intention, but that end up entwining in a daunting final denouement. Steadman's skilful and resplendent prose leads the reader easily into villages, manses and cottages, festivities and day-to-day lives, with amazing detail and descriptions of a past age that jump off the page of the novel. The historical research is rich; scenes and spaces, deliciously visual, and the language employed by the protagonists and throughout the narrative is authentic and consistent, transporting us back in time just by virtue of its ancient tonality. A great read, not to be missed. Susana Aikin, *We Shall See the Sky Sparkling and The Weight of the Heart*

For Oliver and Leon

To the little gentleman in black velvet.

Eigtheenth-century Jacobite toast

Acknowledgements

Special thanks to: Tom Mole – descendant of Hermann Mohll – a charming man who was pleased to tell me about his family, and I hope I've done justice to his ancestor; to Ann Bell, descendant of Adam Oligh, a lovely woman who told me some fascinating stories about her family, and to her sister-in-law, Audrey Ternent; to Malcolm Hill, descendant of Adam Oligh, who was kind enough to show me a blade from Solingen and also a piece of grindstone and clinker from Shotley Bridge; to Marie McNally for inviting me into her beautiful home, for her hospitality and for sharing with me lots of information and artefacts, one of which helped inspire the 'Start with a Nail' chapter; Michael Murray for sharing a photo of his grandmother outside her swordmaker cottage in Wood Street; John Stafford for sending me photos of his swords; David Wright for his advice and encouragement; and Keith Fisher for making me aware that Solingen didn't join Prussia until later.

Thanks also go to the following guardians of treasure: in England, to staff at Tyne and Wear Archives, Durham County Record Office, Northumberland Archives and the National Archives; in Scotland, to staff at the Marischal Museum in Aberdeen; in Germany, to staff at Deutsches Klingenmuseum, Balkhauser Kotten, Schleiferei Wipperkotten and the Historisches Archiv der Stadt Köln. In particular, I'm grateful to: Hannah Clarke, Curatorial Assistant from Museums and Special Collections in the Marischal College at the University of Aberdeen for letting me hold the Jacobite sword; Jörg Schulz-Deike from the Stadt Köln Historisches Archiv for helping me to view the Solingen indictment and for politely tolerating my reliance on Google Translate; Iben Muriel from the Worshipful Company of Cutlers for providing pictures and information about Cutlers' Hall in Cloak Lane, London, where the candle auction took place, and for the kind invitation to visit the current Cutlers' Hall in Warwick Lane; to Noel Adamson from Land of Oak and Iron for the informative and fascinating tour of Derwentcote Furnace and the workers' cottages; Jeff Singleton and Andrew Thompson from Shotley Bridge Village Trust for information about Shotley Bridge and its history, as well as a tour of historic buildings (and also to Jeff for putting me in touch with Tom Mole); and Elizabeth Finch of the Northumbrian Jacobite Society for taking the time to advise me about William Blackett and for providing book recommendations and biographies of key rebels in the 1715 Jacobite uprising.

I will be forever grateful to the University of Aberdeen for granting me an Elphinstone PhD Scholarship, which enabled me to carry out my research at such an august institution and also for providing the grant that enabled me to carry out swordmaking training with Rod Hughes at Butser Ancient Farm in June and July 2018. Without this grant, and without Rod's skill and patience, I wouldn't have been able to test my method-writing approach and I wouldn't have understood the swordmaking process in such detail.

I'm indebted to the following smiths and profoundly grateful to all of them for the contributions they made to my knowledge about blademaking, and for their help in making various metal artefacts, most notably a sword. To Mark Constable (bucketforge. co.uk), who taught me some blacksmithing when I first began my research and taught me about the properties of iron and fire. He advised me how to make a bucket forge so I could practise at home and helped me to make a rat-tailed poker and a firesteel (I take full responsibility for the badly burned pendant that I made all by myself). He also recommended I read *De Re Metallica* by Georgius Agricola (sound advice). To Rod Hughes of Golden Eye Forge: historian, bladesmith, designer, sculptor, film and

TV adviser and presenter (History Channel, BBC, Discovery Channel), who helped me to make a sword. Rod is possibly the most Zen person I've ever met – eternally serene and spotless at the end of each day. If you go to Rod's website, rodhughes.org, you will see me with my (almost) finished sword. Rod has ambitions to play a role in a major production that uses both his acting and swordmaking skills, so if anyone wishes to turn this novel into a film, TV series or play, Rod would make a marvellous Hermann Mohll. Next, to Wes Cole, blacksmith and armourer from Fire Drake Forge (firedrake.co.uk, but at the time of writing, Wes's website was still on the anvil). Wes helped me with the forging and hammering, and he kept up a running commentary about why I was doing what I was doing, as well as filling my ears with tales of dwarves and gods. I was amazed by his phenomenal energy and also for being magnetic to carbon. To Francis Hobday, an excellent woodsman and volunteer at Butser Ancient Farm, for showing me how to use basic implements such as vices, for encouraging me to touch wood until I could learn to tell the difference between types and for telling me about some elderly men who could feel whether metal is 'out' by a minute fraction, purely by touch. I'm also grateful to everyone I trained alongside: in particular to Graham Dawson for helping me, especially with filing down the bronze handle, for letting me borrow some of his tool collection and for warning me of the perils of vibration white finger. Also to Ben Halfon, who, as well as having envy-inducing peacock-blue hair and despite his tender years, also had an endless supply of knowledge about swords and was happy to share it with me. Thank you to all other swordmaking trainees for being so friendly and helpful: Will Scanlan, Nir Halfon, Brendan O'Doherty, James Cartwright, Jeremy Spencer, Alistair Aston and Nick Leech. I would not have managed to make my sword without all of these men's help. When I made my sword, I was more tired than on any other day of my life and I was struck by everyone's energy, tenacity, patience and good humour – there was no problem that could not be solved. I hope these qualities have been infused into my version of Hermann Mohll. Now that I've made a sword, I'm honoured to be a member of the Dwarves of Zennor and I'm grateful to my fellow dwarves. Metalwork is, by turns, hugely exhausting and fascinating and I take my hat off to anyone who smiths, whether for money or love (or both). It's also a complex business. I had a great deal of help and advice from some very experienced smiths but any errors are purely my own and I apologise heartily for them in advance.

I'm also grateful to the people who've helped me to be a better writer and researcher. First and foremost, my PhD supervisor, Dr Helen Lynch, author and Reader at the University of Aberdeen, who challenged me at every turn to try new ideas and perspectives. She also went above and beyond the call of duty, providing pastoral care, setting up book launches for me, driving me about, attending my first launch and smoothing my feathers beforehand (ably assisted by soothing emotional support dogs, Jasmine and Loki). Also to Dr Wayne Price, Dr Elizabeth Elliot and Dr George Green. To my untiring critique partner, Marita Karin Over, novelist and poet, who's travelled alongside me and Messrs Mohll and Tipstaff. Her eye for detail, her demands for description and her ability to spot when author voice overtook character voice have all helped to make this a better book. Thanks also go to critique partners who provided feedback on a couple of early draft chapters: again Marita Karin Over but also Jodie Baptie, Zöe Feeney, Fin C. Gray, Jane Masumy, Eleanor Moore, Chris Price, Sue Smith and Kate Woodward. I'm grateful to all at Impress Books for their continued support of my writing and in particular to Julian Webb and his excellent editing skills. Once again, he's saved me from my seemingly incurable habit of repeating myself. He has the enviable skill of being challenging while remaining kind. Thank you also to Katherine Collyer for her careful proofreading and to Madison Castle for her help releasing this book into the wild. I am especially pleased with the beautiful cover, which was designed by Heike Schüssler from Judge By My Covers.

Thanks must go to everyone who's written about the Shotley Bridge swordmakers. I've focused on only one element of the swordmakers' history, but truth always being stranger than fiction, there are still many curious tales in some of the non-fiction books about them. There is a full list of references at helensteadman.com but these should get you off to a good start: Richard H. Bezdek, *Swords and Swordmakers of England and Scotland* and also *German Swords and Sword Makers: Edged Weapon Makers from the 14th to the 20th Centuries*; Douglas Vernon, *Thread of Iron*; John Ryan, *History of Shotley Spa and Vicinity of Shotley Bridge*, John. G. Bygate, *The Hollow Blade: The German Swordmakers of Shotley Bridge*, David Richardson, *The Swordmakers of Shotley Bridge: Their Strange Story*. (Please note that many are out of print and either hard to find or expensive, so you may need to access them through libraries.)

Huge thanks go to the small army of brilliant book bloggers for being so supportive of my writing and spending so much time reading, reviewing and talking about my work with no thought of reward. Thanks to my friends, who've listened to my ravings about people who lived over three-hundred years ago with kindness and indulgence. Extra special thanks to my family, who've become used to seeing the top of my head and who've tolerated a house filled with random pieces of metal, clinker, blacksmithing tools, sandpaper, sword parts and even more books than usual. Finally, to everyone who has already read my books or who will ever read my books: thank you.

Contents

SILVER THREADS

Solingen, 1687

*T*he secret hovered over the town at night. Five-score dreaming sleepers emitted sighs that clustered, crow-like, above their heads. No storks perched on chimneys. Only sighs and dark thoughts seethed above the rooftops, and their gathering force caused those not leaving to wake in the night, as if made uncomfortable by the stretching of the silver threads that joined all kinsmen. When the swordmakers left, they would go lightly but they would sever the ties that bound them. Deep inside, the townsfolk felt the force of families pulling away. Children tossed and turned, crying out single words heard at the end of whispered conversations: king, boat, bridge. These words flocked over the houses alongside the sighs and dark thoughts, writing messages to be read by anyone with the eyes to look.

And what were these dark thoughts? Out of the night came the dream thieves, their beady eyes roving over sleeping forms, judging how much effort was needed to pierce baby flesh and rip out a still-beating heart, how much guile to lift a sleeping eyelid and pluck out a tear-ridden eye, how much force to part soft lips and pull out milk teeth. The dream thieves tiptoed back into the night, pockets rattling with their harvest. To the observer, the plundered bodies were just sleeping. There was nothing to see here. Easier by far to shut the book of dreams and look the world in the eye.

So, the dream thieves had set the swordmakers running towards the promise of gold. For gold is what lit their fevered dreams – gold and far-off shores. A hundred dreamers would soon slip downstream in the night. One heart plucked from a town might go unnoticed but a hundred hearts would leave bloody wounds behind them, and once gone, there could be no coming back. The strongest of locks and bolts would not keep the dream thieves out. They would slide underneath doors, as slender as shadows. They would flow down chimneys like air. They would slip through knots in the wood as if made of moonlight. There could be no coming home.

To Hermann Mohll, the decision to leave Solingen was as huge as jumping off a mountain. No fall could cause more pain than creating a chasm in the family. To cross the water to England and never see one another again. There was no way to make it kind, this leaving. But staying wasn't kind either. People had started looking over their shoulders and whispers took on greater meaning than in times past. Some had vanished. There were mutterings of purges. There were dark tales with sharp teeth. Tales of people flung in deep pits. Tales of people imprisoned. Tales of people silenced. All for the use of one word over another. No one knew for certain how many had boarded ships and left, or why. A terrible darkness must stalk the borders of their dreams to make men tied so fast to this town move away. Was there a dark hand at work? Or was fear of a dark hand enough to cause men to run? And what were they running from?

Fear is what they were running from. Fear of having no work. Fear of losing the roof from over their heads. Fear of losing the gold from their pockets. Fear of losing the bread from their tables. Anyone with half an eye could see there were too many swordmakers in Solingen. They would sail to England and the islanders would wonder why the Germans had left their own land. Well, let them wonder.

⌒

Early in the evening, night had begun to cover the earth, and in the sky, the slender crescent moon tipped a horn to bright Venus. Every day, Hermann had walked this riverbank with the Wupper singing in his ears. The river rushed towards him, hurrying towards the Rhine, the great river that would take them to the German Sea, the expanse of grey water that would separate his family from their birthplace. For this, they'd leave a warm hearth in a cosy town. A town that had become less cosy lately. Still, it was a necessary journey and if they were to make it to their new home, they must let the sea take them there on its back. Hermann was ready.

When he came to the old elm tree outside home, he stopped and stood, hands on hips, leaning backwards and staring at the trunk.

Liesl appeared at the door, clutching her one-eared pup, and called out, 'Father! Look! My tooth has finally come out. Griselda nearly ate it.'

She walked towards him, holding up the tiny pearl, which the grey pup lunged at.

'Ah, well, you must leave it out for the mouse one last time,' Hermann said. 'Give that fat pup a bone to work her teeth on and stop petting her all the time. She's meant to be a forge hound.' He smoothed his beard and moustaches and turned his attention back to the tree.

'Mother says supper will be ready in half an hour.' She followed his gaze upwards. 'Have you lost something?'

'Lost? Only my youth. Look.' He pointed. 'See that heart and those initials. That's me, HM and your mother, KG. I carved it when we were courting. The tree was a bit smaller in those days.'

'It's too dark to see anything.' Liesl peered up into the branches. 'It's too high up. A tree can grow a lot in a few years.'

'And so may a girl.' Hermann patted his daughter's flaxen hair. 'You must stop growing soon or you'll overtake your mother and even me.'

'I might stop.' She grinned. 'And I might not. Don't forget to come in for supper soon. Grandmother Mohll says she's in danger of fading away.'

'The sun will fade before your grandmother,' he said. 'Tell your mother I'll be in soon. Go on.'

He listened to the waterwheel turning for a while and slid down to unclog some fallen blossom before going into the forge to sort out his tools. The smaller pieces would go with them but the grinding wheels and the anvils would stay behind. His mother might sell them, unless the guild beat her to it.

The sorting of possessions was a death of sorts – the death of their former life and of all they'd known. Each family could take a few choice belongings with them. Of course, people wanted to take more than permitted and there'd been endless trading but there was no need for more than one of each item, so hard choices were made between this copper pan and that one, this grandmother's quilt and that one. And so it went on. The choosing, the packing, the gathering in of the corners of the cloth that held their lives. These meagre belongings their sole talisman against the great unknown.

He would take his favourite hammers, and those that had belonged to his father, but to take even half of what he wanted would sink a ship. If only there were enough work for every family, they might be spared this heartache. Once over, the forges ran at full capacity and when there was too much work it was passed from one family to another. But change came, bringing with it gaps between orders and with the gaps, uncertainty. Orders were gobbled up, making tiring days to complete work, ready to snatch the next order. Tempers frayed and the families of even kind men found their ears burning from harsh words and those with less kind men suffered more than words. And so, like barber-surgeons, blademakers must follow war, this time to England. Twenty families would vanish into the night and sail to that small island.

'Resting on the long bench again, Mohll?'

Hermann turned to the doorway to see his friend, Adam Oligh, a man as fair as Hermann was dark.

'Stealthy as ever, big Oligh. You've caught me pondering what to take and what to leave behind.'

Oligh laughed. 'Careful, if you're left behind, who'll show the useless English cutlers how it's done?' He hefted a hammer. 'Are you taking this?'

'Not that one,' Hermann said. 'Ach, they've some decent-enough jewellers and hiltmakers, I suppose, and importers.'

'Not like you to be so kind to inferior workmen.' Oligh replaced the hammer. 'Imagine the shame of having to import your blades.'

'The tariffs likely pain them more than their incompetence,' Hermann said. 'English protectionism at work, short-sighted as ever, with one hand of government working against the other to spare their tradesmen at the cost of their soldiers.' The English were a funny breed.

His friend ran a thumb over a chisel and began sharpening it. 'Thousands of blades they've had from us,' said Oligh.

'So?' said Hermann. 'It lines our German pockets and if Englishmen want our sharp swords to pierce their neighbours' hides all the faster, so be it. When you've finished sharpening the chisel, pass me that peen hammer.'

Oligh passed the hammer. 'Your father's?'

Hermann nodded and weighed it in his hand, remembering the hand that had made it. Both sides of Hermann's family had worked with metal. They'd bought metal, forged metal and sold metal. Commerce was the rusty silt in their blood that attracted them to all types of metal: steel for his father and gold for his mother. He smiled to himself. Father had always argued that his swords helped people defend themselves, their families and their lands, but Mother always had the last word, 'Blades are no defence against the dark wolf who devours the sweet breath of our children. The wolf who pulls at their bedclothes and leads them down wending forest paths into the heart of hell.' Hermann grimaced at his mother's description of poverty and put away the memory as he tucked the hammer into a leather roll and secured it tightly.

English purses were said to be as deep as their thirst for war and he wondered how their purses had become so richly lined when they were such a small nation. Still, an Englishman's gold was as good as a German's, even if his blades weren't, and it was a short step from importing blades to importing bladesmiths. There was little holding the swordmakers here beyond love of the land and their families. By leaving, they'd break their residency vows but they might manage to keep their guild oaths in England. Twenty families were going out. Would that be enough to build a new Solingen? They should bear enough children to keep the forges running and keep their secrets but eyes would wander and hearts with them. Fine intentions wouldn't keep their secrets when the human heart was so fallible.

Oligh tapped a file on the back of Hermann's hand. 'Wake up, Mohll. I asked if Katrin feels any better about going.'

'No. Not really.' His wife was still upset about being taken away from her mother and sisters.

'When are you going to tell your mother? Old Anna won't like it and you can't leave it any longer.'

Hermann tested a knife blade with his thumb. 'Tonight,' he said. 'I'll do it tonight.' He ran the blade down his forearm where it shaved away a swathe of dark-brown hair. 'If I can find the right words.'

'I doubt such words exist where Anna Mohll is concerned,' said Oligh. 'May God go with you.'

⌒

Hermann's mother sat by the window with her cherrywood chest open before her, sorting her latest lot of broken gold rings, bracelets and chains into its numerous compartments. She glanced out on her stunted juniper tree.

'It's time you told me what's going on, Son.' She looked up at him. 'Katrin's eyes are red all day and Liesl is as pale as the moon.'

He sat next to her and took her hand. 'The English king has bought our blood and we're packing up and sailing to his island. Will you come with us, Mother?'

'It's not right for man to be on water. We're not fish.' She shook his hand away and swept a dozen rings into her hand before placing them in a tiny drawer. 'Our maker put us on earth to breathe air. Next, you'll want to fly like a bird.'

'If you won't put to sea,' he said, 'we'll have to leave you here.'

She smoothed her skirts across her knees: thin hands and thin knees always, but thinner now. Brown hair gone to silver. Bones visible, and veins. Her skin was fading – her last boundary in life before merging with the earth.

'So leave me here. I see you looking, Son, I know it as well as you do: my hair is silver and my skin is thinner than Bible paper. Not long left to me.' She waved a hand above her head, a dismissal. 'You go. I can always make broth from old bones and the church will bury me when my time comes.'

He was used to this stoic act, and although she was ageing, her eyes were still bright amber and her mind was sharp enough.

Leaving wasn't an easy choice but it was a good chance and he couldn't change his mind because he had to do right by his wife and daughter.

'I believe the church *would* bury you, Mother but it won't come to that.'

'Oh, it will come to that, and soon, but don't let me spoil your plans,' she said. 'Most of my life is behind me now. My bones are old but they'll serve me well enough for the years left to me, which can't be many. Besides, I have steel in my spine and I must stay to tend my juniper–'

'Mother! Not that infernal tree again. Don't go dipping your ladle into the past and serving it up within earshot of Liesl.'

'You coddle that girl, Hermann. If you're going to take her away, she needs to hear my tales and carry them with her so they're never forgotten.'

Was he coddling his daughter? His mother was barely older than Liesl when the shadow wolf had visited her. If his own mother was old enough to live through the rage that came to her town that night, was his daughter old enough to listen to the tale of it? It was a tale that needed telling again and again until the poison left his mother but he didn't want it leaching into Liesl. He caught himself drumming his fingers on the table.

'Look at you,' she said. 'Never able to sit still from being a boy. Yours is an energy best tamed in the forge.'

'We'll miss you if you won't come to England with us, Mother, but we'll write.'

'Don't bother,' she snapped. 'Paper can't hold love, the heat of tears or the crack of laughter.'

The worst half of him was relieved. He loved his mother, of course he did, but her eyes were never still and always sweeping her grandchild for smuts, poor tailoring or pallor so she might castigate his wife through pointed glances and remarks. Still, there was nothing to stop his mother's thoughts taking wing over the sea and nestling in his heart, or worse, in his family's hearts, bringing more coldness and spite.

'We'll send you cakes, Mother. Love can be baked into a cake that might survive the weeks at sea.'

'But not the nibbles from needy teeth and no cake tastes as good as when eaten under the eye of the one who baked it,' she said. 'No letters. No cakes. But I'll carry you all here.' She thumped her heart.

Knowing his wily old mother, her heart was probably also made of steel. What was this? A ruse to keep them here?

'Mother, I ...'

'Don't "Mother" me, Hermann,' she said. 'I'll survive but this decision has sharp edges. It will cleave families – some together and some apart. Life can change in the blink of an eye and shortages of food or work create hate. Where hate bides, war follows, which might be needed for trade, but while you're a grand smith, you're no soldier.' She paused for breath. 'Don't look at me like that because you know I'm right.'

His mother was right. He wouldn't fare well in a fight for his life. Of necessity, he could wield a sword and knew its balance, its edge. It must be fit to kill but he wasn't a killer. He was no soldier and couldn't march off to war, sword at his side, ready to plunge it into his countrymen. He lacked the hate necessary because that part of him was hammered out into the metal to speed the soldier on his way. He wasn't a warrior. But now, poverty was at the gate, which meant hate was coming again, and with it, the spectre of the shadow wolf. They should take the chance, step into the waterways and bleed out of Germany, into the sea and onwards to a safe harbour.

After a while, he agreed. 'You're right, Mother,' he said. 'Leaving will be a deep cut to the heart. It'll be hard for Katrin's mother, and for you, but my main worry is breaking our residency vows and our guild oaths–'

'Pah! Vows and oaths.' His mother waved her hand in front of her face. 'Don't feel bad about taking secrets to England,' she said. 'They're not ours, anyway. Not by rights. Our knights stole the blades from the Holy Land, but that wasn't enough, so they went back and stole the men.' Her eyes narrowed. 'Milked their secrets from them.'

This was an uncomfortable truth. Everything he knew about sharp edges and pliability had been plundered. In much the same way as the running wolf blademark had been plundered from Passau. Now he'd continue the fine tradition and steal the mark away to England.

'Families have been leaving this town for centuries,' she said. 'The Mohlls weren't the first and they won't be the last.' His mother poured a handful of knotted chains into a drawer and closed it before locking her chest of gold. 'Now, tell me which side you've chosen.'

'Side?' He glanced at her. 'I hope not to choose a side.'

'Spoken like a true arms merchant.' She laughed. 'England is at war with itself. It's a land divided and the people there love their neighbours only to hate them.'

He blinked at this but didn't point out that his mother had lived most of her life in a country determined to tear itself apart from the inside. 'It's the same the world over,' he said, nodding at the cherrywood chest. 'Who can blame us for following the gold?'

'I suppose you must,' she said. 'Now, when you choose a side, choose the one that looks least like losing and keep your choice to yourself. Don't even think about it. Thoughts can be plucked from the air and have your neck stretched. Don't pull such faces – it makes you look like your father.'

He considered this awhile. There were Solingen men already in the south of England – some had followed the old king and there were rumours they'd been slung in gaol for their trouble.

The thought made him shiver but they'd lived to tell the tale. He was roused from these thoughts by his mother poking him in the side.

'Hermann, pay attention. What's the temper of the land set aside for you?'

'It lies next to the bend of a fast river in a deep valley not far from Scotland–'

'Scotland?' She snorted. 'A barbarous nation, their men are nothing but mercenaries, take it from me. A deep valley may be useful for secrecy but not for safety. Always keep marshland to your back. Horses don't like it so they seek out firmer terrain. Sucking bogs have saved many a town.' She nodded to herself. 'Many, but not all. You must sleep with one eye open.'

'Mother, you worry too much.' Hermann smiled but it was a smile worn to mask other feelings. 'We're going to a place of safety.'

'Near to Scotland? Don't be so innocent, Son. You come from the marches. Living on a border means living like a pendulum. First one ruler and then the next. First one religion and then the next. Be ready to swing whichever way you need to. You have steel running through you but you must bend to survive. Take it from one who knows.' She smoothed her apron over her knees. 'Now, how will you break it to the girl that her pup must stay here with me?'

Roasting Jack

Morpeth Gaol, 1703

The kitchen porter came all the way to Morpeth from Wall-ington Hall in the middle of the night, supposedly to lumber me with a lame turnspit dog. Reckoned it was an arithmetic dog – puts down some legs and carries others – and laughed himself giddy. The daft creature had leapt from the kitchen wheel when his partner wasn't quick enough to spell him off and he's no good to the big hall now. Daft of the dog to risk his neck for freedom but dogs have no fear of the wrath of God. No such luck for the likes of me.

Long-bodied he is, black-backed and grey-bellied, curtailed and with stumpy legs. Ugly, miserable and lousy. He'll fit in here well enough. Roasting Jack, I've called him, and he was easy enough to fix. A matter of binding his hind leg to a lat with a strip of linen. He was a good lad and scarcely whimpered. Won't make much of a ratter with that limp but he'll do till the county can get another man in and he'll make me a canny footwarmer for the dark nights. Won't be well fed like at the hall but he was happy enough to share my potted char.

Turns out the porter wasn't only here on an errand of mercy. No surprises there. Who'd come all that way at that hour just to fob me off with a lame dog? He could barely wait to tip me the wink, 'Glad tidings, Robert,' he said. 'There'll be no rest for the wicked this side of Candlemas so best prepare yourself for a busy Yuletide.' *Robert*, indeed. Such a smirk on him. 'That's Mr Tipstaff to you,' I told the fat wastrel. Likely broke the little dog's leg himself to give him an excuse to gallop over here with his juicy titbits. Thought he was rubbing my nose in it and hoped to ruin my Christmas. Little does he know that hardly a penny piece goes in a keeper's pocket till the prisoner puts it there so the laugh's on him. I'm not like that lazy lump, drawing his monthly crown for lugging a few turnips about.

A lean month for gaolers, December, because no man enjoys prison at this time of year. They'll move heaven and earth to get surety and go home. So the porter's news means plenty of bread and ale for me this Christmas and it's good news for the turnkey as well. Bit extra coin never goes amiss with all those mouths to feed. Not a problem I have anymore.

Porter reckoned the whole coast is up in arms – east and west – with dozens of paid men out hunting some foreign fellow. Sailed into Jarrow Keys from Rotterdam along with a boatload of Scots and Irish soldiers. The main roads are under guard, fast horses are galloping from county to county, the big houses are under watch and innkeepers are under orders to check every stranger beneath their roofs.

We've not had so much excitement since last month when Farmer Thompson found his prize heifer in the branches of a cherry tree. That's the Great Tempest for you. Never known weather like it. Ships blown off course and hundreds of sailors killed. The south's borne the brunt of it by all accounts.

All those good men killed and yet this naughty foreigner survives and has us running about after him in the middle of winter. This chasing around comes at the command of the queen's right-hand man, the Earl of Nottingham: Dismal Daniel, the most funereal of all the black Finches. Dismal might well have the great and good dancing after his pipe but all this gadding about has to be hurting him deep in the pocket. Or hurting Queen Anne, more like. The foreigner must be very interesting to set so many important hares running in the heart of winter. What's he done to cause such a hue and cry?

Pity help this foreign chap when they catch him, especially if he's from warmer climes. Winter in gaol soon saps a man's strength and spirit. Morpeth's colder than a witch's tit even in the summer months. Beyond me why they do it, these men, risking their necks for heaven knows what reward. They never get away with it. I'll get some clean straw in ready for him and he can take his chances in with Walter the coiner. Old Walt will be glad of some company in his final days. Still, the cold might save the county a length of rope in the long run.

the great and good cheering after his pipe but all this padding about has to be hurting him deep in the pocket. Or hurting Queen Anne, more like. The foreigner must be very interesting to set so many important hares running in the heart of winter. What's he done to cause such a hue and cry?

Pity help this foreign chap when they catch him, especially if he's from warmer climes. Winter in gaol soon saps a man's strength and spirit. Morpeth's colder than a witch's tit even in the summer months. Beyond me why they do it, these men, risking their necks for heaven knows what reward. They never get away with it. I'll get some clean straw in ready for him and he can take his chances in with Walter the coiner. Old Wulf will be glad of some company in his final days. Still, the cold might save the country a length of rope in the long run.

GINGERBREAD

Shotley Bridge, 1687

*H*ermann hadn't seen a soul for miles as they followed the meandering river. Finally, in the heart of the hills, they passed a big house, a mill, an inn and a couple of hovels. Along the road from the port, people had come out to cheer or jeer at the caravan of wagons going past, but their new home looked bereft of anyone. After the busyness of Newcastle, the tiny hamlet of Shotley Bridge was entirely quiet, apart from the rushing river.

When the wagons slowed, the drivers leapt down to unshackle the horses and led them to the water. A terrace of houses followed the sweep of the river. Built from blond stone, they were wholly different to the half-timbered home they'd left behind with its black shutters and deep roof. These English houses had two floors, with small-paned windows on each, and doors that faced onto the road. As far as he could hear, there were no waterwheels nearby, so their forges weren't joined to their homes. In the middle of the terrace was a chapel that was plain, even by Lutheran standards. At least the English had kept their word and his countrymen would be free to follow their own worship. It might please Katrin.

A dog barked in the distance and Griselda gave an answering bark.

Liesl hugged her pup. 'Listen to you, *Hündchen*, making new friends already. You hounds must speak the same language the world over.'

Katrin clicked her tongue. 'At least the hound will have some friends.'

'You've got me, Mother.' Liesl leant forwards. 'And don't forget Grandmother Mohll. She's here, too. Shall I wake her up now?'

'No, you should not,' Katrin said. 'We've enough to do without her causing mischief.'

Hermann widened his eyes at his daughter and shook his head. There was no winning with his wife when she was tired like this.

Katrin inspected their new surroundings. 'There's nothing here. A bridge, and that's about all. It makes my heart feel quite hollow. Have we really agreed to come to such a godforsaken place in the name of gold?'

'For now, Katrin, let's try to find our feet.' Hermann took her hand. 'We have each other. In time, your heart might fill with love for this new home.'

'I doubt it.' She ran an eye from the doorstep to the ridge of the roof, measuring their new home with her eyes. 'See how short the door is and how low the ceilings – the English must imagine we're dwarves.'

Liesl giggled and waved at the Schimmelbusch boy as his family's wagon arrived.

'Dwarves?' Hermann looked at his wife. 'Katrin, if you could hear yourself sometimes.' He stepped down from the wagon and stood in front of the houses. They weren't bad. Just different to home. Smaller and more huddled together, a bit like the English. 'Scrimping on stone, most likely. It can't be cheap.' He glanced through the window at the small room inside. 'Besides, none of us are so tall we're in any danger of scraping our heads on the ceilings.' He laughed and turned back to his daughter. 'Except you, Liesl, if you don't stop growing soon.'

But his wife's arms were folded and the set of her mouth spoke of her determination not to like the place.

Katrin tossed her head and a blonde ringlet sprang free from her hood. She caught it and tucked it back in. 'Tears would well even in your mother's dry eyes at the sight of such ugly houses.'

'Hush, Katrin, please.' He glanced at his sleeping mother. 'Not so loud or the drivers will hear you.' The folks hereabouts looked to live in cheap shacks that must have taken three or four hours to build. How would they feel, hearing his wife griping about their new house? It wouldn't do, giving the English any cause to resent them more than they already must. He held out a hand. 'Here, let me help you down from the wagon.'

Katrin ignored his hand and climbed down by herself.

'They won't understand us anyway.'

'I suppose you're right,' he said. 'Liesl, stop sitting there like one o'clock half struck and take your hound to the river for a drink. Try not to get under anyone's feet – especially any feet wearing horseshoes.'

At the end of the terrace, a sandy-haired man with long moustaches came out of a house and spoke to some of the wagon drivers. One of them pointed at Hermann and the man waved and started walking over.

'Wait, Liesl.' Hermann pointed towards the man. 'See, that must be the Newcastle swordmaker, Herr Carnforth. Stay a minute and say hello to him. Katrin, I know you're worn out but please try to be pleasant.'

The sandy-haired man came towards them, beaming, and introduced himself in curiously accented German that made him hard to understand.

'Here you all are, bone weary, seasick and thin from your voyage, with a one-eared pup to boot. Good day to you, little grey one.' He began rubbing Griselda's ear so thoroughly it was a wonder her head didn't fall off. 'But you're here at last to help the

English despatch their enemies: also the English.' He grinned at his own wit. 'How does it feel to be in our beautiful valley at the behest of the English king, eh?'

Before Hermann could speak, Katrin got in before him.

'The Catholic king, you mean?'

The Englishman's eyes widened at this remark, 'King James, yes–'

Hermann raised a placating hand. 'We're happy to be here, Herr Carnforth,' he said with a glance at his wife. 'Some of us are a bit overtired.'

Carnforth raised a brow. 'Your lady wife doesn't honey her words.'

Hermann laughed to himself. If Carnforth expected honeyed words from Katrin, he'd be left wanting. 'Like I say, overtired, it was an arduous voyage.'

Carnforth nodded and smiled. A man without malice. 'Of course Frau Mohll is tired. You must all be exhausted. And here's me jabbering away when you'll want to settle in and get a hot meal inside you.' He held out an arm by way of a flourish. 'Built from the same sandstone as our castle and cathedral so you can be sure these houses will withstand the insult of time and element.'

Hermann considered the houses and wondered what kind of elements this stone was expected to ward off. 'Are the winters here very bad?' he asked.

'They can be, but they're better here in the valley than up on the hills. Go on, Herr Mohll,' Carnforth said, pointing at the nearest house. 'That one there is yours. Why not take your womenfolk inside? Here, let me help you.'

Before Carnforth could open the door, a red-haired woman and boy, both severely thin, started walking down the hill towards them. They called out to Carnforth, who waved and beckoned them over.

Liesl raised her fur-trimmed mitten and admired it.

'Father, why are their clothes so drab?'

'Hush, Liesl,' Hermann replied. 'They must be poor, but take care not to insult them.'

When the woman stopped to cough, the boy waited quietly next to her until she was better and they stepped forwards together.

Carnforth introduced Rose Leaton and her son, Joseph, translating back and forth as he went. The boy dropped to his haunches and held out his hand, palm up, to Griselda. When he received a sniff of approval, he rubbed her chest and she thumped her tail in return.

Liesl frowned. 'Griselda, you're being far too friendly towards these Englishmen.'

Rose bobbed a curtsy and passed a small loaf and a flagon to Katrin, who smiled and passed the gifts to Hermann before unfastening a tin from the wagon and giving it to Joseph. He opened the tin, grinned and held it up to his mother, who hesitated before plucking a star-shaped biscuit for herself and slipping it into her apron pocket.

The boy took a crescent moon for himself. 'Thank you,' he said.

'Danke.' Liesl smiled and pointed. '*Pfefferkuchen.*'

The boy paused for a few seconds. '*Pfefferkuchen?*' He took a bite and chewed thoroughly before replying, 'Gingerbread.'

'Gingerbread.' Liesl laughed. 'Mother, Father, my first English word!'

Hermann nodded. It was fortunate the locals were friendly. Judging by the lack of buildings, there were many more Germans than English here now. A whole village of swordmakers overnight.

The thin woman pointed along the river and addressed Carnforth, who translated, explaining that the Englishwoman wanted to warn them about their neighbour, Ralph Maddison, who lived at Hole House, which was the big house on the other side of the river. He was notorious for causing mischief by lighting fires and suchlike. The madman could be recognised by the burn mark on his hand from when he'd been tried a few years back. Fires sounded more than mischief to Hermann, and both his wife and daughter looked shocked by the news. Hermann reassured them they'd be quite safe in a stone house when they had Griselda to guard them. He'd always had buckets of water ready in the forge and now he'd have to do the same at home.

Carnforth continued. 'You've another near neighbour. Well, yon side of the woods, so mebbes not so near. Witch Wilson.'

Katrin's head turned. 'A witch is permitted to live here?' she asked. 'We burn them in Germany.'

Hexe. Too many had been destroyed already on the wings of that word and Hermann dreaded to hear of witches. Liesl crept closer to her mother, peering into the trees that lined the riverbank.

'Oh, no, Frau Mohll, no burnings. Some hangings a while back …' he glanced at Rose and her son before turning again to the Mohlls, 'but never a burning. There's no bother around here with witches, anymore. You leave them in peace and they'll leave you in peace.' He bent down to speak to Liesl. 'If you ever come across a witch, keep your eyes to the ground and your fingers crossed. Never turn your back on her. As long as you fill your pockets with iron, your mortal soul will be safe. That should be easy enough for a swordmaker's girl.' He straightened up to address Katrin. 'Sorry, excuse my little joke, Frau Mohll. Witch Wilson's not a witch at all. He gets called that because he's handy with all manner of things and he's as skilled at engraving as he is at healing. You should go and see his collection of little machines. He can draw an accurate likeness of any plant you care to mention.' He turned to Hermann. 'Now, Herr Mohll,' he said. 'Rose isn't well and must go home but Joseph's a strong lad who can make himself useful. Go on, Joseph, give the drivers a hand to lift down some of those trunks and help these good people get settled in. They'll be wanting their beds.'

Liesl helped her grandmother up the stairs to bed and soon returned, heels thumping on wood as she ran downstairs. 'Mother, Father, my room's a cosy garret overlooking the river and the woods and Grandmother Mohll is next to you two and she's fast asleep again so I've put your quilt over her because I can't find hers.'

On hearing this breathless news, Katrin's brow furrowed. 'Thank you, Liesl,' she said. 'Don't worry. I'll find it.'

Hermann closed the door and shut out the street sounds. He began unpacking and hanging pans on hooks over the fire. The sooner they got unpacked, the sooner they could go to bed, and Katrin would feel much happier after a proper sleep. The voyage had been difficult for her.

'I like our new home.' Liesl drew Griselda to her. 'That boy, Joseph and his mother, they were kind.'

Katrin took over the pans, rearranging them to suit herself.

'I'm sure the madman will also be kind. We can call on him in the morning with some *Pfefferkuchen*. After all, we need all the new friends we can get now.'

'Mother, what about Rose?' Liesl asked. 'She was friendly. Might she become your friend?'

'That scarecrow of a woman?' replied Katrin. 'She's scarcely more than a beggar.'

'Then perhaps you might befriend the witch,' Liesl said, but this was whispered into the thick fur at Griselda's neck and hopefully Katrin hadn't heard her impertinence.

Hermann wagged a finger at his daughter and turned to his wife. 'Try to decide where you want things to go while I fix this shelf. Liesl, find my smallest hammer and some nails. You can give me a hand.'

Liesl picked up Grandmother Gerner's salt-glazed pitcher and ran a fingertip over its bearded wildman before reading out the inscription: 'Drink and eat and don't forget God.' She put the brown pitcher on the sill.

'Please take it off there, Liesl,' Katrin said. 'It's too narrow even for such a little pitcher.'

'Don't worry, *Igelchen*,' said Hermann. 'I'll soon build some new shelves where it can sit quite happily, but perhaps it's best to move it for now, Liesl.'

'Where to?' Liesl asked, turning sharply. There was a crash. 'Oh! Sorry, Mother.'

'My mother's pitcher.' Katrin ran over and knelt next to the broken pieces, gathering them to her. She gasped as she pricked her finger and stared as a drop of blood bloomed.

'Come, Katrin, I can mend it,' Hermann said. 'Not well enough to hold cream but well enough to look at and remember your mother. The wildman will have a broken nose from now on but that's not too bad—' Hermann stopped when he saw his little hedgehog's face and decided to keep his own counsel. He took the pieces from her and placed them on the table.

'Liesl, bind your mother's finger and take yourselves to bed, both of you. It's getting late. I'll finish up here. Try to get some sleep, eh?' He crouched down, clasped his wife's shoulders and kissed her forehead. 'Tomorrow will be a better day, you'll see—'

'Sleep? And let you put all our belongings in the wrong place?' Katrin waved him away and stood up. 'I can bind my own finger, thank you, and I'll sleep when the work's done and not before.' She tied her kerchief around her finger, held it in the air and instructed Liesl to lay the mat and hang the curtains.

The dutiful girl unfastened the knotted twine from their mat and rolled it across the floor, where its rose hues were warmed by the dying sunlight. Griselda circled the mat and sniffed furiously before curling up in the middle to lick her paws.

Liesl knelt on the mat and hugged the pup. 'Oh, Griselda, you can smell home. But trust you to lie in the worst place possible so we can trip over you at every turn.'

'Griselda,' Hermann said. 'Your place is by the door, keeping out draughts.' To say nothing of this mad Englishman, Maddison. The hound was growing at an alarming rate and Hermann wondered if she wasn't half wolf. That might be no bad thing.

'Liesl, let the hound alone, please,' Katrin said. 'Those curtains won't hang themselves. They're over there, on top of that small trunk. Your father can help you.'

Hermann unwrapped their golden curtains and held the chair while Liesl climbed up to hang them. Not the most even of floors. When she stepped down, the curtains were a good foot too short. Katrin ran an eye along the window frame and a hand along the hem. She sighed.

'Have they got deep hems, Mother?' Liesl examined the stitching. 'All the frocks you've ever sewed for me have deep hems.'

'Children need deep hems because they grow so fast – especially you – but never windows. They'll have to do until I can tack something onto the bottom. Oh, what ridiculous long windows. How can this place ever be our home?'

Hermann opened his arms. 'It just needs fire and a broth bubbling. You'll see, *Liebling*, you'll see.'

Katrin stepped into the ready circle of his arms and leant her head on his shoulder. 'I hate it. I hate it all.'

'Don't hate it,' he said. 'If you set your heart too hard against it now, it might never soften.'

Over Katrin's shoulder, he watched Liesl open a trunk, lift out their table clock, listen to it and smile. Good. It was still ticking.

After he'd sat their brass and ebony clock on the shelf, Hermann wound it with a key so they could live on Solingen time for ever if they pleased. When he came across their Bible, he sat it next to the clock. At least the shelf was up straight now, even if the walls weren't true. In the bottom of a trunk were Katrin's small paintings of field mice, which he took out and hung on the wall above the table. Seeing them would make his wife feel happier and more at home. Next, he found a box of cutlery and passed it to Liesl to add to that provided by the English. The girl picked up an English knife and balanced it on one finger until it tipped and clattered to the floor.

Katrin took down the picture she was straightening and rubbed her temples. 'Liesl, what on earth are you doing?'

'Sorry, Mother. I wanted to check if it's well made.' The girl picked up the knife. 'They must think we have no cutlery.'

'Put the English knives at the back of the drawer,' Katrin said. 'Hermann, light the fire and I'll prepare supper.'

Logs and kindling were piled up ready. Hermann knelt and stacked the firewood before striking the firesteel on the flint. Night was falling, so once the fire was going, he lit a rush light and set it on the table. Finally, they'd eat and might start to feel more content.

By the time the trunks were unpacked, a ring of sausage and a wheel of cheese sat on platters, and pea soup bubbled over the fire. Katrin cut slices of bread from the loaf given by Rose.

Hermann unstopped the flask and inhaled. 'Ale. Not like your beer, Katrin but we'll drink it and be glad of it.' He shared it out and raised his tankard. 'Here's to kindness from strangers.'

'Come, both of you, we'll eat the cold food while the soup cooks.' Katrin set down her ladle. 'It's too late at night to be eating soup, but we need the warmth. Besides, the scent of ham and peas in the air reminds me of home.'

There was a waver in her voice and her hand trembled as she

took a scoop of salt. Hermann took the spoon from his wife and clasped her hands between both of his. 'Life will get better, Katrin, you'll see.'

No Master of Disguise

Morpeth Gaol, 1703

Whatever misadventure is at play in the north, Dismal's efforts have come good after a Newcastle innkeeper found a strange man under his roof and reported him to the good Earl of Nottingham. The constables fetched the stranger here this morning. An Irish man, they reckoned, but said it with a wink. He's a funny-looking sort by anyone's standards: a fleshy man of middling years but lanky and lardy at the same time. For reasons best known to himself, he has a blond peruke plonked on his fat head, curled up at the sides, its long tail tied with a ratty black ribbon. Hardly a master of disguise in this get-up. Every head in Newcastle must have swivelled to get an eyeful of the dew-beater lurching down the street. Naught to me. We get all sorts in here but can this really be the man Dismal seeks? Bluntest knife in the drawer by the looks of him. No matter. He was sent here to be seen to and seen to him I have.

His tongue didn't take long to loosen. Never does when a man has gout and I should know, me being a martyr to it these last ten years. My new guest calls himself John Burke and swears he's been in Newcastle for months on end. Dallied awhile when his gout started playing up. Worst town in the world for a man with gout to dally in, filled as it is with fleshmarkets and alehouses. If the man had an inch of sense, he'd have gone south long ago and saved himself a stay with me.

The queer lump had some papers about his person that I couldn't make head nor tail of. I'm no judge of the written word but a pound to a penny it's Latin or French. We all know what that means. Never good news having a papist under my roof as it always sets the others off. It's as well Walter's in such a bad way or I'd be tearing them apart all night. Walter might be a master forger but he's a good church man and hates the old religion with a passion.

Very teary Burke was, promising he was in no ways working against Her Majesty. Clinging to a book. Kept it clutched to his heart, all the while insisting, 'My book is of some consequence to me.' During my efforts to wrest the book off him, his Irish brogue fell away. The strangest thing. Burke's a Scot pretending to be Irish. As if that would help his cause. There's something badly amiss in that fat head of his. Promised me faithfully there were men of good standing from his kingdom who would speak up for him and the names fairly started tripping off his tongue.

From where I'm standing, there's only one reason for Burke hanging around these parts. Looks to be a papist Scot and likely a Jacobite agent. Newcastle's swarming with the villains. There's been no rest in the north since Queen Anne took the throne, what with her so sickly from being a lass, and left with no heir after her lad died. Poor Brandy Nan – no one's tried harder than her to breed heirs. One bairn after another she's lost down the years. Eighteen, they say. Little wonder she drinks her eyes out. The papists like to think she's just keeping the throne warm for her dead father's little lad, the Pretender. Wishful thinking. As if our good Protestant queen would sully her hands with Catholics.

As for Burke, I've sent a message with a fast horse to Edinburgh to ask if the men of good standing will speak up for him. Once I'd prised that blessed book free from him, it was packed off to

Whitehall to see what Dismal makes of it.

Turns out Burke's good for silver. Just as well since I'll need it to keep Roasting Jack filled. For such a short dog, he can eat his own bodyweight twice over without blinking. The little cur must have worms, so it'll have to be the red-hot poker for him, I don't doubt.

FIRE AND WATER

Shotley Bridge, 1687

*T*he sunlight shone under the too-short curtains and woke Hermann up. After so long on water and wagon, it was strange to wake up on a bed that wasn't moving. He winced as he searched for his schnapps, over-reaching in the unfamiliar bed, his right shoulder still asleep and not yet ready for the strain. He rubbed it awhile and watched Katrin sleeping.

When he sat up, the morning air was cold. Autumn must arrive more quickly this far north. Still, being more northerly would mean lighter nights and he'd be able to work on into the evening without straining his eyes. It was tempting to pull the heavy quilt back over him and sink into sleep until his thick head left him but he was wide awake so he slid from bed, smoothed his hair and beard, pulled on his shirt and breeches and crept downstairs, cringing at each creak. It would take a while to learn all the sounds of this new house and where to set his feet to avoid waking the entire household. When he reached the bottom, the hound raised her head.

'Save your mournful face for those who care, Griselda, I'll set the fire once I've had a smoke. Come, I'll refill the pitcher and you can get a drink from the river.'

There was a little black ball floating in the water pitcher. A dead spider, whose legs had furled. He tipped it outside and was surprised when the spider unfurled its legs and sprang back to life, scuttling back in to freeze beside his bare foot. He saw himself through the spider's eight eyes: a terrifying column. Rain must be coming but hopefully not until after he'd walked the river with Oligh this afternoon. He picked the spider up and put it outside before the hound ate it. Once the spider was out of the way, he lit his pipe and puffed until it got going.

Outside, birds were singing but they sounded different to those at home. Was that because he'd left behind a busy town and come to live in the middle of nowhere or were they different birds? Beneath his pipe smoke, the air smelt of summer roses dying and of apple, pear and oak undercut by damp with a hint of badger, fox and deer. His industry would soon change that, with the burning of charcoal and sulphur surging from the steel. With Katrin's beer fermenting and spices rubbed into meat and dough, Shotley Bridge would soon start to smell like home and they would all feel much more settled.

As Griselda lapped from the river, he smelt something new: a whisper of smoke in the air. A quick glance at the new houses proved no chimneys puffing. This wasn't forge smoke, or forest fire either, since he knew the smell of oak, beech or ash burning. This was a lighter, sweeter smell. Hay? He turned towards the hills in the west and looked up to the high pasture, where a small fire was blazing. The fields were so dry it would take hold in no time. Heart thumping, he started banging on doors and shouting, 'Fire! Fire!'

There was no time to lose, so he waded across the river and raced uphill, with Griselda far ahead of him, barking. In the distance, a spire of smoke spiralled against the blue sky. The fire was too big to stamp out, but if he was quick, he could stop it spreading. Surely this was no accident. The sun was nowhere near high enough to cause it.

When a new flame kindled further up the pasture, it told him this was no accident. There in the shadow of a third haystack was a man, frenziedly hacking at a piece of flint with a firesteel. It had to be Maddison, the madman. Hermann crept towards the third haystack. Maddison was head and shoulders above him and so there would only be one chance to tackle him. He jumped Maddison from behind, snatched the firesteel and hurled it away. Maddison bucked and threw Hermann to the ground with a thump that knocked the wind out of him. Griselda lunged at Maddison, received a kick for her efforts, yelped and slunk out of the way. The man bayed and lifted his booted foot. Hermann feared for his hands and tucked them under his oxters.

He was saved when big Oligh came roaring towards them, brandishing a hammer. Maddison threw back his head and laughed, pausing to give Hermann a swift kick in the guts before lumbering off towards the river, waving his fists at the line of men snaking their way uphill towards the fires. Hermann doubled up and vomited.

Oligh held out a hand and hauled him to his feet. 'You'll be bruised but your innards will soon mend,' he said. 'At least your arms are unbroken.'

Hermann staggered to his feet and bent over, hands on knees, trying to get his breath back.

'You took your time.'

'Grateful as ever, Mohll. What were you thinking?'

'To spare the hay,' Hermann replied. 'What possessed this Maddison? Why would a grown man delight in setting fire to another man's crops?'

'It's beyond me,' replied Oligh, 'but promise you won't chase madmen on your own again. Wait for me next time.'

'If I'd waited for you, Oligh, all this would be blackened and burnt.'

'You stay put till you can straighten up and I'll help Wupper and the others put out the fires before they spread.'

While Hermann caught his breath, an elderly man made his way uphill towards them, inspecting the damage as he walked. He stopped to examine Griselda, running his hands over her ribs, and spoke to Oligh for a while. The farmer? He'd be better employed in saving his own crops. The man gave him a wave and came over.

'The pup will survive,' the old man said. 'Sturdy young creature by the looks of her. Mohll is it? I'm Johnson.' He shook Hermann's hand. 'So now you've seen Maddison's handiwork. The man's a menace. I'm grateful to you for saving my crops. Fast asleep I was till I heard the commotion. You did well to raise the alarm but I wish you'd not set after him by yourself.'

Hermann wiped his mouth on his sleeve. 'I'd do it again in a heartbeat.'

'Hopefully there'll be no need,' Johnson said. 'I'll set young Joseph Leaton on. My wife's friendly with his mother. There's no man in the house since his father passed and Rose will be glad of something coming in.'

'Will you summon the constables, Herr Johnson?'

'It's a fruitless endeavour with Maddison being district warden and all,' the farmer said. 'They've already let him away with murder—'

'Murder? The madman has killed?' asked Hermann. This must be what Rose Leaton had tried to tell them. Why hadn't Carnforth mentioned this? Had he been worried they'd turn tail and run back to Solingen?

'Aye, you do right to be shocked,' Johnson replied. 'Maddison killed his first son-in-law and tried shooting his replacement. Burnt down any number of houses over the years. Always stealing other men's livestock. There's something not right with the man but the authorities' hands are tied. He got burnt on the palm once over for fire-striking and larceny. They fined him handsomely for murder but that's about all. Odd times when he's had a skinful, the innkeeper shoves him in his cell for safekeeping till the morning. Never a whit of remorse, mind.' The farmer spat. 'Come down to the Bridge End tonight with your neighbour and I'll stand you both a pint by way of thanks. I'll send my wife down to visit yours, if you don't mind, she's itching to see what you've all got.'

Johnson raised his hand and went on his way. The farmer was fortunate to have any crops left standing. Hermann knew how he'd deal with a man prone to murder: let the punishment fit the crime. But this wasn't his place. He was in another country and must abide by its laws or at least be seen to do so. This Maddison appeared to do whatever he pleased. Clearly, he'd never been sanctioned so he knew no bounds. No doubt he'd kill again before long and the law would have to act, though by the looks of him, Maddison would laugh as they strung him up. There was something badly wrong in a man compelled to kill. Katrin would never sleep at night when she heard this. What were the company men thinking, putting them so near this dangerous man? He watched the farmer walking about his meadow, checking all the fires were out. While they'd saved much of his hay, there was nothing to say Maddison wouldn't return to finish the job. Would young Joseph Leaton be any match for a man bent on destruction? He doubted it. A guard on the crops might force Maddison to go after softer eggs. Something must be done. The madman needed a lesson.

Oligh returned, sweating and stinking of smoke. 'Have you got your wind back yet?' he asked.

'Just about,' Hermann replied. 'Time to realise I'm not so young anymore.'

'You were fortunate the madman didn't flatten you, Mohll.'

Hermann laughed without humour. 'I only jumped him because I knew big Oligh was on his way.'

'Odd timing, though, don't you think?' Oligh pointed back up the hill to the stacks. 'They must have been there for days, if not weeks. Why set fire to them now?'

Hermann pondered this, wondering whether Maddison might be lunar and ruled by the moon as some men were. Even the best bread could turn mouldy. 'Oligh, who seldom asks a question without already knowing the answer.' Hermann rubbed his side and blenched. 'You think he was giving us a warning?'

'Undoubtedly,' said Oligh. 'He's had the run of the place for too long. He can't have liked a hundred of us appearing overnight. Something's rattled him and he's lashed out.'

'You might be right. Still, now that he's made his mark, he might leave us in peace.'

Down in the valley, the women were now milling about at the river's edge while children shrieked and ran in and out of the water.

Oligh nodded towards their terrace. 'I see your mother's up and about. How's she taking to her new home?'

'About as well as Katrin took to the news of my mother coming with us.'

'You and your womenfolk, eh?' Oligh clapped Hermann on the back. 'Now, will you be well enough to walk the river this afternoon?'

Hermann snorted. 'Dare say I might even be well enough to withstand a pint of English ale.'

⁓

Hermann rolled up a sleeve, knelt at the side of the River Derwent, thrust in his left hand and let the clear water run through his fingers. In truth, he was built for life on the river. He knew its currents and liked planting his feet on the riverbed, even if he was sometimes chest-deep in rushing water. The river had purpose, just as he did. On the day he'd quenched his first blade in the river, he'd felt reborn. No longer a boy who could only rake out ashes and watch the men, but one of the men, and more importantly, a swordmaker. That moment had filled him with more pride than the day he became a master. Becoming a master had been the end of a gradual process, but the plunging of hot metal into rushing water was the beginning, the birth of his life's work.

'Still enraptured by the water, Hermann?' Katrin smiled down at him. 'Don't you think it looks a bit sluggish?'

'It's certainly fast enough now,' he replied, 'and the runoff from the hills should keep it that way.' Despite the spider in the house, it hadn't rained. The mill races should keep the water flowing but they'd need to keep an eye on dry spells. He scooped up a handful of water and tasted it. 'Here, try some. Soft water, clear and sparkling.'

'I've tried it already,' said Katrin, 'and it's not as soft as the water at home.'

'No lime in it, see.' He let some fall through his fingers. 'If anything, it's even softer than the water at home. Perfect for swords.'

She sniffed. 'But not so much for wives.'

'Oh, come, it's not so bad, Katrin,' he said. 'Can't you think of *one* good thing about our new home?' Perhaps he should mention that Frau Johnson would soon pay a visit.

She smiled fleetingly. 'Well, I do get to see your mother every single hour of every single day and it's wonderful living near a madman.'

Hermann rubbed his eyebrow. There was no helpful response to this and so he said nothing. Perhaps now was not the best time to mention Frau Johnson. It could be a pleasant surprise for Katrin. He took one of his wife's hands in his, placed a kiss in her palm and closed her fingers over it.

'It'll be alright,' he said. 'I'll make it alright.'

'Easy for you to say, Hermann when you're in the forge every day.' She opened her hand. 'I daren't leave the house for fear it'll be burnt to the ground.'

'You can leave the house whenever you like,' he said. 'My mother's here, don't forget.'

'As if I could ever forget. Aren't you worried, Hermann? It's one thing having to live on this wretched island,' she said, 'but it's quite another having a killer living barely a heartbeat away from us. We could die in our beds and never know a thing about it.'

'It won't come to such a dire end. We don't know all the circumstances yet. Katrin, you can't live your whole life in one day in your head. No one can guess what lies in the future. It'll make you worry and worry will make you unhappy without solving anything.'

She turned away from his clumsy efforts at comforting her and Hermann watched her go, pausing to speak to Oligh as he passed her.

Oligh strode towards him. 'Come, Mohll, boots off. If you've finished fighting with the beautiful Frau Mohll, we may as well get the lie of the land.' He kicked off his clogs, rolled up his breeches and slid into the Derwent.

Hermann watched Katrin go back into the house, took off his boots and slipped down beside his friend. 'She's worried about that Maddison man.'

'Can't say I blame her,' Oligh said. 'We'll need to keep an eye out. Something of the devil in him unless I'm much mistaken. I'm beginning to think we've made a big mistake coming here.'

'Already?' Hermann asked. 'Give it some time and you'll see.'

Oligh could be right. Nothing so far had lived up to what they'd been promised but they couldn't go back. This Maddison man worried him, though. Perhaps a show of strength might deter him.

Together, the two men walked the river, which for the most part was narrower than the Wupper, only faster. Here, the defiles were steep and the valley plunged to the river and straight up again. The valley at home was broader with useful flat expanses of land to either side of the river. Here, the cottages followed the sweep of the river but flat land was sparse. Otherwise, it was the same as home, although it would never be home for Katrin without all her loved ones. Would she ever adjust to her small sandstone castle when her mother was hundreds of miles away?

They continued upriver, and while Hermann's feet were numbed by the rushing water, his thighs burnt with the effort of walking it. He glanced up at the crags. Deep bands of gritstone, so they'd not be short of grinding wheels.

A sudden current took him by surprise and he flailed for a moment until Oligh grabbed his arm to steady him.

'The river certainly falls fast enough,' Oligh shouted. 'The laughing water, Carnforth called it.'

'Flaying water more like,' Hermann retorted. 'It's almost taken the hide off me. The Derwent is rather fiercer than the Wupper in that respect, is it not?'

'Hard to say,' replied Oligh, 'because I'm relying on my memory, which is hardly better than imagination.'

'You saw the Wupper a matter of days ago. You can't have forgotten it so soon.'

'It feels like a lifetime ago,' said Oligh. 'I'm trying my best to forget the old life otherwise this new one will be all the harder …'

His friend's words were soon lost in the rushing water, so Hermann considered the drop from the moor to their new valley. The river crashed down in a thundering rush, peat-brown with foaming crests. They could easily harness its might to power their hammers, bellows and grinding wheels. When it wasn't in spate, it'd be a much gentler creature. Would the mill races be up to the task? He hoped so or he'd never hear the end of it from Katrin.

He watched Oligh examining the crags and waded towards him. They'd need to cut some grinding wheels. It was a shame to think of those left behind at home. Carnforth was seeing to the necessary licences but it all took time and no one was earning any gold in the meantime. It was a shame, when here they were, surrounded by millstone grit. Hermann climbed out of the river and rubbed the water off his bare legs before rolling his breeches back down. He waved his arm at the riverbanks.

'Why don't we cut some grindstones ourselves?' asked Hermann. 'No one would know—'

'God would know and so would I,' said Oligh. 'Do you want to wind up in an English gaol, Mohll?'

Hermann watched Oligh duck his head as he entered the inn next to the bridge. The dying sun gleamed dully in the windows and a log fire burnt in a grate at the far end. Farmer Johnson was clutching a tankard and talking in low tones to the burly innkeeper. In the corner nearest the door sat Ralph Maddison, sooty-faced and furious-looking. Hermann's fists clenched at the sight of him, but Maddison threw back his drink, thumped down his cup and stormed past them. The door slammed so hard behind him that pitchers and cups clinked and the innkeeper had to put out a steadying hand.

'Good evening, friends,' said Farmer Johnson, waving them over. 'Here's to the heroes of the hour.'

He introduced them to the innkeeper, Blenkinsop, a florid man who looked as though he hadn't smiled in a few decades.

'Order whatever you like,' the farmer said, 'as long as it's ale or rum.'

The innkeeper frowned. 'There's a bit more than ale or rum. What will you have, gentlemen?'

Oligh peered at the barrels. 'We'll each take a half-pint of ale.'

Hermann blinked. A set of cracked ribs should be worth at least a pint of ale and a measure of something stronger but he said nothing and mutely accepted the small tankard. He raised it to Johnson and nodded before taking a drink. The English might enjoy this but it was like cow's piss compared to Katrin's beer. He glanced at Oligh, who angled his eyes towards the innkeeper's hands. They were the size of shovels and so Hermann decided now was not a good time to share this opinion.

Oligh sipped his ale and leant nearer to Blenkinsop. 'What do you make of Herr Maddison?'

The innkeeper poured himself a generous measure of rum and blew out his cheeks. 'You mean my best customer?' He laughed a hollow laugh and knocked back his tot. 'Went in for wild horseplay as a lad and was never checked by his father. Man's a law unto himself.'

'But even so,' said Oligh, sipping his ale slowly. 'How might a man guilty of murder be allowed to roam at will?'

The innkeeper glanced sharply at the farmer, who shrugged.

'It's hardly a secret, Blenkinsop, and if you want my opinion,' Johnson said, 'they've a right to know about their neighbour.'

Not for the first time, Hermann wondered why they'd been placed so near a madman. There was barely a soul along the length of the river and yet the company men had set them here. They must have known Maddison's history.

Oligh shook his head. 'He would have been executed at home.'

'Aye and he would have been executed here and all.' The innkeeper picked up a jug of rum and held it out, eyebrows raised in question.

Ah, so this was the game. If they wanted to know more, it would cost them. Hermann nodded, held up four fingers and handed over some coins. He could hardly blame Blenkinsop, whose livelihood must depend on passing trade and there couldn't be too much of that. Maybe that's why they'd been placed here, to keep the inn going. They clinked glasses and drank. Hermann breathed deeply through his nose until his eyes stopped watering and wondered what misbegotten shipwreck this rum had come from.

Oligh swirled his measure and nursed it to him without drinking. 'So, tell us,' said Oligh, eyeing his glass suspiciously, 'how did Maddison save his neck?'

The innkeeper leaned towards them, glancing from one man to another, not bothering to hide the fact that he enjoyed having an audience. 'How do rich men ever get away with anything?'

'Sorry, Herr Blenkinsop, but we're none the wiser,' said Oligh.

Hermann wondered if this would hurt him in the pocket again but the innkeeper smiled the smile of one glad to impart knowledge to a lesser mortal and rubbed his fingers and thumb together.

'Silver.'

'Sorry,' said Hermann, 'he bought his freedom?'

Blenkinsop scratched his head for a minute. 'Aye. Cost him plenty, mind. Had to sell off most of his estates. Same again when he tried to finish the magistrate. No silver left and he's hardly more than a tenant now.'

Hermann looked at Oligh, who shrugged. 'So rich men get away with murder?'

'Aye, exactly right,' said Blenkinsop, 'and not just murder.' He leaned in close. 'They say he murdered his son-in-law after he'd accused Maddison of debauching his own daughter.'

So grave was this news that Oligh took a sip of his rum and flushed immediately. He was much too well-mannered to cough but his eyes streamed with the strain of holding it in.

The innkeeper roared with laughter. 'Of course, the man's hellbound.' He shared a look with Johnson, who was sipping his rum and looking as though he wished he wasn't there.

'Blenkinsop,' Farmer Johnson said, 'look what you've done to this fair fellow. He's gone purple. Stop your gossiping, man.'

Chastened, the innkeeper put down his glass. 'It's not gossip. It's what they said at the assizes.'

'Mebbes,' said Johnson, 'but think of the lass. She's enough of a cross to bear as it is.'

'So,' said Hermann, interrupting Johnson and Blenkinsop, 'you're telling me a man might get away with murder providing he can pay?'

'Aye, that's about the size of it,' said Blenkinsop, 'but he's no silver to pay the next time, and there will be a next time, you mark my words. Maddison can't help himself. Aye, he'll slay another man before long and then we'll see the bugger swing.'

A Queer Kettle of Fish

Morpeth Gaol, 1703

A queer kettle of fish landed on me the day. This one had
jumped ship, straight into the drink and washed up in the
Tyne. He was blue with cold and no wonder. Bad enough time
of year to be sailing, let alone swimming. The constables sharp
fished him out. A man swimming in these conditions is bound
to be up to no good. Must be hard as the hobs of hell, mind.
Most men would've perished in the blizzard on the way here,
even if warm and dry to start with. He's a foreigner. Not the man
Dismal seeks, though he might take us a step nearer. This one
is master of the ship from Rotterdam, one Cornelius Soldart.
The customs men have dragged their heels long enough catching him. How hard can it be to catch a man on board a ship at
anchor?

Soldart's best kept apart from Burke in case they're known
to one another. A job easier said than done since prisoners will
talk and pass messages behind my back. They think I cannot
understand thieves' cant but I've been here longer than any of
them. The ship's master is in with the local lads for now but he's
none too suited about being under my roof and clammed right
up.

Lucky for me there's more than one way to skin a cat. For

Soldart, it took no more than a loaf, a flagon of ale and a jug of rum. He's another huge man. Blond as well but not built like Burke. This one hasn't an ounce of fat about him. No gouty old sea captain, this. Weather-beaten and toothless as a babe but a happy enough talker for being such a mumblecrust.

Soldart reckoned he'd arrived in England sixteen days earlier. Said he was held up in Rotterdam while the queen's men were seeking ships to carry the King of Spain and his family. If he's to be believed, nearly five-hundred hangers-on, and all with horses. Some family! He means *our* King of Spain, of course, the Archduke of Austria, and not that French plague-sore, Philip. Fancy having two royal arses trying to sit on just the one throne.

Full of himself, the captain was, saying the queen's men were past themselves, scurrying about and trying to find passage for all the royal personages. By all accounts, the king looked ready to board Soldart's own vessel and bed down with his crew. Seems the king wasn't fussed how he travelled and was all for getting on board till some of his fine friends had a fit of the vapours at the thought of such humble conditions. Well, what a yarn to be spinning. The man must think I was born yesterday. Likely trying to keep me talking so he can keep crooking his elbow at my expense.

Counted himself lucky for surviving the Great Tempest when plenty didn't. Said he'd had the sense not to leave port till the worst of it had already passed. Dreadful business but the pamphleteers are still doing a roaring trade. Ships made into so much kindling in the English Channel. Thousands dead. Our King of Spain still missing at sea. Windmills turning so fast they burst into flames. Half the chimneys in London down. Even poor Queen Anne had to huddle in her cellar for fear of falling masonry. They also say the wind blew the lead off the roof of Westminster Abbey. That'll be the cockney starts to blame, though, never mind the weather.

Still, if even half the pamphleteers' tales are true, it's quite the adventure Soldart's had. Refused to be drawn on what he's doing in England when there's so much fighting in his own country. Sailed in on the *Eufro Angelique*, a vessel of war. Queer name for a ship. Told me she was laden with ballast, flax and sail-duck. Also let slip about some mysterious bundles belonging to a passenger. All put up in straw, wrapped in brown paper and tied with string. Soldart claimed to have no clue what these bundles contained. As if any ship's captain worth his salt wouldn't inspect every ear of grain fetched aboard his vessel – especially a man o' war.

The captain's tankard needed topping up a fair few times. There's not so much seawater running in his veins as rum. Finally, the cat was forced from the bag and he told me all about his human cargo. Four crew and nine passengers: six soldiers and a foreigner who had his wife and girl with him. The woman and girl went aboard at Jarrow Keys but Soldart made no mention of the foreigner getting off. He could recall no names, no matter how I plied him. What kind of captain has the best part of a dozen folk on his ship without knowing their names? But those names would come to me by and by.

AT THE SIGN
OF THE CROWN
AND CROSSED SWORDS

Shotley Bridge, 1688

*N*ow they'd been in England for almost a year, life had settled down and there was plenty of work to keep all the swordmakers busy. Most of their new customers were paying their bills on time, apart from Henry Benson, the London cutler. Having bought hundreds of beaten blades, the swindler had sent an insulting letter, insisting on deducting a shilling for every dozen blades, without recourse to discussion or negotiation. Sheer disgrace. Instead of being courteous in his petition to reduce the bill, Benson's letter was merely line upon line of falsehood. It made Hermann furious and he'd planned to ride to London to show the blademonger his true mettle. Fortunately, Katrin had pleaded with him to stay his hand, else he'd have cheerfully demonstrated how sharp his blades were on the man's guts and been hanged for the pleasure.

Liesl had settled in well. She was happy with her grandmother and Griselda for company and she'd made friends with Joseph Leaton and his mother, Rose. Katrin had made their new house into a home. She still missed her mother but she was smiling again and had started brewing her own beer, hoping to convince the innkeeper to buy it from her. As if he'd need asking twice. Frau Johnson had turned out to be a pleasant woman and Katrin got along with her, sharing recipes and sewing patterns. They hadn't much common language between them and perhaps that was why they got along so well.

The swordmakers had become regular visitors to the Bridge End and Blenkinsop always welcomed them heartily, which was hardly surprising when Shotley Bridge was so deserted. It was a miracle the man had managed to make both ends meet before the Germans came. Hermann had yet to meet Witch Wilson and the innkeeper had confided that Wilson wouldn't darken his door because Maddison was terrified of witches, even though he'd been told dozens of times the man was no witch. Since Maddison was the inn's best customer, Herr Wilson didn't want to scare him away for Blenkinsop's sake. Although the ale there was inferior to that at home, and the rum rough enough to dissolve teeth, the inn was a welcome meeting place and made a pleasing change from the church.

Life was good and the only lion in their path was the madman, Maddison, who was determined to make a nuisance of himself. In the spring, he'd almost succeeded in making Oligh lose his temper by stealing two webs of linen set out to bleach by Frau Oligh. He'd first taken one web, and after Oligh told him he'd pay dearly for his sins one of these days, Maddison came back and snatched the other, calling over his shoulder that he may as well hang for a hog as a ha'penny. For a godly man, Oligh had used some very ungodly language.

When Maddison was at the inn, he was usually outnumbered by the Germans and so contented himself with pulling faces and waving a fist. Blenkinsop had counselled the swordmakers to speak English when Maddison was present, suggesting their own language aggravated the madman. That hadn't sat well with

Hermann's countrymen and especially with Oligh. His friend was adamant they had a perfect right to speak their own language wherever they liked and protested at being forced to mangle his mouth around a mongrel language that had run its tongue across the earthly globe and dabbed up a dozen other languages. Oligh thought Maddison too eccentric to care what language they spoke, arguing that Blenkinsop was the one to benefit if they spoke in English as he could hardly pass along gossip if he couldn't understand it. Hermann thought this unfair as the innkeeper struck him as a decent man and one trying to keep the peace. Maddison aside, life here was good and Hermann was certain they would prosper in England.

⌣⟶

Amidst the sound of hammers ringing on metal from the surrounding forges, Liesl held a finished blade before the firelight and traced one finger across the running wolf inscription that told the world a Solingen blade was at its throat. She frowned as she ran her finger along the fuller and over the Mohll blademark.

'What troubles you, Liesl?'

She paused, her finger still in place near the tang, where the guard would one day cross the blade.

'Nothing, Father. I was just thinking about our mark. Don't you think it's a bit plain?'

The family mark didn't seem so plain to him. Three chevrons to stand for the crown and two upswept lines that crossed to represent swords in battle. What could be better than blades being used for their intended purpose of fighting to protect the crown, rather than being an ornament in a scabbard? Clearly, his daughter had other ideas.

He pinched her cheek but she twisted free. 'What else have you in mind, girl?'

His little swordmaker was too ready with her answer.

'Something more like the Schimmelbusch mark.'

'Schimmelbusch, eh?' Hermann suppressed a laugh. 'What's so striking about his mark?'

Did Liesl blush or had he pinched her too hard? At any rate, she spoke too quickly.

'Well, it's quite pretty,' she said. 'You know with scrolls and flowers and a picture of Herr Schimmelbusch.'

'If I were blessed with Herr Schimmelbusch's fine features, I might flaunt myself on our blades.' Hermann smoothed down his beard and hair. 'What say you? Do I pass muster?'

His daughter rolled her eyes and continued attending to the blade.

'Well, my girl, isn't it quite vain to make a self-portrait and put it on a blade?'

'A little,' she said, 'only the scrolls and flowers are so pretty.'

'But you know why the mark is there, Liesl?'

'Of course, so people know whose sword they buy.'

'Exactly,' he said. 'Although Mohll swords can be recognised by their qualities alone, to the extent we need not brand our blades.'

'What?' asked Liesl. 'Are you saying we need have no family mark at all? It's barely there as it is.'

'Take my word, Daughter, it'll never happen, but our mark is barely there because the brand must never outshine the blade. A point you need not make to Pieter if you wish him to remain your friend.' He hoped she'd absorbed the lesson that it wasn't a pretty mark that mattered but what the mark represented.

'Very well,' she said, 'I'll not upset poor Pieter.'

'So now he's poor Pieter? No longer the object of your envy but of your pity?'

'Stop teasing me, Father. He's my friend and I do still like the scrolls and flowers but I'm not envious of them.'

Her earnest expression made him smile. Envy had to live in swordmakers' hearts because that's what created the urge to be better at their craft. He tapped the line drawing.

'See how the brave wolf is ready to run along the blood gutter towards the blade's point–'

'So she's running into battle.' Liesl grinned. 'You've told me this a hundred times already. It's been drummed into me from birth.'

Hermann raised his brows. Who was this cheeky young woman who'd taken the place of his little girl? He put down the blade and squeezed the bellows, staring at the flame as he adjusted the air flow. 'Liesl, you're too near the flame with those lacy sleeves. Your mother will never forgive me if you singe them.' Katrin was already unhappy at the thought of their daughter getting forge-burn and ruining her fair complexion. 'Why don't you get yourself home to help your mother? She'll have a busy day ahead of her.'

'Can't I stay here, Father? Please? Swords are so much more interesting than kitchen knives.'

'Then you should have been born a boy.' Hermann ignored her pet-lip. 'Stop wheedling. Go and help your mother. Go!'

When she'd left, Hermann turned to draw a piece of steel from the shelf. He held it up to the firelight, examined it and weighed it in his hands. Satisfied, he plunged the blank into the yellow heart of the fire, turning it as the metal began to move through rainbows of colour, the grey melting away into the flames, changing to orange and becoming part of the fire. He slid the blank from the fire and rested it under the water hammer. The mighty hammer fell onto the metal until it began to change shape, with orange sparks flying around in the dark forge. As soon as the blank lost its colour and began returning to grey, he put it back into the fire, rekindling the flame in the metal before hammering it out again and again and again. Sweat haled from his brow and ran into his eyes, making them sting and he swiped his forearm across them, making matters worse.

He felt bad for giving his daughter such short shrift. She'd always been fascinated by forge work. No son meant no one to hand his life's work on to. Half of him wished he could apprentice her but it would do no good to give her false hopes of becoming a swordmaker. Who'd want to marry such a girl?

When the blank began to take on the form of a sword, Hermann moved it to an anvil and struck the blade quickly with a hand hammer, watching the orange fading to grey. He continued to heat the steel and beat the orange out of it, hammering a bevel on each side.

Once satisfied with the overall shape, he examined the length of the dull, grey blade, squinting at it through first one eye and then the other. It was straight enough and it would soon be sharp but that would have to wait. For now, he had another task ahead of him.

Hermann led the white mare from the paddock down into the river. She must have been magnificent in her youth but her best days were behind her now and Maddison had replaced her with a grey mare. The madman had been reluctant to part with her, even though she was good for no more than flattening grass and making manure, but gold had a way of persuading men against their better judgement. Maddison had taken the money offered and Hermann had taken the mare. The beast's brown eyes followed the lure of a rosy apple and she came quietly enough, if uncertainly. It was best not to look into those eyes.

While the morning was cold, with a light frost coating the grass, she pulsed with heat, and Hermann pressed himself against her, sharing her warmth. He led her through the water, and after they'd climbed the riverbank, they approached the clearing where his neighbours were massed. The old mare snickered and trembled. So now she knew her fate, as all living creatures understood their fate. He stroked her nose.

'Ach, horsey, it comes to us all and you're too old to earn your keep anymore. It's a better end for you this way. Take it from one who knows.'

But she wouldn't take another step, pulling her head to gaze back at her old master and the safe paddock. Not even an apple was enough to persuade her to part with this sweet life. When big Oligh ran forwards to take the rope, the mare shied.

A shout came from across the river, 'You cruel bastards!'

Hermann turned just as Maddison fired a stone at the mare's rump, causing her to rear so she had to be pulled down by a half-dozen men heaving on her rope. Her eyes bulged. Foam appeared on her flanks and at her nose and mouth. Finally, the men got her to the ground and fastened her legs, although she redoubled her efforts to rise, cutting her legs on the bindings as she thrashed. The men and boys took out their flenching knives and the women and girls came scurrying with dishes. The mare panted, great plumes of steam rising into the cold air.

'Come, horsey,' Hermann said. 'Enough.' He placed a hand on the pulse at the mare's neck, feeling the life pounding through her. She was old but she didn't know that. She'd worked hard by the looks of her and deserved a better ending than this. He held his breath, braced himself and drew his knife quickly across her throat. Hot blood coursed from the wound. The mare tried to gain her feet and had to be pinned down by the men, her legs thrashing as the lifeblood left her. Once Hermann had wielded the knife, his mother held the pail to catch the nourishing blood, her eyes gleaming. The old woman never faltered from this work and even relished it. A line of women stood behind her, ready to take the full pail and pass an empty one, the men straining to hold the thrashing creature down.

Finally, the great heart seized and the mare lay still, awash with blood and gently steaming in the cold air.

'Now!' he shouted.

At Hermann's word, the men set forth with knives to skin and gut the animal, removing her organs and bowels into pails before quartering her. The smell of the rich, dark meat made his mouth water and he cut himself a cube of hot flesh from the heart and swallowed it without chewing. Living flesh. No meat quite like it. He turned at the sound of sobbing to see his daughter and Pieter Schimmelbusch holding hands, and beside them, the English boy, Joseph. Liesl was fair-haired, Pieter dark and Joseph ginger, but all three were pale faced. The madman stood across the river, rubbing his eyes and shaking his fists, his black hair standing in spikes.

Hermann haled his daughter, who ignored him and turned her back on the butchering. So Liesl and her friends were in sympathy with the madman. Good meat and yet here was his own girl turning up her nose. It wouldn't do for Liesl to take on these English ways.

Hermann blinked at his wife. 'It will cost how much?'

'Don't say it like that. It's not so very much …' Katrin lifted a pan of boiled sausages from the flame and placed it on the waiting trivet. 'Not when it's in the praise of God Almighty.'

Liesl sat cross-legged on the mat, Griselda's head in her lap, working on her sampler. His mother dozed before the window with the sun on her face but it was hard to tell whether she was asleep or not. The last thing he wanted was for her to wake up right now – she loved causing trouble more than she enjoyed napping – but the old woman staged a yawn and sat up, eyes glittering with spite. Hermann cursed himself for handing his mother the perfect opportunity to cut Katrin down to size.

'Ah, Katrin Gerner,' his mother said. 'Never afraid to invoke God if it will help your argument.'

'Anna Mohll, you're not helping,' Katrin said. 'Besides, the name Mohll is as much mine as it is yours.'

'My job isn't to help but to make sure we do what's right and best for our family.' The old woman smiled and reached for her snuff. 'Well, Hermann,' she said, 'you're right to be concerned about the cost. It's good to proclaim our faith but we don't need gaudy carvings to do it. After all, aren't we supposed to be humble Lutherans and not vulgar papists, although they say the Catholic king won't see out the year.'

'Don't wish ill on King James, Anna, Catholic or not,' Katrin said. 'And yes, we're humble Lutherans so that means we have to proclaim our faith.'

Mother cleared her throat, which always signalled war. Hermann dreaded what was coming next.

'You see, Son,' his mother said, 'this is what happens when wives have too much time on their hands. They get ideas and these ideas cost gold. You're not working her hard enough.'

Katrin set down a dinner platter so hard that the pea soup slopped over the rim and soaked into the embroidered tablecloth. 'I'll thank you to stay out of matters that don't concern you, Anna.'

His mother eyed her half-empty platter and Hermann got up to fetch his own soup.

'That's right,' his mother said, 'you fetch your own dinner or it might end up decorating the table, too. Your fault for choosing a wife with such a temper on her.'

'Mother. Stop trying to provoke war and eat your dinner. This is your favourite and you must admit that Katrin is an excellent cook.'

The excellent cook picked up a cloth and began dabbing at the spilt soup. 'Never mind flattery,' Katrin said. 'If you don't want to proclaim our faith, Hermann, you've only to say so.'

But his mother wasn't finished yet and brandished her spoon.

'Son,' she said, 'don't let her browbeat you into going against your will. You don't know how to stand up for yourself properly. This is what comes of growing up without a man in the house.'

Ah, so it was time to play the suffering widow. Now he'd be reminded of all she'd lost and all she'd given up to raise him after his father died and how it was a miracle he'd turned into such a decent man with no father to influence him since the age of twelve.

Hermann blew on his soup and took a spoonful. 'Are all the families to have these stone tablets?' he asked.

'Those who can afford them, yes,' replied Katrin.

'Those who can afford them? So hardly any amongst us,' he said. Hermann certainly wouldn't want to waste money on something so expensive yet so useless and he marvelled at the idea that any of his neighbours could afford such vanity. 'And who's the carver?'

'A Newcastle mason.'

'And will this Newcastle mason grasp our language?' he asked. 'Anyway, since each German already knows the faith of the family next door, shouldn't our proclamation be in English?'

'Of course not,' Katrin said, 'how would we read them if they were in English? Most of us women can scarcely read our own language let alone another one.' She ladled more soup into his bowl. 'You know, we have to think about Liesl and her future.'

Hermann glanced at the girl, whose head was bowed, wisely keeping out of this skirmish.

'And when we can't afford to feed our daughter, who pretends to work on her sampler but who is really eavesdropping,' he said, 'she can kneel on the doorstep to admire the lintel instead and say her prayers.'

Liesl's head jerked up, showing a pink face. 'Father, I was never eavesdropping.'

'Hermann,' Katrin said, 'you can never give in graciously, can you?'

'No.' He grinned. 'Now, are those sausages ready yet?'

Liesl pulled a face. 'I'm not hungry.'

His mother threw up her hands. 'We've not been in this confounded country two minutes and already it's started,' she said. 'What's wrong with you, Liesl? Why aren't you sitting at the table enjoying your dinner?'

'I'm too busy, Grandmother Mohll, because I'm making a cushion for Father's Christmas present.' The girl held up her embroidery. 'Besides, I can't possibly eat horseflesh.'

'Why not?' asked Hermann, eyeing her needlework, which showed the outline of a family of three deer. There were no more than two lines of stitches filled in so he wouldn't be receiving that present any Christmas soon. He wondered which Christmas he would receive it. 'You've eaten it all your life and you love it best of all with green cabbage and white sauce.'

'But that was before today,' replied Liesl. The pasty child turned her wide blue eyes on him. 'Pieter Schimmelbusch said that Joseph Leaton said that horses aren't food animals.' She pulled the hound closer to her. 'And he said that Joseph Leaton would no sooner eat a horse than a dog.'

Hermann wiped soup from his moustaches. Judging by his thinness, the poor English lad would eat whatever was put in front of him. Doubtless his mother couldn't afford to put such good meat on the table. 'Of course he wouldn't eat a dog,' he said. 'We wouldn't eat a dog. They're flesh eaters.'

'Well so are pigs, Father.'

'They are, girl, and they're more intelligent than dogs,' he said. 'Even more so than Griselda there.'

'Indeed,' his mother said. 'More so than many boys, especially English boys. Your trouble, Liesl, is that you've never known hunger. When I was a girl, the townspeople killed the starving horses fetching newcomers to town, often before they'd dismounted–'

'Mother ...' A note of warning crept into Hermann's voice. His daughter looked fit to faint as it was. He leant over the table. 'Come, Liesl, your mother worked hard today and it's a shame to allow good flesh to waste.'

But his spoilt girl shook her head. 'I can't eat it,' she said. 'Not now I know what it is ... after seeing what I saw today.'

Katrin set out platters of sausage and cabbage. 'Well, I'll keep some in case you change your mind,' she said. 'When you're hungry enough.'

His mother cut into the dark meat and dipped it into the rich sauce. 'You don't know what you're missing, Liesl. You young people. You won't drink schnapps. You won't eat horse. No wonder you're all so lily-livered.' She raised her glass and quaffed its contents. 'Get some of this inside you, girl. You're old enough now.'

'Mother, you will not give Liesl schnapps.' Hermann snatched the glass away. 'And stop this daytime drinking before it finishes you off.'

Katrin raised a brow and smiled. 'We can but live in hope.'

But his mother wasn't to be deterred. 'Son, Liesl's easily big enough,' she said, 'I was weaned on it.' She held up the bottle to the girl, who dipped her eyes.

'Thank you, Grandmother Mohll, but I'll stick to beer if I may?' Hermann leant down and patted his daughter's arm.

'Sensible girl.'

'Father, your hands are shaking,' said Liesl, looking up at him. 'How do you ever grind a straight fuller?'

His mother grinned and pointed at the confiscated glass.

'With this enchanted potion, of course. Once swallowed, his hands magically stop shaking.'

Hermann put down the glass with a thump. 'Mother ...'

'It can hardly be a secret from the girl,' she said. 'So many secrets. So many lies. How am I meant to keep track of them all?

It's not my fault if some slip from my mouth now and again. I can't be on guard all day every day, can I?'

⌒

Hermann returned from the forge to find Katrin out and his mother in fine fettle, pacing back and forth on the mat, filling Liesl's ears with tales of the old days. He stood close by, ready to stop the old woman if she went too far.

'There were such sights for me as a girl,' she said. 'Each year, Liesl, all the men had to go and swear fealty to the elector: my father, my grandfather, my uncles, my brothers. My mother gave birth to many sons. Not like your mother.'

Thank God Katrin wasn't here to be stung by this barb.

'And not like my own mother,' Hermann said. 'Liesl, you are blessing enough to us.'

His girl wrinkled her nose, smiled and went back to her grandmother's story.

Certainly, this tale belonged to Hermann's father but his mother had woven it into her own memories to replace those that had fallen out of her head on that terrible night all those years ago. The old woman went on to tell her rapt granddaughter about the castle gates being opened to admit throngs of people, who were showered with pieces of silver and gold as they entered. Best of all was the stone eagle spouting great gouts of wine – red and white. Such tales. He'd heard them time and again as a boy.

The old woman turned on her heel. 'But my proudest sight was to watch our men kneel,' she said. 'Now, Liesl, do you want to be the elector or his subject?'

How many times had Hermann played this game with his mother as a boy? He'd badly wanted to play the elector but the gleam in his mother's eye told him she'd be nobody's subject.

Liesl sighed. 'I'll be the subject, Grandmother Mohll.'

'Good girl. Come, kneel before me.' His mother pointed to

the mat. 'Now, fold your arm – yes, like so – place your left hand across your chest, over your heart, yes. The right hand, you must raise above your head. No. Here. Like so.' She arranged Liesl's hands to her satisfaction, oblivious to the fact that the girl looked weary of the game. 'Now hold up your thumb and the next two fingers. Tuck the others away.'

Hermann found himself folding his own fingers. It was hard to keep the two smallest fingers tucked down as they strained to stand up. His mother tapped his daughter's thumb and told her what it stood for: God the Father. Next, she tapped Liesl's pointing finger: God the Son. The middle one was God the Holy Ghost and the trembling ring finger was the sacred soul. The pinkie was the body, because it was smaller and less important than the soul.

The girl examined her ring finger. 'Really? So how does the soul stay in place when it's bigger than the body?'

'Quite simple,' his mother said. 'The soul is one of two things. In some people, it's folded over a thousand times into something small and mean, with many dark corners and sharp points. In others, it's a cloud floating around them, which lights them and keeps them warm.'

'Which am I?' Liesl asked. 'What kind of soul do I have?'

'Oh, your soul is like that of all children,' his mother said, 'a soft cloud. Only you can decide how it will be when you're grown up.'

His daughter looked so solemn swearing fealty to his mother. How well he remembered this moment from his boyhood. He'd sworn never to become a man with a folded soul, determined that his would contain not so much as a crease. Mother had rubbed his hair, saying that he'd have the biggest, most precious soul of all. Her eyes had twinkled but they held a shadow. Now, as a man, he wondered how many times his mother had folded her own soul to get through life.

A SCURVY LOT

Morpeth Gaol, 1703

*T*he four mariners from the *Eufro Angelique* were dragged
in today. What a scurvy lot. No doubt found within striking distance of the fleshmarkets. Roasting Jack nearly bust a
gut barking at them. Running backwards and forwards he was,
dragging his splinted leg behind him. At least one old salt's foot
tapped with the itch to kick him. Sharp thought better of it,
mind. Nothing wrong with the little dog's teeth.

Not a single travelling paper between them. Lost at sea by
all accounts. A likely tale. Their true names are anyone's guess
but they called themselves Robert Jacobsen, John Cornelius,
Thomas Roberts and John Harrison. Never a Cornelius across
my threshold in twenty-odd years and now two in as many days.
I wondered if this one was related to Soldart in some way but the
mariners' lips were buttoned. Cannot say there was any family
resemblance shouting out to me but blood doesn't always show
itself in height and complexion.

It was a mistake to keep them together with their non-stop
shouting and jabbering away in two tongues. They've seen some
sights these mariners, what with Holland bearing the brunt of
the war. Hard to get them to talk about much else. It took a
while, and it took a lot more than liquid persuasion, but I finally

got the mariners talking about the soldiers on board their vessel. At first, there was some carry-on about how many redcoats were on the ship. At the finish, they settled on six soldiers, but they were hard pushed to remember more than one name between them. Sergeant John Ross was the only name I managed to get. A beardless swain who'd left his regiment overseas and come home recruiting. They'll need all the men they can get now that half the world's at war and with no sign of it ending. All those lives wasted for the want of a Spanish heir. What's wrong with these kings and queens who cannot make a bairn or keep one alive? Pray God we put the French in their place soon and bring our lads home safe and sound.

For all the mariners knew plenty about Sergeant Ross, they knew not a jot about the other redcoats. Still, one name was enough for now. If I could get my hands on Ross, he'd give me the others soon enough. The mariners reckoned Ross haled from Morpeth. A bit too nice and handy, but a warrant went out to fetch him in sharpish and we'll soon find out if the Jack Tars are spinning me a yarn.

When it came to the foreign passenger, these water dogs weren't much more talkative than their master. What are they trying to cover up? They did let slip that their foreigner was a German. This must be the rogue that has half the north in pursuit of him. To a man, the mariners denied knowing what kind of booty was hidden in the straw bundles – even when pressed. The ship could have sunk under their not-so-watchful gaze. Never in all my born days have I met a bunch of swabbers so uncurious about their own cargo. They'll be having their fists greased. There's not a sailor on the high seas who doesn't have the heart of a privateer. All it takes to reveal it is the glimmer of gold. Well, I can do no more to them now and only time will tell.

It gave me a headache working out where to put everyone. All this shunting prisoners back and forth, with not so much as an extra shilling for my trouble. The mariners couldn't go in with Burke in case they were known to one another. Not in with their master in case they thought he'd named them and did him some harm. So Soldart went in with Walter as they share the same flavour of religion, which meant the mariners could go in with the local lads. What the locals lack in years, they make up for in fighting spirit. Fighting's bred in the bone in these parts. With any luck, they'll all be evenly matched and not bother tiring themselves out too much.

THE LETTER

Shotley Bridge, 1688

*H*ermann came in, freshly washed by river water, put his arms around Katrin and kissed her behind the ear. 'Something smells delicious.' He hoped it was beef now they'd finally finished eating Maddison's mare. 'Is it *Leberknödel?*'

'Yes, with broth,' she said and wriggled free to lift a liver dumpling from the pot before pointing at the mantel with her long spoon. 'There's a letter.'

'From Henry Benson, about his unpaid bill?' he asked.

'No, it's from home. In my mother's hand.'

Hermann wedged a knuckle in his ear, rubbing it round and round, before picking up the letter and running a fingertip over the seal. 'But why has she addressed it to me?' he asked, turning the letter over and holding it up to the light from the window.

'Aren't you going to open it?' Katrin asked.

'After supper.' He put it back onto the mantel and came to sit at the table. 'Liesl and my mother not back from the market yet?'

'Not yet,' she replied, 'and I'm starting to get worried.'

'When there's so much to see and so many people to gossip about? They'll not leave until they're forced out or the sun sets. They'll be fine,' he said, 'so stop fretting.'

Their daughter wasn't the real cause of his wife's worry. This letter staring down from the mantel had to be bad news. Why would Frau Gerner write to him and not to her own daughter? Someone must have died. One of Katrin's sisters, perhaps, or one of their children. But in that case, the letter would've been addressed to her. Hermann had no family left in Solingen so whose death would warrant a letter being sent overseas to him?

It was still light and the sun wouldn't fall for another hour. His mother and daughter would be back soon. Liesl would make certain of that as she didn't like being away from home after dark. 'Shall we wait until everyone's home?' he asked.

'To open the letter?'

'No, to eat,' he said. 'Better to dine as a family.'

'And let my best broth spoil? Liesl will have filled herself up with savouries from one barrow or another, no doubt. And she'll have to roll Griselda home as it is.' Katrin got up to fetch bowls from the dresser and ladled out beef broth. 'We'll eat now and your mother can warm some if she wants it.'

Hermann sniffed. 'I hope there are plenty of dumplings.'

'You'll be a dumpling yourself if you keep eating this way.'

'Is there something sweet for after?' he asked with a wink.

'There's a cherry tart that Frau Johnson fetched down this morning, although it's beyond me how you can think of eating, with that letter glowering down from the mantel. In any case, it may be good news.'

When did letters ever bring good news? 'Whatever it is, it'll keep until we've finished.'

He sat down and patted her chair until she joined him. They began to eat, but after a mouthful, Katrin put down her eating knife and pressed one hand to her sternum.

'What's the matter, *Liebling*?' he asked. 'Has something stuck? Here, wash it down with beer.'

Katrin took the proffered tankard and drank a sip. 'It's like a vice has gripped me and the dumpling has stuck near my heart.'

She pushed away her bowl and breathed out deeply. 'Please open the letter, Hermann. My meal is ruined as it is.'

'Cut from the same cloth as your father, aren't you?' he said. The man had suffered nervous digestion all his short life.

Hermann leant back in his chair to pluck the letter from the mantel and weighed it in his hand. The thickness of the letter didn't bode well. Still, it might set his wife's mind at rest. He wiped his knife on his breeches, slit the letter open and drew out some papers. Katrin came and held back the curtain to offer extra light. He shuffled the pages and drew out a folded leaf of paper, smoothed it out and read it twice before looking up. He tugged his beard as he read to the end.

'What is it?' she asked. 'Has something happened to my mother or sisters? Hermann, don't even think of lying to me. You're much too honest. I can see your face contorting at the thought of misleading me. Spit it out, word for word, or I'll read it myself.'

'No, no, nothing like that,' he said. 'It's not about your family.' He jabbed at some words with a soot-marked finger. 'It's just a notice that was pinned to your mother's door – to all the families' doors. To our door.'

'*Just* a notice. Oh, this can't be good. What does it say?'

'It says …' He drew in a breath and leaned nearer to the window. 'It's from the court, from the lay assessors. They accuse us of absconding even though we're bound to Solingen.'

Katrin let go of the curtain and sank into the chair next to him. 'Not even the guild. It's the court. That's much worse.'

He placed his hand over hers. 'Shall I continue?'

She nodded at him.

He ran his finger down the indictment until he found his place again. 'Here we are. It says our leaving has become notorious and see here … it lists all our names.'

Katrin pointed to his name on the notice. 'Why are you

mentioned first?' she asked. 'Do they think you're the main culprit?'

'If you'll let me finish, *Liebe*.'

'Who else is named?'

He placed his thumb on the page and read out their neighbours' names.

'Oh, what a muddled list,' she said. 'It's hard to tell who's who. They can't even get half the names right.' She moved his thumb out of the way. 'But you're mentioned first. That must signify they hold you more responsible than the others.' She held her hands up to her mouth. 'This sounds bad. Is it?'

'It may not be as bad as it sounds—'

'Of course it's bad.' Katrin's voice rose. 'What else does it say?'

In future, he'd have their post delivered to the forge to avoid this kind of upset. 'Are you sure you want to hear it?' he asked.

She nodded. 'I must hear it, no matter how terrible.'

'It goes on to say that we need to return in the next six weeks and three days or give sound reasons for our defection ...' He paused to work out how much of that time they had left. The notice was dated the twenty-sixth day of September 1688, which was more than a year after they'd left. Frau Gerner had sent the letter straight away but the long sea voyage and the journey by horse and foot to their door had eaten into the time. By the looks of the notice, they'd already had three warnings and this was their final one. How had they not had wind of anything sooner? What was afoot?

Katrin nudged him. 'Go on,' she said. 'Stop wondering whether to spare me the next part. Finish it. I can see in your eyes that there's more to come, *worse* to come.'

Would it be possible to make something up? Something that might spare his wife unnecessary worry? She could read a little but he could toss this letter on the fire as if it were trivial. 'I think it's nothing much to worry about.' He saw her face and

held up a hand. 'Alright, alright, I'm getting on with it. It says …
it warns us that if we don't go back, they will carry out … legal
proceedings against us.'

'Proceedings.' she said. 'What proceedings can they possibly
mean?'

Hermann slid the paper in front of her so his wife could see for
herself. Her reading was much slower than his and he tried hard
not to drum his fingers. Of course, Katrin would imagine the
worst. It was as well his mother wasn't here to add fuel to the fire.

'Hermann, we have to go back home.' She stood and turned to
face him, face pleated with worry. 'Will they punish our families,
do you think? Will they execute them? Is it possible that …?'

'No. No, Katrin, you mustn't foresee catastrophe everywhere.
This is Solingen we're talking about, not England, where they
hang urchins for stealing halfpenny loaves.'

'Don't you dare make light of this,' she said. 'Our families
could still be punished … my poor mother. Remember Johann
Knechtgen! They caught him and look what happened.'

'Oh, *Liebe*, that was, what … seventy-five years ago? They
don't do that sort of thing anymore. Besides, they caught him.
They can't catch us if we don't go back …' But he was talking to
himself. There was no point arguing with Katrin when she was in
this mood. It was in her nature to jump to the worst conclusion
possible. 'I'm sure they won't be punished.'

She ran a fingernail across her top lip, pushing all the blood
out of it. 'You *hope* our families won't be punished,' she said. 'You
don't know for sure they're safe.'

'You're right, of course, but I'm sure your mother and sisters
will be fine.' He opened his arms and drew her towards him,
breathing in ginger, cinnamon and rose water. Why on earth had
the court issued this notice a whole year after they'd gone? It
made no sense at all. 'I'll go and speak to Oligh about it and see
what might be done.'

She jerked back from him. 'Oh, because Adam has all the answers, does he?'

He took a deep breath before answering her. 'No, *Liebe*, but he has a different way of seeing things and it can't hurt to hear what he thinks, can it?'

'Well, you might as well eat your meal, Hermann, because nothing will keep Adam from his meat.'

He smiled a half-smile and took the notice from her. 'This might well keep Oligh from his meat. No need to give me that look, *Liebe*. You're right. I'll let the man eat before I disturb him but my appetite's gone now.' He put a hand over his heart. 'I'm sorry.'

She sniffed and passed him his pipe. He took out his small knives and set about cleaning it while he read the notice again.

When Oligh joined him on the riverbank, Hermann handed over the letter and while his friend strained his eyes to read it in the dying light, he drew on his pipe.

After a long while, Oligh folded the pages and handed them back to Hermann. 'Will you share this with the others?' he asked.

'Of course,' Hermann replied. 'Do you think it warrants a meeting?'

Oligh wrinkled his long nose, inhaling sharply. 'It might well do and it would be best to let everyone know at the same time,' he said. 'Shall we say in ten minutes at the church? The men should have finished eating by now. Come, let's get knocking.'

When all the men were gathered and the candles lit, Hermann read out the indictment. There was a hush in the church as the news was digested.

Finally, Heinrich Wupper broke the silence. 'Why's it taken them so long to get around to it?' he asked. 'It can't have taken them all this time to realise we're missing, surely?'

Hermann shook his head. 'More like there's a slow hand cranking the machinery of the law,' he replied.

Schimmelbusch stepped forwards, took the notice and sat down to study it, with Tiergarten looking over his shoulder.

'These notices were put up to frighten any other men who might get ideas about leaving,' Hermann said. 'Solingen wouldn't do so well if all the workers left, would it? You'll see I'm right. This indictment is just for show and has no teeth.'

Tiergarten jabbed the air with a forefinger. 'Easy for you to say, Mohll,' he shouted. 'But you can't know that for sure. Remember Knechtgen! Oh, I knew it was a bad idea coming here.' He turned to appeal to his countrymen. 'We must go back now. They gave us forty-five days from the date of the notice.' He counted on his fingers. 'Leaving us a bare thirty-three days. There's no time to lose. I wish we'd never come.'

Trust Tiergarten. He could always be relied on to be gloom-laden but Hermann worried he might set the other men off if he wasn't calmed down fast. 'It's a mere rap on the knuckles,' Hermann said, reasonably. 'The Solingen authorities have to be seen to be doing something. The guild was glad to see the back of us. Less contest for work. If we were to roll home on wagons next month, they'd no doubt pin notices to our doors telling us to get out again.'

This raised a few half-hearted laughs but Oligh glared at him. 'Mohll,' he said, 'you can't make this a laughing matter. It's serious. Potentially, deadly serious.'

'True, very true, Oligh, old friend,' said Hermann, 'but this is the officials justifying their positions and the taxes they steal from the working man. All they're doing is showing us their sabres.'

Tiergarten's leg was joggling up and down, moving of its own accord, as if he wanted to start running home already.

'Yes,' he shouted. 'Showing us their sabres in readiness to cut our throats.'

Hermann ignored the hysterical man and turned to address his countrymen again.

'Look, they're most worried about what?' he asked.

'What are they most worried about?' Wupper replied, wriggling his brows and grinning. 'Us giving up the secret of our famous hollow blade, of course.'

Good old Wupper. He could always be relied on for support. 'Exactly,' Hermann said. 'This is a reminder and nothing more. The burghers are rattling their chains to remind us that we're still under their watch. These notices are nothing more than empty threats.'

Tiergarten piped up again. 'Aren't you worried by the fact they've nailed a notice on our doors and our families' doors?'

'On the doors,' Hermann replied, 'it's the usual way. Nothing to lose sleep over.'

But Tiergarten wasn't to be convinced. 'Little point when they know we're not behind the doors. It sounds to me as though they've taken inventory of our properties, preparatory to seizing them.'

Hermann scratched his brow and caught Oligh's eye. Was that fear he saw there?

'Tiergarten,' said Hermann, 'I'm willing to wager in twenty years' time, when you're six feet under, your property will still be in your family.'

'Twenty years?' asked Tiergarten. 'You don't measure me much time left on earth, Mohll.'

Tiergarten's voice had taken on a whine and Hermann's blood began to boil. This problem could best be solved by putting the nervous man out. Or knocking him out.

Oligh gave him a guarded glance and stood to join him – no doubt to save Tiergarten from a well-deserved blow. The big man pointed at the letter, which Schimmelbusch was still poring over. 'For safety, I'll send the notice to Carnforth and ask him to speak to the company men. Get them to make some enquiries,' Oligh said. 'No doubt, we'll all receive similar letters in time. For now, there's nothing we can do.'

It was doubtful the Newcastle swordmaker could achieve much but there was no harm in Oligh having a word with him. Carnforth had the ear of the company men and they had friends in high places.

Tiergarten refused to be soothed and shook his head.

'You're wrong, Oligh,' he said. 'There is something we could do. We could go home. We have thirty-three days and if we hurry, that's just long enough to get back home. This notice has been carefully calculated to give us time to return,' he turned to leave the church, 'and don't tell me we have to honour the contract with the English king.'

Tiergarten was wrong. They couldn't ignore their contract even if they went back to Germany because King James' influence stretched across the sea. Even without any threat from the English king and his emissaries, Hermann was damned if he would go back to Solingen with his tail between his legs and he had to make sure the others stayed here. Tiergarten wasn't going anywhere. The man wasn't stupid and understood the weight of their contract as well as Hermann did. It was merely panic but it could soon infect the others and make them start to think about leaving, which would make it impossible to meet their orders.

Hermann had to try a different tack. He yanked a hand in the air. 'So, Mother Government pulls on her apron strings and we all obey like simpering babies?' he asked. 'No, I vote we stay–'

But it was too late. Tiergarten had gone and slammed the door behind him.

The noise must have disturbed Schimmelbusch, who now stood up and planted himself squarely in front of Hermann, waving the notice in his face. 'Mohll, you're too quick to speak for other men,' he said. 'Let's wait to hear from our own families before we decide what to do.'

Hermann had known Schimmelbusch since they were boys, fighting with their first swords. He rubbed his right thigh where he still bore the scar inflicted by his childhood enemy when they were seven. Was Schimmelbusch here to deal him another blow? Hermann squared his shoulders.

Oligh edged in front of him and spread out his hands.

'Schimmelbusch,' he said. 'Yes, you're right to wait for news from your own people. For now, brothers, let us pray together for our families in Solingen. They're closer to the source of this woe and must feel the worry far more than us who are distant. Come, let us pray.'

Hermann bowed his head. Oligh was so skilled at bringing peace, being every man's friend and always knowing the right thing to say. And such stentorian tones – perfect for prayer and politics in equal measure. Truly, the man was born with gold in his mouth.

QUITE A KNAVE

Morpeth Gaol, 1703

S eems the mariners were telling the truth. Sergeant John
Ross got dragged in today with a face on him like a bairn's
smacked arse. Cannot say I blame him. No man wants to be
away from his loved ones at Yuletide. It's the best time of the
year. For those with family, at any rate.

He's a bonny-enough lad, the Morpeth sergeant, still shiny-
faced and not much in the way of whiskers. Well brought up,
though, and knows how to behave. Showed his furlough papers
right off and rubbed Roasting Jack's breast. The lad's a grenadier
in the Scots Fusiliers, quartered in Brabant at Flanders. That's
a canny way to come when he has no sweetheart to put in the
family way. Released for a quarter by his major to recruit more
men for the Duke of Marlborough. Ross was lucky to make it
across the sea and I don't like his chances of making it back in
February with so much war at play. His papers looked in good
order to me but they still had to be horsed down to Whitehall so
some London wiseacre can give them the old say-so.

Ross reckoned he'd sailed into Jarrow on Soldart's vessel and
set away home to Morpeth as soon as he landed. Swore he'd seen
neither hide nor hair of his shipmates since Newcastle. A tough
lad but I'm nothing if not perseverant and I finally got some

names out of him. First was Joseph Heron, bagman to Captain Ramsay from Brinkburn. Serving in Colonel Colyear's regiment and stationed at Bergen-Op-Zoom. Sounded a made-up name to me but Ross promised it was a real town in Holland. This Heron was due to land his master's baggage at Howdon Panns at Wallsend. I'd give a limb to know what was in that bag. Not coal or salt, I'll warrant, but it'll be long emptied by now. Then there was one Robert Dodsworth, a volunteer in the same regiment as Heron. The best of pals, no doubt. He was coming home to see his sweetheart in Framlington. So she's most likely in the straw by now. Third was Captain Robert Carr from the Earl of Orkney's regiment. This Carr had been given his discharge and was away back to Scotland. Aye, hurrying homeward to sign up for the other side, I'll wager. Fourth was an Irish man, Christopher, but Ross had a failure of memory – or imagination – when it came to any family name. Another one given his walking papers from Orkney's regiment. They must like to travel in twos these redcoats. Fifth was John Granger, a carabineer in Colonel Wyndham's Horse. The cavalry man was on furlough as well, going home to Barnard Castle down in the bishopric.

So many men coming home to recruit. Marlborough must be fairly grinding his way through young lads. All this fighting from one end of the continent to the other just to keep a French arse off the Spanish throne. All those lads' lives wasted, dragged from their mothers' tits half of them, and sent to die on foreign soil. Well, good luck to Ross and Granger getting their neighbours to part with their sons. Must be a blessing to have daughters these days. God knows when this war will end. I might see the end of it but I doubt young Sergeant Ross will if he goes back over there.

For all he gave me the redcoats' names, it took some doing to get Ross to talk about the German. But I have my ways and he finally gave him up. This man was aboard the ship with his wife and a tall, blonde lass of marrying age. Strikes me that Ross had high hopes in that direction. The German worked as a swordmaker at Shotley Bridge down in the bishopric and was on his way back there. So the bundles must have been swords. Now all the commotion adds up. That Soldart's a born liar, claiming he'd no notion of what was fetched onto his ship. Bundles of straw, my backside. Swords are hardly as light as straw. Ross must have bad eyes as he hadn't seen them either but at least he managed to remember the foreigner's name, 'A fellow by the name of Hermann. Imagine it, Hermann the German!' Had himself a right good laugh at his bit joke. Won't laugh for long in here.

So, nine passengers all told. A right funny little party to be sailing the high seas through winter, war and tempest. What kind of man would take his womenfolk on an arms-smuggling venture? Quite a knave this German must be, quite a knave.

The Grey Mare

Shotley Bridge, 1688

*T*he river was high after all the rain and the rushing sound disturbed Hermann in the half-light. He woke with the word defection in his mouth and shook his head to rid himself of it. Their forty-five days had run out but they'd hear no more from Solingen. Hermann would bet his life on it – had already bet his life on it. The notice was no more than a ruse, simply the guild wanting to make sure no more men left. More worrying than empty threats from back home was the fact that Thomas Carnforth hadn't been successful and there'd been no help forthcoming from the company men. There were days when he wished they'd never left home.

The sun wasn't fully up yet but he was no longer tired and could hear Katrin stoking the fire downstairs, so he got up. The floor was cold to his sleep-warm feet and he shivered as he went to check on his mother. Her bed was empty again. She'd be in the forge, no doubt, praying over the swords, shivering and half-famished.

Downstairs, Katrin had her back turned, kneading dough to make their daily bread, and Liesl lurked in the corner, running a finger over the face of the clock. He sat down at the table and began putting on his boots.

'Father, the clock sounds slow,' said Liesl, her ear pressed against the dark wooden case. 'Might I wind it?'

'No, *Liebchen*, in case you overwind it,' he replied. 'It's been temperamental since we moved here. It must be wound once a day at the same hour so the time from Solingen is never lost. See, whenever we look at it, our thoughts can wander back home. If it's Sunday at seven o'clock, Grandmother Gerner will be at prayer.'

Theirs was the only clock in the street, a treasure from the old country, so it had to be held in keeping for all. The tick of the clock slowed his heartbeat and breathing as he imagined his countrymen, heads bowed in the cool interior of their chapel. But that same clock might have another story: it might count the seconds remaining in a long sentence or the seconds remaining in a shortened life. He shook these thoughts away and pulled on his boots. This was the indictment making him mawkish.

Katrin looked at the clock. 'Is our time up now?'

'Yes,' he said. 'Today, the clock has run down on our forty-five days. But don't worry, *Liebe*, I promise you, that indictment holds no power.'

His wife didn't speak and continued staring at the clock, perhaps expecting it to stop, but soon turned back to kneading the dough.

He knew Katrin was still worried sick and nothing he could say would convince her otherwise but now she'd see that nothing bad was going to happen. His wife wasn't alone in her worrying, of course. Many of the swordmakers were still fretting. Tiergarten mostly, but even Oligh was concerned in his quiet way, although that was mainly because he wasn't a natural rule-breaker.

'Liesl,' he said. 'I'm taking Griselda out to seek your grandmother. She's out wandering again. If your mother doesn't need you to help with the bread, do you want to come?'

Katrin nodded her assent and the girl put on her clogs. Hermann called the hound and they wandered along the riverbank. The sky was blue and the trees were still clothed but winter was in the air and the leaves would fall before too long. The river was in spate and flowing fast so he pulled Liesl back from the edge.

Overhead, there was honking and he pointed to the sky.

'See, the geese, Liesl? They bring their young to gentler climes to feed.' He watched their V formation and wondered if that's what he'd done but decided he was different to a goose. Geese always had elsewhere to be and no one place was their home, whereas man built nests of stone and his possessions weighted him to the earth.

'Come, let's see if we can find your grandmother.' The hound followed at their heels as they walked alongside the river. 'Derwent. It means sparkling water, or laughing water, you know.'

'It's sparkly *and* laughy,' she said. 'Is this river joined to the Wupper at home?'

He considered this. 'I'm not so sure, *Liebchen*.' Certainly, it carried a different scent.

'Do you think it might be a silver ribbon, wrapping itself around the world, leading from me to Grandmother Gerner? I miss her. Do you think she misses me?'

'Of course she does.' Hermann smothered a smile. As if his own mother wasn't enough grandmother for one lifetime. 'But I don't know about your silver ribbon. Rivers emerge as springs and run towards the sea.'

'What if the silver ribbon runs through the earth as well?'

He patted Liesl's head. 'That's a lovely thought and I'm sure Grandmother Gerner thinks of you and your mother whenever she's by the river.' Had he done the right thing splitting his wife and daughter from Frau Gerner? It had felt right at the time but now he wondered.

Liesl skipped at his side. 'Father, can we speak in English, please? Me and Pieter have been teaching Joseph German and he's been teaching us English.'

He frowned at this request. Whether at his daughter wanting to speak English or Joseph learning German, he couldn't be certain, but it was no good trying to stop her now when her ears had filled with English already and her tongue would wind around it easily enough, but Katrin wouldn't take it well, to say nothing of Oligh.

The hound dropped a stick at Liesl's feet and barked.

'Griselda, wait a minute,' she said. 'Please, Father, let's speak in English. Can we?'

'Alright but not for too long and don't be in too much of a hurry to learn any local customs. The English have strange ways, you know.' He rubbed her head and loosened the flaxen braids encircling it.

'Father don't mess up my hair or Mother will get cross. What sort of strange ways?'

'Maybe not strange.' He patted her worried face and smiled. 'Just different.'

Liesl shrugged at this, picked up the stick and threw it into the river. Griselda chased it and landed with a mighty splash, sending chevrons across the water. The hound swam out into the middle of the river and returned bearing the stick between her teeth, shaking the water from her and showering her mistress with sparkling droplets.

'Oh, Griselda! You'll have to learn some manners.'

'Now, what shall we choose for our English topic?' The language was too soft to be of much use in the forge where fire and metal did battle but it would do to help Liesl make friends. 'Shall we start by talking about food and see how we go from there? We can practise while we hunt for your grandmother.'

Griselda's hackles went up. 'Hush, girl, what's wrong?' Hermann caught a movement on the opposite bank – a white mastiff running upriver – and put a hand on Griselda's scruff. 'That beast would eat you.' There came a grey mare, carrying a big man with curling black hair, his head jutting forwards like his dog. On the back of the horse, clinging for dear life, was a skinny old woman.

'Father, why is Grandmother Mohll on the horse behind Herr Maddison?'

'I've no idea.' He strained his eyes to see his mother. 'She's not safe with that heartless swine.'

'He must have a heart,' she said.

'I doubt that,' he replied.

'But, Father,' she said, 'Herr Maddison cried when his white mare was slaughtered.'

'Never mind that now, girl. Come.' He began running along the riverbank, calling out, 'Mother. Mother!'

Either she couldn't hear or she was too scared to speak. Did Maddison realise how precarious his passenger's position was? Did he care? If Hermann attracted the madman's attention, he might slow down.

'Maddison,' he shouted. 'Maddison!' But the man gave no greeting in return, instead, kicking the mare, putting down his head and pressing on. 'Come, Liesl, we must catch them.'

The mare was going at such a gallop now, there was no way of matching her speed. His mother would fall off and break her bones. They started running again but stopped when they heard a splash near the ford. A shriek followed the splash and Hermann ran to the river's edge where two arms waved like sticks above the water. 'Liesl, go home,' he shouted. 'Bring blankets.' He took hold of a young branch above his head, twisted it back and forth until it broke and leapt into the water, holding it out. The current pressed against his thighs and his feet shifted on the riverbed as his waterborne mother raced towards him. Could she grab the branch? And would she have the strength to cling on? If he didn't stop her, the rocks near the bridge would do the job. He shivered, realising she might not live to tell the tale.

'Hoy there,' he shouted. 'Hoy!' Mother's head appeared above water and her terrified eyes met his. She grabbed the branch but the combined force of the water and his mother took Hermann off his feet, and he floundered, trying to keep both their heads above water.

The old wife was frail but still a heavier catch than any he was used to. He gripped the branch and wedged his leg behind a rock. Pain shot through his hip and he strained with the effort. Mother was screaming and white eyed but she clung to the branch and he dragged her safely to the riverbank, pushing her up the slimy mud.

Liesl came running. 'Oh, Grandmother Mohll, have you hurt yourself?' She held up a blanket and wrapped the old soul, who was spluttering and shaking from head to foot.

'Come, Mother, let's get you inside and next to the fire.' He scooped her up and carried her towards home.

The old woman raised her head. 'Liesl, run ahead and fetch my warming medicine,' she said. 'You'll find a bottle in the larder.'

Hermann placed his mother on the chair nearest the fire and pulled a rug around her thin shoulders. Liesl fetched the bottle and fed spoonsful into her grandmother's toothless mouth until the old woman's shivering subsided.

'What were you thinking?' Hermann asked. 'Getting up behind the madman? You saw how angry he was when we slaughtered his old mare.'

'I wasn't thinking straight,' his mother replied. 'I'd been in the forge all night blessing the swords. It was easy enough to cross the river in the night when it wasn't so high but it was a raging torrent this morning.'

The blessing of the blades. Not content that Hermann's sharp edges were enough, Mother blessed the blades in the hope they might one day slit soldiers' gizzards. All soldiers were one in her mind: one Catholic soldier, wearing the rig of the emperor and carrying his seed. His mother gave no quarter and she didn't want peace. She wanted revenge.

Katrin widened her eyes at Hermann as she walked past carrying a bowl of hot beer. She put it down and whipped the bottle from Liesl's hands. 'What were you expecting after all the rain, Anna?' she asked. 'It must have fairly swept down from the hills.'

'Well, I was standing on the riverbank wondering how to get back across when a man on a grey mare appeared,' his mother said. 'He was handsome and quite the gallant gentleman.'

'Mother, didn't it occur to you that this "gentleman" was Maddison or that he was far from being gentle? Instead, a madman and one made madder by us slaughtering his mare.' Hermann smiled grimly. 'Did you not consider where this tale might end?'

'I was still half asleep,' his mother replied. 'It'd been a long, cold night in the forge and I'd taken a bit more of my warming medicine than usual. These English berries are too small and weak.'

Mother and her warming medicine. An oily spirit distilled from the berries growing on her juniper tree. She used to take it from a spoon while hiding in the larder. As a boy, he'd often wondered why no one else took their medicine in this way.

'Anyway,' she continued, 'the man lifted me up on his mare and I was glad of the ride. It was a bit worrying when he set off down the riverbank at a gallop but I thought he must be going to the ford so I clung on to him.'

She paused to drain her hot beer. Hermann took the empty

bowl and passed it to Katrin, who crossed her eyes. He winked in return. Mother enjoyed a drama and wasn't above creating one if life became too staid.

'When we reached the midst of the river,' his mother went on, 'the man turned his head and he was no longer handsome, gallant or gentle, just wild-eyed and grinning. I dug my knees into the horse and clung to his cloak but he swept me off the horse with one arm. Such a drop, it's a wonder it didn't smash my bones. Then the river nearly did away with me,' she said and pulled the rug closer. 'Oh, I thought him a gentleman but all along he was a demon. He should suffer the breaking wheel, trying to kill an old lady like me.'

Katrin turned from scrubbing the bowl. 'Anna,' she said, 'I'm beginning to feel some sympathy for Herr Maddison, who can't have been pleased at having an old crone on his back, talking without ceasing.'

Hermann's mother ignored his wife and fixed her amber eyes on him. 'I owe you my life, Son,' she said. 'Bless you, for intervening in God's will. As my saviour, you're responsible for me for the rest of my life.'

'Intervened in Ralph Maddison's will more like,' Katrin said, 'and just look at your reluctant saviour's face, Anna. Being responsible for you is an unfair reward for good behaviour. Next time, Hermann, let the querulous old woman take her chances on the rocks.'

RIVER RATS

Morpeth Gaol, 1703

A wearing day for me after being up half the night seeing to the rowdy mariners. Those curse-mother fellows
will have me in an early grave. Must think they're still at sea,
demanding rum and ale at all hours. They'll sharp get used to
going without. No rest this morning either. Right in the middle
of sharing my bacon with Roasting Jack, I was, when a constable dragged in a waterman, one Tommy Davison from North
Shields. The constable was full of news. He'd taken sworn state-
ments from a couple of other river rats, two coblemen from the
fisheries, John Chambers and William Arsbit. Now there's a lad
whose mother must hate him. The constable loved the sound
of his own voice and was falling over himself to tell the tale,
'Minding their own business at the South Shields salt pans, they
were, dragging up mussels for bait, when they pulled out the
strangest looking mussels they'd ever seen.' The constable almost
split his sides laughing at his feeble joke. Took him a while to
get around to telling me Arsbit and Chambers had pulled out
three sword blades and reckoned they'd have got more if not for
the bad weather. As if I need telling about bad weather up here.

Funny swords they've pulled out by the sounds of them. Some
kind of three-edged hollow blade. The constable said they looked

to be English-made, though that cannot be right if they've been fetched in from Rotterdam. Colonel Henry Villiers, Governor of Tynemouth Castle, is putting up five shillings for every score of blades handed in. Once folk got wind of this, half the coast-dwellers were at it, by all accounts. Three coalmen from Shields had turned fishermen. They got a rattling great bundle done up in paper and twine as far as the water's edge but it sank and they had to go dragging till they fetched up the blades. This German knave must have been trying to dodge the duty on his cargo. As for this Tommy Davison, he must be making money hand over fist. They do a fair trade on the Tyne, these watermen, what with Newcastle having the busiest port after London. I daresay he makes a prettier penny smuggling than he ever does from his honest toil. Who can blame him?

Newcastle must have the richest customs men, as well. They'll take your eyes out as soon as look at you. Half of them are bound to be papists, filling their pockets with bribes for turning a blind eye. And as for his high mightiness, Colonel Villiers, what does he do all day? He can't be catching many smugglers. Couldn't tell you when I last had any behind these walls. The government lies at fault for all the smuggling going on. Get rid of the duty, I say, and you'll get rid of the smuggling, but I'm no more than a humble keeper so who's going to pay any mind to what I think?

Davison's a wiry little runt beneath his fisherman's ganzie. Straight off the Tyne and still reeking of that foul river. A right gnashgab, who complained the tidewaiters have been after him for years. All for no good reason, of course, him being an innocent man. Aren't they always?

Hardened by life on the sea, he had no fear of me and kept his trap shut. But as all men have their breaking point so little Davison had his. Finally confessed to holding forty-six bundles of blades in his waterhouse. Fourteen-hundred of them he was keeping till next tide. Quite a clue. Now where might those swords be bound? Davison wouldn't name any outbound ship, no matter what, and turned tight-lipped again. Not doing himself any favours being so stubborn. More than a case of simple smuggling, this. Bound to be a plot afoot so better for Davison to give up the German. But would Davison give him up? He would not, no matter how hard pressed. Why risk his neck to save a foreigner? I suppose a man who makes his gold from smuggling must take his customers' names to the grave or who would trust him otherwise? Better change his tune or he'll be looking at the thick end of the rope before too long.

MEASLES

Shotley Bridge, 1689

Hermann was in his mother's room, working on her gold. Her eyes were poor and her hands trembled so much of late that the finer pieces were impossible for her nowadays. Her near-drowning at the hands of Maddison last year had affected her more than she cared to admit and of course the madman had gone unpunished. The families' trials were far from over, with the valley now in the grip of a measles outbreak. Someone must have fetched it back from Newcastle as there was nobody else here to speak of. At least his mother had suffered it as a girl so she was safe.

The sun pooled on the table, a warm breeze blew through the open door and hammers rang dully on steel in the distance. He ran his fingernail over the intricate engraving on a ring. Mother's skills had probably saved her life when she'd escaped the clashing metal of her hometown and came instead to the town famous for the blades that had delivered so much slaughter. Solingen had admitted this curious woman, who had nothing to her name other than a precious bundle, wrapped in a red silk kerchief, which had knocked against her heart during her long march west. She'd always insisted Solingen took her in because her beauty brought with it the whisper of a fresh strain of blood but really it was her ability to work gold. Once saved, she'd watched her husband and son forging the earth's metals into shapes that would bring death to other men, trusting that her menfolk would be spared the sword because of their work. Could she be right? Did something of Hermann's soul enter the steel along with his sweat and blood? A hoarse breath interrupted his thoughts.

'Liesl? Is that you under the table?'

'Yes, Father.'

'Shouldn't you be outside in the fresh air?' he asked.

'Mother won't let me out,' she replied.

'In that case, would you like to come out from under the table and sit up here where it's airy and more pleasant? You can help me.'

'No, I like it under here where it's dark and the sunbeams cut through the shadows and make the dust sparkle.'

Sparkling dust? Had his mother been filling Liesl's head with her tales again? When he was a boy, she'd tell him the room was full of gold dust, which would line his lungs when he breathed in. For years, he'd believed that he sparkled secretly on the inside and had golden breath. He'd saved up this precious breath and delivered it in a mighty roar the next time Schimmelbusch came at him with his sword and his young enemy had left him alone ever since. Hermann rubbed his thigh at the memory. Not such a bad tale to tell small children after all.

'Liesl, why are you really under the table?'

'So the sun can't jab me in the eyes,' she replied.

His heart lurched at these words. 'Let me close the curtains so you can come out.'

The door opened wide and his mother entered the room.

A feeble croak came from under the table. 'Mother?'

'No, it's me again,' the old woman said.' Your mother needs to stay away from you in case she gets sick. You can save your pitiful act for one who might be taken in by it. Hermann, you shouldn't have the girl in here in case you get sick as well.'

He waved her away. 'Ach, I'm made of sterner stuff. It'll take more than a bout of measles to finish me off.'

His mother wagged a finger at him. 'Always tempting the gods, Hermann. Will you never learn? Now, Liesl, come out from under there. You'll be better off resting in bed.'

Hermann ducked his head under the table but Liesl wouldn't reply. 'My girl is now too hot and weary to talk, it seems.'

'But not too hot and weary to disobey me.' His mother rapped her knuckles on the table. 'Come, Liesl, drink some medicine and off to bed with you.'

Still she wouldn't come out. 'Ugh,' she complained in a muffled voice. 'Medicine.'

'Drink it up,' said his mother. 'It'll put hairs on your chest.'

'Well, I certainly don't want it now,' said Liesl. 'I'm not well as it is.'

'Well enough to back-answer means well enough to take your medicine. Come, it'll make you cooler.' His mother crouched down. 'Liesl, get out from under there or you'll bump the table leg and jolt your father's work, and his nerves.'

'But, Grandmother Mohll, the light makes me feel sick.'

'Wait,' his mother said, 'and I'll fetch something cooling. As if my old knees have nothing better to do than creak up and down these blessed stairs all day long. Hermann, get her onto the couch while I'm gone. I can't lift the great lump of a girl.'

Hermann leaned under the table and drew Liesl out.

'Come, you heard your grandmother, she's not in the mood for disobedience. Lie down on the little couch here and close your eyes.'

'But grandmother's couch is all scratchy and smells of old cats.'

'Cats? No cats have been in here. Griselda would see to that. Lie down, girl and don't, for heaven's sake, challenge your grandmother. Don't mention cats to her, either.'

While they waited, he scrutinised his daughter's face. She was pale but her face wasn't yet marked by a red rash.

When his mother returned, she was carrying a cucumber and a knife and began shaving off thin slices and laying them across Liesl's eyes.

'There, that'll take the light away,' she said. 'How are those cucumber spectacles?'

'Like pale-green stained-glass windows,' replied Liesl. 'It's still light but it's fuzzy and it doesn't make my eyes so sore. Thank you, Grandmother Mohll.'

Hermann tapped on Liesl's door and went into the darkened room, breathing in the scent of lemon, ginger and hot sugar wafting from the platter in his hand.

'Mother?' she asked.

'No, sorry, you'll have to make do with your father,' replied Hermann. 'Your mother's finished baking so I've fetched some *Pfefferkuchen* for you.' He put the platter on top of the chest of drawers and perched on the bed. 'You seem sad, Liesl. Will your smile ever come back?'

'One day.' She turned to face the wall and he heard a quiet sob. 'But not today. Poor baby.'

So, she'd heard about little Adam Oligh, the second child to die locally, but the first German. Further along the valley, Farmer Johnson's great-nephew had gone blind. No doubt Liesl had overheard her grandmother gossiping. Instead of talking, the old woman shouted and her voice carried for miles, despite considering herself a great keeper of secrets. So Liesl would no doubt also know about Rose Leaton and Joseph. The poor soul hadn't lasted long, even though Frau Johnson had been down to minister to her. Joseph had taken seizures but was still alive and in God's hands now. As he went to and from the forge, Hermann was looking in on the distraught lad and taking broth from Katrin. He smoothed the quilt over his daughter and tucked it under the mattress, fastening her arms by her side. She'd loved to be swaddled as an infant and it used to help her sleep but she wrested her arms free and propped herself upright.

'What about Joseph?' she asked. 'Will he live?'

So the girl did know. He couldn't bear to see her so distressed. 'Joseph's a strong lad and we're watching over him,' he said. 'Concentrate on getting yourself better.'

'Well, I can't get better if I'm sad,' she protested, 'and I can't stop being sad when there's so much to worry about. What if Joseph–'

'Joseph will be fine.' He hoped that would be true but who knew what years of poverty had done to the lad.

'How will he be fine when he has no mother? Where will he live? What will he eat?'

'Settle down, Liesl, don't get worked up. Once he's better, Herr Johnson will give him work bringing in the harvest and he can bed down in the byre. Joseph would not want to see you sad. Come, I know a way to get rid of sadness. Do you want to try it?'

Liesl bit her lip. 'I don't know if I want to let it go or keep it tucked inside.'

'I'll fetch something to help.'

He left and soon returned carrying his mother's jewellery chest. Out of it, he took a handful of tarnished and sticky gold bands.

'Now, this gold has lost its shine but your grandmother's special polish will make even the dullest metal gleam again.' He took out a tin from his pocket and prised off the lid, letting out a sharp smell that brought water to his eyes. He dipped a ring in it and passed it to his daughter, along with a small piece of cloth. 'First you must pick a ring and gently rub it all over, inside and out, until the gold is polished and shining again. Do you see, *Liebchen*?'

Liesl held the ring up and sighed. It was a breath made jagged by tears and he worried she might start weeping again. 'Come,' he said, 'keep rubbing the ring.'

She rubbed the ring until it shone and took another from the chest. By the time she'd polished six rings, there was a change in the rhythm of her breathing.

The door opened and his mother came in, a grim expression on her face. Before he could signal her to leave, Liesl dropped the ring. 'What's the matter, Grandmother Mohll? Tell me, what's wrong. Is it Joseph?'

'Joseph is well,' his mother said. 'His blood heat is almost back to normal.' She glanced at Hermann and whispered. 'It's the Schimmelbusch family—'

'Pieter?' Liesl began getting out of bed. 'Surely not Pieter?'

His mother shook her head and tucked Liesl back into bed. 'Worse,' she said. 'His father. That's two of our number to die. Tiergarten is saying it's a punishment from God for ignoring the indictment—'

'How can that be worse, Grandmother Mohll?' asked Liesl. 'Herr Schimmelbusch is old. Pieter is just a boy.'

'Because the whole family will struggle now, my girl,' his mother said. 'The other families will help but it'll be a hard life for those left behind.'

'I'm sorry for baby Adam, for poor Rose and for Herr Schimmelbusch.' A hitch in the girl's breathing before she picked up the ring and continued rubbing. 'Mostly, I'm glad it wasn't Pieter but what if he dies as well?' Her chin quivered, heralding a spurt of tears. 'What if it *is* a punishment from God?'

'There's no such thing as a punishment from God,' Hermann said, eyeing his mother. 'At least not in this world. It's bad fortune. No more and no less.' A punishment from God. Wait till he got his hands on Tiergarten. It was beyond him why the man hadn't just upped and gone back home if he was so worried. But no, here he still was, along with all the others. Hermann rubbed Liesl's hand as if she too were precious gold until her tears began to dry. 'Don't you go worrying about Pieter. It's quite rare to die from measles. Rose Leaton was weakened by poverty, the baby was very young and we don't know about Herr Schimmelbusch. He might have had some underlying ailment.' This was all cold comfort, though.

'Your father's right, girl,' his mother said, 'it's plain misfortune, that's all, and I'm sure that's an end to it. Now, let me be for a few hours. I'm not cut out for nursing.'

They watched as his mother left the room.

'Oh, Father, Pieter must miss his father so much and one day I'll have to miss you and Mother and both my grandmothers. It'll be unbearable.'

'*Liebchen*, many years, scores of years, will pass before you have that to face so don't worry.' He leant over and hugged her to him. 'By then, you'll have your own family and they'll keep you comforted.'

'Where will Pieter live now that he has no father?' she asked.

Hermann looked at his daughter's blue eyes, reddened from crying. 'Well, that's up to his mother. They may go back to Solingen to their wider family or–'

'He can't go back to Solingen. They'll all perish on a ship. If his mother goes back, we must take him. Please, Father. We're the smallest family here and we could offer him a home.'

'Hush, girl. Pieter's mother needs him now. As the man of the house, he'll have to work and keep his family.'

'But, Father–'

He held up a hand. 'Enough, Liesl.'

The girl went too far at times. It was his own fault for indulging her. Hermann pitied the Schimmelbusch family. Life was starting to become hard for all the families, with the promised gold being rather scarce of late. It might be better for Pieter's mother to take her family back to Solingen, where they'd have the protection of the town. The guild would take pity on a widow and her family. He picked a pile of snarled-up jewellery out of the wooden chest and began untangling clumps of chains from broken brooches.

'Is any of this your gold, Father?'

'No, it's all your grandmother's and it was her grandmother's before that. It was often said *she* attracted so much gold to her that it adorned her hands and wrists, neck and teeth.'

'Teeth?' Liesl shuddered.

'Oh, yes,' he said. 'Your great-great grandmother had a set of teeth entirely made of gold. They used to terrify my mother so much when she was a girl that she dreaded being kissed by her.'

Liesl laughed. 'I can't imagine Grandmother Mohll fearing anything.'

Hermann waggled his moustaches. 'When I was a boy, your grandmother insisted she weighed more at the end of a working day than on the Sabbath because she was coated in gold flakes. I used to shadow her to see whether she shimmered in a certain light.'

'She told me that as well.' Liesl went quiet for a while. 'Grandmother Mohll told me she can turn lead into gold. Like magic. Could that be true?'

'What do you think?' he replied.

'I can't grasp it.' She scratched her head. 'My head's too hot. Can't you just tell me?'

He laughed, though not unkindly. He could tell her but he wouldn't and she'd thank him for it one day. Instead, he'd give her a clue. 'How much gold do you think is in this room?'

'Not too much.' Liesl studied the rings, the chains, the brooches, the medals. 'A pound or so.'

'What does that tell you?'

She bit her lip for a while but then her eyes lit up. 'If Grandmother Mohll could do magic, she could make as much gold as she wanted.'

'At least until the lead ran out,' he said. 'Go on.'

Liesl grinned, seizing the idea now. 'She'd live in a golden castle and dress in cloth of gold and dine on gold-dipped *Pfefferkuchen*.'

'Precisely.' He smiled at the thought of his mother the alchemist living in the lap of such luxury. 'It's an impossible dream.'

'So it's just another one of Grandmother Mohll's tales,' she said. 'It's hard to tell sometimes.'

'But, like all tales, based on a grain of truth.' He held up a ring. 'When gold was first smelted from stone, it must have seemed like magic.' He picked up a clutch of knotted chains and untangled a slender chain that slithered free.

'I like to watch you working with tiny things,' she said. 'You handle them as gently as robins' eggs.'

'Are you well enough to help?'

She nodded and he passed over a heap of chains to show her how to unknot them, how to work with the metal, how to listen with her fingers so she could hear its rhythms pulsing with her blood. 'All metal yearns to escape. It's not meant to live above ground and longs to slip back beneath the earth,' he said. 'Try to feel which way it's pulling and the knots will flow open for you.'

Liesl stared as she unpicked tight knots from the bundle in her hands. 'When you do it, the chains seem glossed with butter and the gold melts through your fingers into strands.'

'It'll come to you with practice and patience,' he said. 'You have nimble fingers, which is good and you have sharp eyes, which is also good.' He watched her tugging at the fine chain. 'But there's not much patience in you, is there?'

'I do have patience.' She yanked at a fine chain and it snapped.

'No, you need to be a much larger vessel first. Patience pours out of little pepper-pots like you. Don't worry, girl. You can never break gold.' He put the broken pieces in a box to fix later. 'Watch again, more carefully this time.' He eased his thumbs through a muddle of chains and handed them to her. 'Feed the ends under, over, through.' He guided her hands. 'Repeat. Under, over, through. Repeat.'

'I'm tired now, Father.' Her eyes were drooping and she put down the gold. 'I need to go to sleep.'

He gathered the chains and kissed her on the forehead. Her little face was flushed and she was hotter than ever.

'Sleep well, Daughter. Goodnight. May God keep you safe until morning.'

A Fish Out of Water

Morpeth Gaol, 1703

*T*he language out of Tommy Davison through the night made the mariners sound like missionaries. For a small man, he has some lungs on him, shouting and bawling the odds all night. Had all the others rattled and set Roasting Jack howling along with him. Davison took some fettling and now there's been another prisoner fetched from the same neck of the woods. Another short-arse, this time a wherryman from North Shields, one Anders of Surinam, by way of Africa. Light-blue eyes, name and tongue courtesy of a Dutch father. In this job, there's no such thing as coincidence so I'll be keeping a close eye on him.

Fancy leaving the warm climes of the New World and coming all the way to Newcastle. Must have been quite a shock fetching up on the cold Tyne. No wonder he looks such a fish out of water, twisting and turning his cap in his hands as if wringing seawater from it. Fretting about losing his pay. The man wants to be more worried about losing his head.

The constables told me he's a freeman but had no clue how he'd managed to buy his way out of slavery. Mebbes his Dutch father bought his son's freedom and helped him hot-foot it from the sugar plantations. Good for him. Must have been like hell on earth and Surinam will have himself a kinder home here.

They're said to be cruel masters, the Dutch, though I doubt our English slavers are any kinder. Lucky to make it here without being pressed into service in the Dutch army.

He swore down he was haled in the early hours by several men on a ship near Jarrow Keys. That'll have been the mariners and redcoats, most likely. He said it was a vessel of war and when he spied a man going overboard, he rowed towards him in case he got into difficulties. This one's a natural storyteller! Reckoned our German friend was a stowaway who took a lend of his good nature and forced him to transport bundles of mysterious goods to Davison's waterhouse. How mysterious can goods be, when the clank of blades is impossible to miss and must have nearly sunk his boat? Yet, the poor wherryman pleaded he was innocent.

Innocent, my backside. These river rats are all working in league with one another, anxious to get their hands on some extra coin. Cannot say I blame them when it's so hard scratching a living from the filthy Tyne. There's not a waterman born who can stomach the customs gang or who doesn't live for the day he can outwit them. But not Anders, who stood there with his eyes cast down, afraid to say boo to a goose. He must think I'm soft-headed. This poor little Anders was rowing his great boat up the Tyne in the middle of a December night. Not a task done lightly. Although short, his arms are like hawsers with enough knotty strength to fell six of me. Yet still he put on a voice like a mouse, which would not be the same voice used to bellow the length and breadth of the Tyne to keep his passengers in good order.

The German never stowed away on that wherry. As if a man working that river would suffer a stowaway. The wherryman was there to pick up a paying passenger, along with his booty. The plan was to squirrel it away at Davison's waterhouse, ready to take away on another ship at next tide. Not hard to guess where she might be bound with her cargo of smuggled swords. North to Scotland, I'll wager. A well-oiled venture to arm the Jacobite rebels and only spoilt by the customs men getting wind of it. Surinam is in it up to his eyes, as is Davison. I wonder what brought them together: a German, a Dutchman and these men of the Tyne? The world cannot be so small. Still no sign of our German friend, though. If he's any sense, he'll have flitted into the night and got himself back to his homeland. I wouldn't want to be in his shoes.

An Ill Wind

Shotley Bridge 1689

*U*nder, over, through. Repeat. Under, over, through. Repeat. The words chanted through Hermann's mind. All he could see was a dizzying array of gold chains. A million links. Insect segments, glistening and tightening around his chest and throat until he couldn't breathe.

The wind made the curtains billow. It was wild but warm and it carried the musk of honeysuckle and roses into his broken sleep until he surrendered to its sweetness. The perfumed night slipped over his skin like the goose-down quilt of his childhood and the aches soaked from his bones into the feathers stuffing his mattress.

He was a hard man, all bone and sinew, but thinking of his dead neighbour, softness slid into him. People died all the time and now Schimmelbusch was gone, his blademark would be carved onto a stone to commemorate his life. It was a cruel turn for him to leave his homeland, travel to England and lose his life so soon after. Now he'd be laid to rest far from home. Why should he die when he was a good man who never did a bad deed in his life? Much better for everyone if Maddison were to die. Hope flared briefly in Hermann but it was bad to wish death on anyone else, even someone like the madman.

Katrin came into the room. 'Hermann? Are you awake? Liesl's getting hotter. Nothing's helping her.' She shook his shoulder. 'I'm worried she'll start fitting.'

He opened his eyes and looked at his wife's worried face.

'I'll go and fetch Witch Wilson–'

'Witch?' Her face hardened. 'You would put our daughter under the care of a witch?'

'Witch Wilson is just a curious name for a local man.' He rubbed his shoulder and sat up. 'A bit of a joke.'

'How can a witch ever be a joke? And is it wise even to associate with a man named witch?'

'Away with you, Katrin,' he said. 'Wilson's nothing more than a skilled engraver who can make medicine from plants. Blenkinsop reckons he can tinker with any machine and make it work – daughter or clock.'

'Our daughter is not a machine. And how can you even think of the clock at this time?'

He could think of the clock at this time because it was important to count the seconds of their lives, what remained of them, however shortened. He stood up and drew on his breeches and shirt. Katrin followed him downstairs and watched him put on his boots, hat and coat.

'Forget your hat,' she said. 'The wind will snatch it in a second.'

'You're right, *Liebe*.' As usual. He took it off and placed it on the table.

'You can hear the trees creaking out there, Hermann. It's like an ill wind from back home so please be careful.'

'It's not in me to be careful.' He cracked a smile. 'If you wanted a careful man, you married the wrong one.'

A wry smile in return. 'This strange storm might ease off,' she said. 'What about waiting an hour?'

'An hour may be more time than is good for Liesl.' He took her hands. 'I must go now.'

She closed her eyes and nodded so he set off, Griselda at his heels.

The wind howled down the leeward side of the hills and leaves streamed around him. The woods were alive and he feared for the forges – there must be felled trees by morning. Katrin was right, it was exactly like an ill wind, bringing with it every ailment from headache to madness. The trees were decked out in green and the wind wound itself into the boughs so their leaves created great sails. The alder and birch swayed in the teeth of the gale but the oaks twisted in a curious dance that must stress the heart of the timber to breaking point. The oak was too stolid to bend with the wind, and if not uprooted, must surely break. Listen to him. He'd uprooted himself but might yet be broken anyway.

Engel Schimmelbusch had always looked like he belonged more to the angels than to the forge and now he'd been struck down at the height of an English summer. The turning of the new year always opened doors into men's hearts and let in all manner of ill but it seemed cruel to be struck down by fever in the middle of the year when the days were so glorious. Hermann hoped there'd be no more deaths. The Germans were so few in number. How much would it take to finish them? They could all fall asleep and not wake up, and who would know? Their skeletons might lie in bed forever more. He laughed, the hollow sound lost in the wind. Of course they'd be missed. As soon as they breached their contract, a company man would duly appear. Well, best of luck to the English wringing a hefty fine out of their dry bones. The Germans would survive this outbreak, but not all of them.

He walked with the wind rushing into his face, taking his breath away, and leaned into it. If he let himself go, would it support his weight? He might let go for a short time and allow the wind to take him. With any luck, it might blow him all the way home to Solingen and he might wake up to discover England had been no more than a bad dream.

When the trees thinned out, Hermann made his way through a clearing to a small dwelling and hammered on the door with the side of his fist.

There was a scrambling sound and the clatter of metal implements falling before a wizened man appeared at the door, scowling.

'Good morning,' Hermann said. 'Herr Wilson?'

'Who wants to know?'

'Me, Herr Mohll.' He held out a hand. 'Hermann.'

'So you're one of the German lot down by the river. Though two less of you, I hear?'

Hermann gave a curt nod. 'Yes.'

'Well, I'm sorry to hear it,' said Wilson, 'but glad to meet you at last.' The elderly man shook Hermann's hand and rubbed Griselda's ear. 'You'll know me as Witch Wilson.'

'Yes, but please let me call you Herr Wilson or my wife won't give you house room.'

The wizened man grimaced. 'Ah, I see how it is,' he said. 'Don't worry, there's no fear of me being a devil-cleper. Now come away in out of this wind. It's got me fair rattled this morning.'

All the flat surfaces were covered with pieces of machinery. Hermann was afraid to move in case he knocked a day's work flying so he stood still and stared at the walls, which were festooned with fine drawings of plants and their parts. They were faithful enough reproductions and it was obvious the man had a good eye and a steady hand.

'Don't mind my herbarium. Each malady has a remedy. It's just a matter of matching the two up.' Wilson tapped his head. 'It's all stored up here, of course, but I won't always be around so that's there for whoever comes after me. I've no bairns and no apprentice so this knowledge will be lost and that mediciner up at Medomsley will charge people through the nose.'

Hermann wondered at his meaning. 'I'm sorry? Nose?'

Wilson waved his hand. 'Don't mind me blethering on. Now, what can I do for you?'

Hermann explained that Liesl was burning up, her breathing was laboured and she couldn't stand the light.

Wilson listened and nodded along. 'Alright,' he said. 'It sounds like the measles. Let me get a few roots together and I'll come directly. I'll soon fettle what ails your daughter. She sounds like a strong lass, not like poor Rose Leaton. I doubt even her mother or her granny could have saved her. God rest all their souls.'

Hermann paused. Katrin would kill him but it would save two trips. 'Herr Wilson?'

'Yes, Mr Mohll?'

'After you've seen to my daughter … there's also an old clock, if you wouldn't mind taking a look at that as well?'

⌣

Hermann's fellow German was lowered into the deep clay and Pieter Schimmelbusch threw a handful of English soil into his father's grave. Such a short time here and now the man had gone forever. The journey must have been a strain for him, along with the worry of the Solingen notice. Liesl was better now, thanks to Witch Wilson, but Hermann supposed himself not too far from the grave. He should make sure his family were provided for, especially as he had no son to keep his womenfolk.

He placed an arm around Pieter's shoulders and while the priest intoned, Hermann whispered the forbidden prayers for the dead. Young Schimmelbusch was bereft and would need to make a life for himself. Whether here or back at home would be a decision for another day. The lad was skilled and could keep his folk but it would be a hard life for one so young. At least Pieter still had his family. Joseph Leaton had no one. If the English boy survived, Hermann would give him a job in the forge once the harvest was over. Katrin would come around to the idea in time.

While the priest went on, a kestrel hovered not thirty feet away, its eye no doubt on some small furry creature. Hermann wondered whether the scurrying creature would be aware of the cruciform shadow above. Would it escape to its burrow in time? He held his breath as the kestrel swooped. There was a shriek as sharp claws snatched up the quarry and the bird flew back into the air, soaring home with its broken-necked prey. At least its young would eat today.

After paying his respects to Widow Schimmelbusch, Hermann made his way home with Griselda at his side. The sun made his eyes ache and it would be light for hours yet so he pulled down his hat to keep out the glare. His soles were too thin so he felt every lump and bump on the riverbank, with every tree root, rabbit hole and fallen twig firing urgent pains around his body. The meadow by the river shimmered with the purple silk of wild oats in the barely there breeze and the air filled with the aniseed aroma of fennel hidden behind the bracken.

After three days of burning sun and three nights of pouring rain, the ferns were way over his head. He battled through them until he reached the open meadow. Griselda ran barking into the oats, where a crow hopped along a path. When Hermann called the hound off, the bird fluttered in fright and made it to the low branches of a young ash.

'Come back, Griselda, give him a chance, he has just the one leg. Come.'

Her hackles went down and she slunk back to her master.

When they passed Hole House, Maddison's white dog barked

itself berserk on the end of its chain. It had the thickset body of a mastiff, with the intelligent eyes and pointed ears of a German hunting dog. When it growled from its deep chest and flung itself against the limits of its chain, Hermann understood that only the chain prevented the mastiff from ripping out any intruder's throat. Griselda pressed herself close to Hermann's leg and he stroked her head.

'Good girl, Gris, pay the beast no mind.' At least Maddison was nowhere to be seen.

The air was still hot and Hermann was running with sweat. The fire in his eyes was blinding and the heat in his blood too great. It was a golden day, but sweltering, and the island air was humid. Living in the slenderest neck of England, just before the great head of Scotland, he was pressed on either side by two great seas and there was as much water in the air as in the river today. He kicked off his boots, sat on the riverbank and plunged his feet into the water, letting his blood cool and carry the chill around his body. This heat was so tiring. It was no good being like this or he wouldn't be able to work and his family would suffer. Katrin would have to start scrimping and he didn't want to do that to her when she'd finally started to settle in here but he was exhausted. He closed his eyes against the bright sun and rested for a minute ...

⌐

Hermann woke with a jolt as something struck him.

'Mohll? Mr Mohll?'

He opened his eyes to see blue sky and a huge shadow looming over him.

'Blenkinsop?'

'Sorry, man,' said the innkeeper, 'I thought you were dead.'

Hermann blinked at the dark outline of the man against the sun and rubbed his brow. 'Dead? No, only ...' but what was he?

'Tired. Hot and tired.'

'Not another one taken bad?' asked the innkeeper. 'Come on, let's get you away home so your womenfolk can tend to you. I'll send for Witch Wilson.'

'The sun's too bright.' Hermann closed his eyes again but was soon jolted awake when urgent hands gripped him.

'Come on, Mohll, no sleeping on the job,' said the innkeeper. 'Let's have you up. Are you well enough to walk?'

As Hermann raised his head, the world moved under him.

'Yes, but not quite yet.' He put his head back down. This wasn't so bad. In the shade, he could lie here and admire the sky. Nightfall would bring cold and make him better.

When he opened his eyes again, it was to see the oak beams over his bed. He sought the memory of how he got there and ideas formed at the periphery of his mind but slid away again. It was too tiring chasing fluttering thoughts that vanished down rabbit holes and sleep soon overtook him again.

In the night, he awoke in the arms of fever, joints aching, blood boiling, sweat dripping and hair plastered to his head. Most of all, his eyes ached, even in the silver moonlight, and he pressed the heels of his hands against his eyes. There was no respite from the heat. His nightshirt was stuck to his back and his joints felt as large as turnips. Alone in this endless night, he wrestled with the quilt. Company was what he wanted but also quiet.

He went downstairs to find the hound and buried his hot face in her fur. When he tugged her scruff she followed, eyes downcast, knowing she wasn't allowed upstairs but doing her master's bidding anyway. The hound was hot and made him hotter but Griselda's greasy fur and the dank, earthy smell of her brought comfort. He imagined himself suckled and raised by wolves, a wild boy of the forest with no parents, except for this she-wolf, as old as the world itself.

When he woke, his mother stood over them, snapping her fingers. 'Griselda, get down.' The hound didn't even reproach him with her eyes but slunk off the bed and skittered downstairs, claws clicking on the bare wood. If Griselda was punished, Hermann would feed her his own dinner. That was the chief punishment for wayward dogs and boys – no dinner or else bound indoors, deprived of the forest and its enticing smells and sounds. Mother placed a cold hand on his brow for a few seconds. If only her hand might stay there so the coolness of her blood could flow into his own. When she opened the curtain a crack, Hermann winced and she shut it again.

'Still sore-eyed, Son?'

The thought of the yellow sun sickened him and he longed for the night.

'Stay in bed.' His mother pressed him backwards and he was too weak to resist. It roused a memory from when he was a boy, crying for his father, but it slipped from him. At his age, he had so many memories, there was no way he could remember them all at once, and there weren't enough beats left in his heart to remember them one at a time. He would remember only happy times and not waste valuable heartbeats on missing those who'd left him behind.

The night air was still warm. Hermann was hotter than ever and turned over in bed to find himself beside the river in the argent night. The world smelt different at this hour. Subtle scents underlined by greenery burning, the acrid smell of vegetation taking its last gasp. The fennel wasn't there tonight. That was a smell only lured out by the warmth of the midday sun. His eye caught a flash of black satin, half-covered by the long grass. He nudged the grass with his foot and saw the crippled crow. Dead.

He plucked a handful of oat ears and sprinkled them: purple shimmering on black. Poor crow. As he walked through the night, there was a lot of death on the path, velvety moles, their pink baby hands grasping at air they no longer needed.

He eased himself down onto a flat rock, running his fingers through the damp moss. Here was a cool pillow at last. He removed his clogs and nightshirt, slipped into the rock pool amongst the fishes and raised his feet off the muddy bottom, rolling in the water as an otter might. There was so much water in the world, covering him and making his scalp shrink until it felt smaller than his skull. The cold water calmed him and drew the fire from his blood as he bathed under the moonbeams, witnessed by a ring of silent badgers, foxes, owls and wolves. They wouldn't hurt him though and bore no him no ill will. To them, he was neither predator nor prey but just another nocturnal creature in torment. Only the fish moved, shimmying past, each taking with it a livid spot from his speckled hide. He let the darkness fold over him in the silvered waters of the night pool, turning under the stars, blood boiling the water and the fish with it.

THE MOLE

Morpeth Gaol, 1703

*A*t last, the constables dragged in the German. An easy catch in the end. Hadn't the sense to flit when he had the chance. After evading half the north country for so long, the numbskull went and handed himself in. He's all but placed his neck on the block to spare the little waterman. What a fool. As soon as he got wind of the blades being seized, he went straight to Davison's waterhouse and owned up. Goes to show, there is honour amongst thieves, or amongst smugglers at least.

Enjoys a drop by the looks of him but don't we all? Hermann Mohll is his name but it strikes me as a flowery spelling for mole because he's as dark and sleek as one. Scarcely over five and a half feet, wearing his own hair, with arms and torso covered in cuts and burns. Wiry, and bent on staying that way judging by how he's pacing his cell and flexing his muscles. Might need to watch my back with this one. There again, need to watch my back every minute in this job. He's a Lutheran, which makes him some flavour of Protestant, so there's another one that can safely go in with old Walter if needs be.

There's been no word of any charges yet but it looks bad for my new prisoner, very bad. When Her Majesty's men take a close interest, it never bodes well. Mute as a fish when he came in.

Thought he had no English but I got him talking at the finish. Not much to say about his associates, and no matter how hard I persuaded him, he refused to mention his womenfolk. Likely fears for their necks more than his own. Mebbes that's how they run their gaols in Germany and he must think us the same here. No harm letting him think it a while longer.

He's a funny tongue on him but his English isn't bad and he's a man of letters. Wasn't here two minutes before he started demanding paper and ink. More worried about his letter than his belly when most in here would sell their soul for gruel if kept hungry enough. Well, hard lines to him. A man with empty pockets might as well ask for a gold ring. No coin? No paper.

A master swordmaker by all accounts. Pointed at my old blade and said a queer thing, 'He who rests grows rusty.' Had himself a right good laugh about that. Some rest he'll get in this place. He got up on his knees for a closer look at my sword and asked to be uncuffed, claiming his hands were more reliable than his eyes these days. I told him to look with his eyes and to be quick about it. He eyed its length before passing judgement, 'This hanger is worth more than a gaoler can earn,' he said. 'It's well enough made but the blade is weighty, warped as wet paper and about as sharp. Your attempts at grinding it have split the edges. The wire on the handle is slack. In short, this sword has not been well cared for.'

None of this was news to me but it pained me hearing it from a prisoner. Still, he knows his bones and he's not daft. Offered to fettle the sword in return for paper. I didn't take the bait on first pass but he had more up his sleeve and fancies his name adds to the blade's value, bragging on that he's famous the world over. Men say all sorts in here. Quite an opinion he has of himself but reckons it's one shared by men that matter. He started pushing his luck a bit then and suggested taking the sword to his forge where he could use his own tools. He must think me born yesterday. I laughed in his face and left him to ponder his fate and the many ways a man's soul might leave his body. The Mole strikes me as a man more likely to welcome death than to give up his secrets. No point hiding them. The justices leave no stone unturned at the quarter sessions. If the Mole is found as a traitor, he'll be hanged, drawn and quartered. If he even lasts that long. Winter in gaol can be unkind. Very unkind.

START WITH A NAIL

Shotley Bridge, 1690

*W*hen Hermann and Griselda entered the forge, Joseph was busy examining the blades and stretched out a finger to touch one until Hermann yanked his hand away.

'Good morning, Joseph,' he said. 'Lesson number one: never touch metal in a forge. Even if it's grey, it could still be hot. To be on the safe side, always assume metal is hot. Now, is that fire going to light itself?'

His apprentice reddened. Too late, Hermann saw the lad had already cleared the grate and stacked fresh charcoal. He should be a kinder master. The lad was an orphan. Nearly a year had passed since he'd lost his mother but the wound would still be raw. Griselda, the traitorous hound, sat next to the lad and leant her head against him, gazing up with clear brown eyes. After rubbing the hound's breast, Joseph picked up the firesteel and began striking the flint until an orange spark caught the tinder cloth and he set fire to the wood shavings placed ready in the heart of the fire. Hermann watched while the lad blew on the small flames and picked up the hand bellows, opening and closing them enough to persuade the fire to breathe.

'You're a fast learner, Joseph.'

'It's because I'm that grateful to have the chance to earn me keep,' the lad glanced upwards, 'and to have a dry roof over me head.'

'Good,' Hermann said, gruffly. Joseph's gratefulness made him awkward, perhaps because the lad filled a gap in his heart where a son might have lodged. 'Though it's only because I sleep better knowing there's someone guarding the forge at night.'

Joseph's smile slipped a fraction.

'And because you've got a bit of catching up to do,' Hermann added quickly. 'Being surrounded by the steel all hours, you might absorb its qualities by breathing it in each day.'

'I hope so, sir. I'm a good guard as well.'

'You earn your keep, lad, you earn your keep.'

Joseph's grin returned and Hermann patted him on the head and ruffled his hair. It wasn't just an act of charity letting the lad sleep in the forge. Maddison had started up his old ways again, burning down a barn over the river and there'd been talk from the innkeeper of him sniffing around the forges after dark. Hermann did sleep better knowing there was someone in the forge at night, though he doubted Joseph would be much use against Maddison. Still, the lad had lived this long and come to no harm. Perhaps the madman only had an aversion to sons-in-law and foreigners.

'Always keep the door barred when you're sleeping,' Hermann said. 'Now continue with the bellows until the fire begins to breathe red.' Hermann watched until the fire took hold. 'Yes. Yes. Switch to the water bellows now and their lungs can give yours a rest.' He pointed out the lever to Joseph, who pulled on it. Good. The lad was strong for all he was skinny. 'Just open and close them enough to coax the fire to spread to the surrounding charcoal – no, too much, too much. Close them down a little. Quick.' Hermann took control of the bellows. 'You see? Now you take over again. That's it. Keep them steady and watch how I pile up the charcoal so the heart of the fire grows hot enough to soften the metal.'

The lad was eager to learn and grateful for his chance. When Farmer Johnson started struggling to find enough work for Joseph, Katrin had eventually agreed they could take him on, providing he lived in the forge. Liesl had railed against it, begging for her friend to be allowed under their roof, but when it came to his daughter's virtue, he was resolute. Joseph struck him as decent but there was no telling and even the meekest boy could become a dog when his loins were alight. He'd do well enough in the forge, which was warmer than any hearth and made for a comfortable-enough nest at night. Of course, Oligh had not taken kindly to the apprentice, protesting that Hermann was breaking his guild oaths by sharing their secrets with an Englishman. Hermann had shrugged it off without a second thought. They'd all broken their Solingen residency vows with no sign of any punishment and this would be no different.

'Watch me now.' Hermann slid a batten of steel from the shelf, weighed it in his hands, eyed its length and passed it to Joseph. 'You do the same.'

The lad followed the instruction but his eyes and hands weren't yet trained to know what they were after. That would come in time.

Joseph squinted. 'It's hard to see in here. Shall I open the door?'

'No.' Hermann took back the batten. 'If you're going to be a smith, you need to get used to working in the dark. We're like moles.'

The lad raised his eyes, uncertain. Hermann grinned. 'It's a joke, boy. You can laugh.'

Joseph gave a watery smile. 'Sorry, sir. I wasn't sure.'

Hermann explained they needed the forge dark so they could see the colour of the fire and the steel. It was too easy by far to burn steel in daylight. Joseph's eyes would soon adjust. But the lad wasn't paying attention and leaned towards a blade.

'This is fine work.' Joseph ran his finger down the length of the engraved blade. 'What is it?'

'It's cold, fortunately for you.' Hermann moved the lad's hand out of the way. 'It's a *Kalenderschwert* – calendar sword – handy to have in battle. See, there's today's date. We can find your saint's day, if you like. When is it?'

'St Joseph's day,' he replied. 'The nineteenth day of March.'

Hermann ran his eye up the sword and pointed out the day and the month but Joseph's face was blank. Could he even read the hundreds of dates? If he was to be a swordmaker, he'd need to learn to make more than his mark. Before Hermann could ask him about his reading, Joseph had wandered off to the corner and raised a cloth.

'And what about this one, sir? Is that St Andrew on the saltire?'

Hermann tapped the side of his nose. 'Learn to keep this out or you'll find yourself on the wrong side of one of these.' He pointed to three blades propped against the long bench, each with jagged teeth down both edges.

'Oh, I see. Sorry, sir.' Joseph swallowed and turned to look at the serrated edges. 'What are they for?'

'Come on, surely you can work that one out for yourself?' Hermann made a sawing motion across his gut. 'Just pray you won't ever have to find out the hard way.'

Joseph blinked and pointed to a finished sword. 'Is that a bronze grip?'

What was it with this lad? So keen but so many questions. They'd never get any work done. But it was early days and he'd no father to guide him so Hermann told him how bronze was nearly impossible to grind, even though copper and tin were soft. He picked some strips of copper and tin from buckets on the floor and bent them to show the boy they were so supple they'd bend under pressure from a warm hand. He handed them to Joseph, who bent them this way and that, smiling to himself.

Hermann glanced at the fire. 'Notice how the tips of the flames are yellow, almost white? That means it's time to start work.'

'Begging your pardon, sir,' Joseph eyed the blades again, 'I cannot believe I'm to be a swordmaker.' He bit his lip. 'Me ma would have been so proud–'

Hermann cleared his throat. 'Yes, she would.' Best keep the lad's mind on his work. 'You'll be a swordmaker one day but not for a few years yet. For now, you can make a key of Hubertus.'

'Keys are useful enough, I suppose.' The lad's face was tripping him up but he was trying hard not to show it.

Hermann put his hand in his pocket and rummaged about before finding what he needed. 'You can use this one as your pattern.' He winked and opened his palm.

'But, sir, this isn't even a key,' said Joseph as he picked up the piece of iron, 'it's just a nail.'

Just a nail? Such lip! Hermann might have cuffed an apprentice in Solingen but Joseph hadn't grown up around forges, weaned on metal and absorbing the craft, learning through the jokes and tricks played by the older lads. He'd endured enough in life and there was no need to add to his burden, no matter how great the temptation to get a rise out of him. Hermann had tricked many apprentices in the past but Mad Maddison's cruelty had taken the joy out of making mischief.

'You must learn to walk before you can run,' Hermann said. 'Even Herr Oligh – the most august of swordmakers – had to start with a nail, and so must you.'

The lad was still putting on a brave face but his disappointment was plain to see and so he'd need the tale. When Hermann was a boy, he'd curled his own lip at being forced to make a nail and he'd needed the tale, although he was much younger. All swordmakers had to start with a nail because it was humbling and because of its importance to all smiths.

Hermann plucked his flask from a pocket and swigged from it.

'Have you heard of Saint Hubertus?'

Joseph glanced at the flask. 'No, sir, I haven't.' His shoulders sagged, no doubt fearing a sermon.

'Hubertus is the patron saint of hunters and metalworkers. He was a hermit who lived in the woods. One day, he had a vision of a stag bearing a glowing cross in his … *Geweihe*?' Hermann put down his flask, held his hands above his head and wiggled his fingers.

Joseph grinned. 'Antlers?'

'Antlers, yes,' replied Hermann. 'He had a glowing cross in his antlers.'

The lad looked askance at him. 'Had the saint mebbes dined on too many red toadstools?'

Hermann tried hard not to laugh. He couldn't blame Joseph for drawing such a conclusion but warned him about mocking the patron saint and went on to tell him how Hubertus fell to his knees at the sight of the stag and swore to a life of protecting animals.

'Now, you might wonder what all this has to do with nails or swords,' he said. 'The best way to learn is by doing, so take a scrap of iron and make yourself a nail. It's not as easy as it sounds and it needs to be true. See, there are no bends or kinks in mine and that's how yours must be.'

'But why is the nail called a key?' Joseph pressed a fingertip onto the point of the nail. 'What does it open?'

This lad must think they had nothing better to do all day than stand around prattling. Hermann picked up his flask and drank until his eyes watered. 'No idea. Something to do with curing rabies so maybe it's the key to life.' It sounded thin, even to his own ears. 'You heat the nail in flame and press it onto the afflicted beast.'

Joseph laughed. 'Who'd press a red-hot nail into the flesh of a rabid dog?' He bent down and patted Griselda. 'Even a lovely natured lass like this would have Saint Hubertus's arm off at the shoulder.'

Katrin had better not hear him taking a saint's name in vain. Hermann put on his sternest face.

'Even so, metalworkers must always carry one, and hunters too, so that's why it's your first job.' Joseph would learn in time that the humble iron nail was a great leap forwards in the mind of man. Nails held together houses and ships, kept horses shod and protected against evil spirits. 'If you can't make a true nail, you'll never make anything.'

'But why heal rabid beasts when it would be kinder to kill them?'

So many questions and so much work to do. It was worse than talking to Liesl. 'The key reminds the hunter of the true way.' Hermann eyed the flame and adjusted the bellows slightly. The lad had grown up with no man to teach him the proper way of hunting and it could be rectified in time but that lesson must wait for another day.

He recalled his own father's voice in his ear, telling him not to kill a mother with young or the orphans would be left to fend for themselves through winter, not out of any kindness, but to ensure enough meat for the coming year. That was the true way of the hunter. One day in the woods, he was lying on his belly downwind of a young buck, when his father placed a hand on his head and turned his gaze towards an old doe that was limping. He was faced with a choice: take the trophy or put a lame animal out of her misery. The buck had to be spared for another day. The doe took the arrow in her neck and was slain without too much suffering so her end was a swift and merciful one and the saint was appeased, but to this day, Hermann regretted losing the trophy. That old doe was tough eating, too.

Joseph weighed the nail in his hand. 'So this is your own key of Hubertus?'

'That's right.' It was the first metal Hermann had ever worked. It was true and sharp, with his initials inscribed on its flat head. While he'd never had cause to cure a rabid animal, the lesson about hunting was lodged in his head. He'd take Joseph hunting in the winter so it might lodge in his head but for now he'd have to begin at the beginning.

'Come, Joseph, do it now. Start with a nail. The devil's favourite piece of furniture is the long bench so stop leaning on it and get to work.'

Still the lad looked woebegone. Would Hermann have to show him what to do? But Joseph took his tongs, picked up a scrap of iron, heated it in the fire and turned to the anvil to hammer it into shape. Hermann let him work for a while to find out what he could manage of his own accord.

'Let me see how that nail's coming along,' he said. 'Show me.'

Joseph held up his handiwork. Hermann had seen straighter twigs but a little kindness might go a long way with the orphaned lad. 'It's not so bad that it can't be made better. We need to beat it straight, take out some weight to lighten it and we need to shift the balance.' The lad glowed under Hermann's lies, may God forgive him. 'It's not so bad for a first effort, and when you've mastered the nail, you can go on to make a sword for a child.'

Look at the lad, trying to keep his face straight. A child's sword was hard enough to make but less hung on it as even the English hadn't started sending infants into battle quite yet. A sword for tiny hands meant a more intricate scale and consideration of whether the sword was for dress or whether it should have some edge since no one wanted tiny fingers cut off. Thought had to be given to the hilt and pommel. A novelty was always welcome, a pretty pommel in the shape of a horse's head, or some such nonsense to amuse a young mind.

'Once it's finished, you can put it away for when you have a boy of your own.'

Joseph reddened. 'Mebbes I could make a sword for Liesl?'

'For Liesl?' Hermann guffawed. 'What would a girl want with a sword?' Joseph had no clue but that blush worried him. He'd better keep a closer eye on the lad, and on Liesl.

THE HUMBLE SERVANT

Morpeth Gaol, 1703

No word from on high about my German guest, no hint of charges and no one in to see about him. Hardly surprising after last night's snowfall and the post road all drifted. It's a bad enough time of year anywhere but colder than death here. A man would have to be mad to come out in this weather if there was no need. Downright cruel to put a horse out in it. My mother's uncle fell down in a blizzard when I was a lad. Never got up again. A man doesn't need to be here long for it to kill him. Not many places in England colder than north Northumberland. Not much warmer inside the gaol.

Thought the Mole would be soft after being in a hot forge all his days. But I found him this morning, laid back, arms behind his head, serene as a cat on the hearth and smiling to boot. What does he have to smile about, with a charge of high treason hanging over his head? It's all play-acting though. I watched him shiver all night, tossing and turning, trying to find a spot without the cold floor pressing into his bones. But no point pretending he's not famished when his guts rumble constantly. He can always feast on rats and roaches. Lucky for him there's plenty to keep him company.

He's a sly one. Refused to fettle my sword, saying he wants his letter first. No give in him at all. I'm not thick-skulled enough to hurt his hands but I pointed to his legs. He threw me a scornful glance and said it was the old way, laming a blacksmith to prevent him wandering. Then he said people in high places were watching out for him. Plenty in here say that and it's just a ploy, the same way all men claim innocence. Kept insisting though, swearing the queen's father fetched him and his brothers of the blade over here because the English can't make decent swords. As if a Catholic king would bother his arse with a bunch of Lutheran workmen. Even if he did, why would he set them in a godforsaken hole like Shotley Bridge? There's naught there to speak of and it's miles from anywhere worth visiting. Little point getting in a toss about it. Might pay for me to play along for a bit and let him win the first fight. There's silver to be made on that old sword of mine. The town smith needs to agree to give up his forge first, though a few bob should encourage him.

So, the German got what he wanted: a mean square of paper and some lumpy ink. Good enough for him. He knelt on the floor, dipped the pen in the ink and wrote, with me breathing down his neck. The man took his time. Best way. No second chances in here. He's a man of few words. Least said soonest mended, I suppose.

DEAREST HERR OLIGH,

FOLLOWING A VISIT TO MY HOME IN SOLINGEN, I HAVE FALLEN INTO TROUBLE ON MY RETURN TO ENGLAND. I AM HELD AT MORPETH GAOL ON CHARGES UNKNOWN. I BEG YOUR ASSISTANCE.

YOUR HUMBLE SERVANT, HERMANN MOHLL

Humble, my backside, with all his talk of royal charters and being sponsored by kings. That servant won't have a reply from his friend any time soon. Who'd brave the roads in this freeze? I'll have to feed him from my own pocket. No softness on my part but he might well have friends in high places. Pays to keep on the right side sometimes.

The Mole didn't look too clever by nightfall. No longer grinning and pretending to be warm. He was shivering and resting his head on his knees. I took pity and sent Roasting Jack in with him, but was he grateful? Not a chance. Started demanding to know whether his letter had gone. It's not in me to bring disappointment to a man already in a bad way so I told him the letter was on its way to Shotley Bridge. Little lies do little harm and can close rifts before they open. Told him not to get his hopes up. Letters move slowly, what with horses struggling to get up and down the post road in this weather. Easy enough to lose a shoe, a horse, a letter. Or a man, come to that.

TABLETS OF STONE

Shotley Bridge, 1691

The sound of heavy horses in the street interrupted their supper. Griselda began barking and Liesl ran to the window.

'Mother, Father! Come quick,' she shouted. 'They're bringing the stone lintels. Oh, may I go and watch them being put up please?'

'Yes, but keep Griselda out of the way,' Katrin said. 'You don't want to cause an accident. Herr Oligh will never forgive you if his stone tablet falls to the ground and breaks. Don't slam the door on your way out in case you wake your–'

The girl grinned and ran out, hound at her heels, letting the door slam behind her. Katrin raised her eyes to the ceiling but no sound came from above.

Hermann pushed away the platter of *Sauerbrauten* and watched the steam rising from it. He had no stomach for the mutton anymore. Besides, it was too hot and could wait. Katrin passed him the letter, which had arrived that morning. It bore the seal of Henry Benson, the London cutler and would hopefully contain a promise to pay a four-year-old debt. He broke the seal and unfolded the paper. To his surprise, the letter came not from the cutler but from his widow. The combination of having to read

English, Hermann's fading eyesight and the writer's frail hand made for slow reading. Although the handwriting wasn't familiar to him, the words were already etched in poison on his heart.

'Katrin, get my correspondence box, please, and find me the first letter from Henry Benson. The one from not long after we first arrived here.'

She raised her brows at him. 'The insulting one?'

He nodded and she lifted the box from the shelf, thumbing through the letters until she found the one he wanted and passed it to him.

'I knew it.' He flicked the letter with a fingernail. 'The widow's letter simply echoes her dead husband's words and it's no less aggrieving for arriving all these years after the original.'

He set the two letters side by side and compared them. Word for word, they were identical and the insult leapt off the pages of both.

THESE BLADES ARE SOFT, ILL-TEMPERED AND STAND LIKE LEAD.

'No blade marked with the running wolf of Solingen can ever be described in these words and less so any blade leaving the Mohll forge. These London cutlers are an obscenity. They want my blades in their thousands but they're not prepared to pay the necessary gold for them.'

'This is nothing to do with your work,' Katrin said. 'More like they can't pay their blade bill. These Bensons call themselves cutlers and yet all they're capable of is taking your blade and hilting it. Playing with fripperies, the work of children.'

Hermann smiled at his wife and patted her hand. She was trying to be kind but she was right about the English cutlers. He folded the letters and handed them to Katrin, who placed them both in the box.

'Let the unskilled English cheats buy blades from their own countrymen at a shilling cheaper but they'll have no more of my work—' A great clatter from outside interrupted him and he twitched the curtain. 'Don't worry, it's Adam's ladder falling and not his stone tablet. Will you come and have a look at Oligh's lintel, *Liebe*?'

'No, Hermann, I will not.' Katrin sat down and began to thread a needle. 'Oh, it's a great shame you didn't see fit to follow suit and declare our faith.'

'Faith? Really, these stones are nothing more than a plea to God to reward our industry and born of a fear that God speaks no English.'

She tangled her sewing thread and tried to unpick it. 'You mustn't make light of our faith, Hermann.'

These stones worried him. This pushing of their religion and language into the faces of the locals might not wear so well. Maddison wouldn't take kindly to it with his dislike of any tongue other than his own.

'I'm not making light,' he said. 'The local people strike me as superstitious and the strange words might be seen as magic or spells.'

'Magic and spells, Hermann? Have you taken leave of your senses? These are God's words. As if a prayer could be witchcraft.' Katrin gave up trying to untangle the thread and bit through it with her small, sharp teeth. 'Once they know it's a prayer, the English will admire them as much as we do.'

'And another thing, the English have very little so we shouldn't flaunt our wealth. We might not have much but we still have more than the people here.'

'All that we have,' she said, 'we've worked hard for and have sacrificed much.'

He got up, took down his mother's jewellery chest, unlocked it and began polishing a small wedding band with his kerchief. The London guild galled him no end. It was too bad trying to force him to sell his fine blades for a shilling per dozen cheaper than originally agreed. He breathed on the ring and held it up to the light, which revealed an ingrained mark. He rubbed at it hard.

Satisfied, he replaced the gleaming ring in the chest and took out another. The English thirst for killing each other was waning and with it the need for swords. That much, he couldn't deny, but for the Bensons to take the blades and cheat him out of his hard-earned coin by spreading lies and reneging on the agreed price was dishonourable. He plucked his flask from his inside pocket and drank. The schnapps burnt his throat and with any luck it might burn out the rage fermenting in his gut.

These past years, Hermann had ignored Benson's complaint and continued sending regular reminders for payment of the retained amount. Reminders that had been roundly ignored. Now, when every shilling counted, when he really needed these bills to be paid, here was the cutler's widow, scratting through her dead husband's effects, seeking excuses to avoid paying for swords that were perfectly well-tempered, balanced and sharp. If the swords purchased were as ill-tempered as described, they'd never been returned to his forge and were no doubt sold on and used in battle. And now the widow came whining about her husband's death following his lying sick with a fever for so many years. Four years for a fever? Four years for an unpaid bill? He took another pull from his flask and coughed. It wouldn't surprise him one bit if the London cutler were still alive and hiding in his wife's petticoats to continue making unfounded slights against Mohll workmanship. Hermann would feel deep shame had he owed money for such an expanse of time. It grieved him to think of the widow still whittering on so many years later because people in London might listen to her harping and think badly of him. Of course, his work stood for him and people knew its quality, but there was no telling what power the Widow Benson's words might have.

Four years ago, when the forges were thriving, life was different. Not like now, when they were all struggling. His neighbours were foolhardy, wasting gold on stone tablets when they had no idea what might lie around the corner. At this rate, Hermann would have to taint his hands by making farm implements and household cutlery. Scythes and knives. It was as well his father wasn't alive to witness this moment. Something would have to change soon. He would have to make something change.

Liesl ran in with the hound, breathless, letting the door slam. 'Mother. Father. Come and see. The lintels are up. They've put them up at last and the Olighs have the best one. Herr Blenkinsop the innkeeper has come to see but I can't tell him what they say. Come and read the words for us, Father. What words can they be? I wish we had one. Mother likes them, don't you, Mother? Will you come and see them?'

'You ask me to come and see something to remind me of what we haven't got?' Katrin snatched up her sewing. 'I'll stay here, thank you, and don't slam that door!'

With a final pleading glance at her mother, Liesl ran out again, leaving the door wide open.

'Griselda, you stay here, girl.' Hermann got up to follow Liesl, closing the door gently behind him.

⌒

The innkeeper had beaten Hermann to it and stood next to Liesl outside Oligh's door, arms folded.

'So,' Blenkinsop said, 'this is what all the noise and fuss was about. A pair of carved lintels set above the doorways. Your little lass cannot read, is that right?'

Hermann nodded to the innkeeper, 'Waste of time teaching a girl to read, isn't that right, Liesl?'

His girl flushed, drew Griselda to her side and walked to Wupper's door to look at his stone.

Blenkinsop peered at the lintel as if reading, while rubbing his hand back and forth across his great chin. 'There's to be none over the Mohll door by the looks of things?'

'That's right,' replied Hermann, 'just one each for Wupper and Oligh.'

'Who did the carving?'

'A mason from Newcastle as far as I know,' replied Hermann. 'Oligh will tell you his name.'

'You must be glad you're not a mason,' said Blenkinsop. 'Now there's some skilled workmanship. See, your iron is malleable and forgiving, but there's no chance of reshaping a slab of stone, so masons need the steadiest of hands.'

Blenkinsop was a fine one to pass comment on who was skilled and who was not. As if pouring cow's piss from a big jug into a littler jug needed any skill, let alone a steady hand.

Hermann snorted. 'If this one's anything to go by, there'll be a pile of ruined slabs somewhere.'

The innkeeper raised his brows at this and swiped at an imaginary fly. 'Has your friend stopped to wonder what the English priests will make of this display?' asked Blenkinsop. 'I can tell you something for nothing. They won't like it. Not one little bit.'

'Since one priest lives at the top of a high hill and the other away along the valley, I doubt they're likely to get wind of them.' Hermann paused to eye the innkeeper. 'Unless someone goes out of his way to tell them.'

'They won't hear it from me,' Blenkinsop sniffed. 'A good innkeeper has big lugs and knows when to keep his gob shut. Well, good luck to your friends is all I can say.' He tipped his hat to Liesl and went on his way, only to turn back and call over his shoulder, 'Of course, it's not the priests you'll need to worry about, is it? Maddison won't take kindly to these queer tablets written in another tongue. Wait and see.'

Hermann watched the man shamble towards the inn before turning his attention back to Oligh's door. The lintels wouldn't weather well and they were bound to darken the doorway almost as much as they darkened Katrin's temper. He had no doubt Johnson, Wilson and Blenkinsop had also worked hard and sacrificed much. It wasn't their fault they had little to show for it.

Now they'd see strangers from another land embellishing their homes with stones carved in a strange tongue. What would the English think? Blenkinsop hadn't seemed too concerned but the innkeeper was right and Maddison might be a different matter. If the madman was angered by the Germans speaking in their own tongue at the inn, how would he react when he saw these lintels and couldn't make out a single syllable?

Liesl slunk back to stand beside him outside the Oligh house. 'Father, it's not a waste of time teaching me to read,' she said, 'I wish you would so I could read the lintels myself.'

'Your husband can teach you one day,' he said. 'If you can find one with plenty of patience.'

Hermann ruffled her hair but she turned her head away from him.

'I'll ask Pieter then. He'll teach me if you won't.' She gazed up at the carved words that held no meaning for her. 'Imagine being greeted by a story or a hymn or a prayer each time you return home. Come and stand underneath it with me.' She tugged at his hand. 'Let's pretend it's ours and that we're going into our home.'

Hermann yielded, following her underneath the lintel. Its mass shaded the doorway and he felt its weight, or at least the weight of the prayer, pressing down on him. Perhaps he should teach Liesl to read. Pieter Schimmelbusch wouldn't have time to give reading lessons. The lad would be too busy trying to keep the wolf from his family's door.

'Come back out, Father, come on. I want you to read it to me.'

Liesl pulled at his hands again and he stepped back into the street, where he started reading the inscription.

'Hurry up, Father. It can't be taking you all this time to work out what it says, surely.'

'Patience, girl. Now let me see.'

Judging by the state of Oligh's lintel, he'd got a ruined slab. The hand that had sculpted this stone couldn't have been too steady. The lettering was a disgrace, with several misspellings, three letters in the wrong case and two back-to-front, but criticism would sound like carping. Perhaps it was the gesture that counted. God wouldn't be concerned whether the letters were the right way up.

He read it aloud, 'The Lord's blessing brings wealth without sorrow so long as you work hard and follow His commandments.' He pointed to the bottom. 'And it gives the year: 1691.' At least the mason had got the year right.

'Is that one of King Solomon's proverbs?' she asked.

'Yes. A plea to God for gold. You know that Solomon's family wealth came from trading precious metals, just like Grandmother Mohll's family?'

'Oh, yes …' The girl's eyes wandered back to their own house. 'I'd better go and make sure Mother's alright.'

To say nothing of Griselda and the fresh batch of *Pfefferkuchen* baked that morning.

'Go on,' he said, 'go back to your hound.' No head for commerce, that girl.

Oligh emerged from his house carrying a pail of cement and a trowel, shouldering Hermann out of his way. 'Ah, Mohll, admiring my lintel, I see. It's a great shame you've chosen not to proclaim your faith.'

'I proclaim my faith each time I set foot in church,' Hermann said. 'It's enough. There's no need for tablets of stone to act as proof.' He reached up and ran a finger along the joint where the stone met the wall. 'Who pointed this up? It's ready to collapse.'

Oligh glared at him. 'I was waiting for the cement to go off so I can fill it in again. Here, hold this a minute.' He shoved the cement and trowel into Hermann's arms and went indoors. He soon reappeared with a ladder, positioned it under the tablet and held out his hands for the cement and trowel before ascending. 'Still, you should reconsider getting a tablet, Mohll. You must consider Liesl's future.'

Hermann put a foot on the bottom rung of the ladder, stuck

his pipe in his mouth and felt for his tobacco pouch.

'You astonish me, Oligh. You can't suggest my daughter's prospect of marriage hangs on whether or not we balance a badly spelt prayer over our heads.'

At this remark, his friend remained silent. Hermann imagined he'd taken the slight to heart. What did it matter, really? Spelling was neither here nor there and he supposed a man might choose the letters that made up each word as he saw fit. God would be able to read what was in their hearts. But in that case, there was no need for any stone lintel. Oligh had bought it purely for his own ends, for his own vanity, to shore up his sense of who he was.

Finally, Oligh stopped sulking and spoke again. 'It helps us remember where we came from and where's the harm in that? We've had more of our life there than here but Liesl will spend more of her life in England than at home.' He began trowelling quickly and running his finger along the joint to remove the excess cement. 'So she needs to remember where she came from.'

As if it were any business of Oligh's. Hermann lit his pipe, puffed quickly to get it going then drew deeply. He'd chosen to uproot his daughter and plant her tender roots in England. She absorbed England every time she took a breath, ate a bite or heard a word. 'I can't insulate Liesl from England and pretend she still lives in Germany.'

'We've created a little Solingen here,' Oligh said. 'If we stick together, there's enough of us to remain true Germans.'

'Ach, Oligh, you live in a land of dreams,' said Hermann. 'Our children have eyes to see. If Liesl takes a liking to an English lad, what can I do? Force her to marry one of our own?'

'If necessary, Mohll, if necessary.'

'And when she's a mother herself, trapped in a miserable marriage, do you think for one second she'll force her own girl to follow suit?' Hermann asked. 'No, she'll push her towards an English husband.'

Oligh must realise this was a situation of their own making. They'd come to England and must accept Englishness. His neighbour should see this tablet as the ridiculous protest it was from a man sinking into foreign soil, and his family with him. They needed to get along with the English. It wasn't possible to pick and choose, to turn to the English when their pockets needed filling, when they needed safe harbour, and then turn away when it was time to marry.

'You're wrong and you must stop this English orphan sniffing around our girl,' Oligh said. 'Forbid her from seeing him anymore.'

So Oligh had finally come out and made his point. Well, it wasn't for his neighbour to dictate who Liesl might or might not marry. It'd be no bad thing if Joseph entered their family because not everyone was blessed with sons. Hermann kept this remark to himself. It would cut Katrin if she were to get wind of it. Not because he meant anything by it but their lack of sons was a source of constant pain to her. While Liesl was a great blessing to them, his wife had always longed for more children. If his friend thought they'd created a little Solingen here, he was much mistaken.

'We live on a river and it has a life of its own,' Hermann said. 'Like all waterways, it'll eventually bring new people to us and also take people away. We don't exist in a locked box and nor should we try to.'

Oligh climbed down from the ladder. 'There's not just your family to consider, Mohll,' he said, passing Hermann the cement and trowel while he wiped his hands on his apron. 'If an English lad takes away one of our daughters, our sons might have to seek English wives.'

Liesl would never consider one of Oligh's many sons, each more pious than their father, but Hermann kept this thought to himself. He drew on his pipe, exhaled a long plume of smoke and watched it move into the air before fading away. Air must take on the scent and taste of whatever it touched, moving around the earth, the wind whipping along from country to country. It would be better to be like the air, carrying a little of whatever he'd touched but constantly moving and blending in. Oligh needed to stop being such a stubborn German and meld with his new countrymen. Hermann laughed to himself. He might as well try to drain the sea with a ladle as change the big man's proud ways. He patted his neighbour on the shoulder and pointed up at the lintel.

'You've missed a bit there, Oligh.'

on the scent and taste of whatever it touched, moving around the earth, the wind whipping along from country to country. It would be better to be like the the air, carrying a little of whatever had touched but constantly moving and blending in. Oligh needed to stop being such a stubborn German and meld with his new countrymen. Hermann laughed to himself. He might as well try to drain the sea with a ladle as change the big man's proud ways.

He patted his neighbor on the shoulder and pointed up at the lintel.

"You've missed a bit there, Oligh."

BUILT LIKE A DURHAM OX

Morpeth Gaol, 1703

*H*ard to say who was more pleased to see me this morning: the Mole or Roasting Jack. The Mole was glad of a bite of bread and ale, and even softened a bite for the dog, but filling his belly didn't soften up the Mole one whit. When asked again what his game was, all I got was gibberish: 'A fight in which I have no dog.' Then he laughed till he coughed and set Roasting Jack away barking.

After he broke his fast, it was time for the Mole to make good on his deal. At the door, he squinted against the low winter sun as he hobbled to the cart, his eyes fixed to the horse's behind. Not so haughty this morning.

At the forge, the smith's metalwork was displayed all around. Like its maker, it was heavy and none too sharp. Great loitersack of a lad, the smith is. Built like a Durham ox but with a bit less wit. Being the only son, his father had no choice but to apprentice him. Fit for fixing shackles, bending horseshoes, making cheap nails and not much more. The master swordmaker took the smith's measure in one glance. The lift of a brow and the wriggle of whiskers gave him away but the size of the smith's ham fists sharp settled him down. The smith might not be quick but he can hoy a hammer further than any man this side of the border so the Mole won't get far if he gets any notions about bolting. Not that the Mole was in any hurry to leave, not with a hot fire blazing. Told him no half measures and not to be all day about it. No good him getting too easy by that fire or it'd make his damp cell all the harder to bear.

Funny to watch the lumpen smith nodding along to the Mole's orders. Thought himself a master even though he was reduced to humping charcoal and passing hammers. Poor lad. Forced to be a servant in his own forge. The smith never minded though and no wonder for the Mole was one to watch at work. Ignoring the smith's mumbles, the Mole never took an eye off the fire or the blade, hammering the orange blade fast till it turned grey. Straight back into the flame. Always turning, turning, turning. A quick man armed with hot metal might do some damage, even if slowed by shackles, but he never once raised eye or hand.

The smith was sent to dip the blade in the Wansbeck, and while the sword cooled, I shared my game pie out, even tossing the Mole a scrap of pastry. The prisoner shut his eyes on it as if feasting on mutton. When it was time to grind the blade, the Mole narrowed his eyes and clamped his lips against the steel dust flying. So much dust made me fret there'd be nothing left of my sword but the Mole had both a practised eye and hand, that much was plain to me.

When he'd looked the blade up and down a few times, the Mole handed over a true, sharp-edged sword with a bit of spring to it. Had the cheek to tell me to watch I didn't cut myself. I clenched my fists but decided to bear the insult. Anyone would think the man wanted to do without his supper. When it was time to go, the prisoner showed no sign of moving from the fire. Hard to blame him when I was quite cosy myself, but a hoof from the smith sharp moved him along, and back to gaol we went.

ADVENT

Shotley Bridge, 1692

*C*hristmas. Their fifth in England. It was only one day a year but excitement took over the household for weeks. The preparation started at Blood Moon with the hunting of venison and ducks in the wild and the slaughter of pigs and geese in the yard. November had been filled with damp mist and the steam rising from the hot blood of slain beasts. Christmas was always a feast of salted meat. To offset the salt, there were many sweetmeats to make: spiced apple rings, raisins dipped in honey and *Pfefferkuchen* moons and stars. At the start of December, there was the Advent wreath to make with holly, ivy, pine, mistletoe and four fat beeswax candles, which Liesl loved to light each Sunday before church. As Advent progressed, the kitchen was overwhelmed by scents from back home as Katrin soaked the Christstollen ingredients in rum: almonds, raisins, cherries, cinnamon bark and lemon peel. Christmas could come every day for those born with greedy stomachs like Hermann but would their customs last any longer than the smell of spice in the air?

He came through the door to find his mother asleep in front of the fire and his wife pushing dried berries and cherries into bottles of clear spirit. He took off his boots and banged them together.

'Hermann,' said Katrin, 'for heaven's sake, shut the door, the snow's getting in.'

He did as he was told. 'Sorry, *Igelchen*. Something smells savoury. Where's Liesl?'

'Out with Pieter and Joseph.'

'Both boys?' He hung his coat near the fire to dry but Katrin gave him a look and he moved it so it wouldn't drip on the mat. 'What are they up to, the three of them?'

'Less mischief than two,' she replied. 'Liesl was all for going out with Joseph alone but I insisted they collect Pieter.' She sniffed. 'Why must our daughter spend time with that English boy when there are perfectly acceptable German boys?'

'Joseph's a sensible lad and Liesl's a good girl,' he said, 'they'll be fine.'

'Well, don't complain to me when we have an English son-in-law.'

If only Katrin would stop worrying about the future and let it take care of itself instead of trying to see her whole life in one blink. Again, his eye fell on the many bottles of spirit.

'Who are these for?'

'All the Solingen families,' she pointed to bottles as she recited the names, 'and one for the Schimmelbusch family although it's a waste with no man in the house. One each for Carnforth and the company men. One for Blenkinsop. This large one is for the Johnsons because they've been kind to me. One for Herr Wilson, of course.'

'That leaves this one. Is it for me?'

'No, it's for the Maddisons.'

'A gift for Maddison?' Was his wife joking? 'The man who almost drowned my mother? It's as well she's sleeping and can't hear you.'

'Feigning sleep more like and that was years ago,' Katrin said. 'It does no harm to reach out to people. Maddison's wife and daughter have done us no harm so why must they suffer? Besides, he seems to have settled himself down lately. He might have seen the error of his ways at last.'

His mother sat up and grinned. 'You think the leopard has washed off his spots?' she asked. 'Not likely. Here, pass me Maddison's bottle and I'll grind some glass into it. Liesl can deliver it. She has the face of a saint and no one would suspect her of dark deeds.'

'Ugh, Anna, you'll leave my daughter out of your wicked plans.' Katrin took off her apron and began counting the bottles again. 'See how impossible she is. Speak to your mother, Hermann. We mustn't make things worse than they already are with that man. Frau Johnson says he responds best to kindness because he never—'

But the old warrior was on her feet. 'Pah! You do wrong to pander,' snapped his mother. 'Stop apologising for breathing. It's not at all like you, Katrin. Grind in some glass and hope the swine dies a long and painful death.'

'Mother ...' There was a warning note in Hermann's voice. 'You will not involve Liesl in your plotting,' he said, 'and stop inciting murder.'

His mother just laughed and returned to her chair.

Katrin turned back to counting her bottles and pulled Hermann towards her. 'The old cinnamon goat is too much. Her sole reason for coming to England was to stir the pot and make my life a misery.'

'I expect you're right, *Liebe*.' Hermann was at a loss. Pandering to Maddison seemed unwise but his mother carried war in her soul. Perhaps Katrin was right and they could bring Maddison's wife and daughter on side to make peace that way. Yet his mother was also right. The man hadn't washed off his spots. Hermann had spoken to Farmer Johnson after this year's harvest, and while his crops had been safe these past few years, Maddison was still as much of a firebrand as ever. Johnson had heard tell of him burning down two cottages away over the moors, saying he'd gone back and forth between the two for days because he couldn't decide which to burn down first. What was wrong with the English? Why wouldn't they punish him properly? The man should be locked up or at least sent away.

Katrin raised a bottle to the light. 'I'll give them this one,' she said. 'It has more berries than schnapps in it. Who knows what the man will be like with German liquor on him? I'll send some of my drunken-man pies as well to soak it up.'

'It's a kind thought, *Liebe*, but it might not be wise to put yourself in his path, even with your kind gift.' Hermann pressed himself to her back and put his arms around her, resting his chin on her shoulder. 'Do we have to give these away? Do all the families need a bottle? Just let me wet my whistle …'

'First you say I must make friends with these families,' she said, 'and now I'm giving them gifts, you say I must not. There's no winning with you, is there? And get off, you're making me shiver.'

'That's good.' He kissed her warm neck. 'I used to make you shiver a lot once upon a time.'

She laughed. 'Hermann, let me get on. There's too much to do and not enough time to do it. Make yourself useful and stopper these bottles, but wash that soot off you first.'

Hermann watched Liesl stamping her feet and clapping her hands. The sky was pinking, the air had ice in it and they'd have to return soon.

'Come, Liesl, time to go before it gets dark.'

'We still need to find some mistletoe or Mother will be sad, and Grandmother, too.'

There didn't seem to be any white berries this year, although there were plenty of pinecones, holly and ivy.

'We might have to manage without,' he said. 'It mustn't grow so well in bad winters this far north.'

Her face fell. 'Oh, but then it won't be the same as our wreaths at home.'

Hermann patted her shoulder. So Solingen was still home.

'Alright, we can search for a while longer. What we need is an old apple tree.'

'Joseph showed me a really old one in the heart of the wood once,' she said. 'Quick, follow me.'

That lad had better watch his step. He'd have a word with him. Just as well he was spending Christmas with the Johnsons. Hermann dropped the sack and followed his daughter deep into the wood, the trees feathered with rime and the snow past the tops of their boots.

'There it is.' Liesl ran ahead and scrambled up into the bare branches of an old apple tree, where she reached out for a clump of mistletoe.

'Careful how you come down, girl. Look, the bark is thick with frost.'

Liesl jumped down from the tree and landed with a soft thump in the snow. He held out a hand to help her up, not that she needed it, and they set off together.

It was getting harder to see now and Liesl ran ahead to the riverbank where they'd left the sack. She opened it to show the brown, green and red, adding the white mistletoe.

'Look, Father, all the elements are there now: earth, air, fire and water. Mother and Grandmother will both be pleased.'

Hermann doubted that but he smiled, hefted the sack onto one shoulder and they began trudging home, leaving a trail in the snow behind them.

When they returned, Katrin was darning by candlelight using quick, tiny stitches. The smell of cloves and wine was heavy in the air as his mother stirred a bubbling pot with a glowing poker.

Liesl raced in. '*Glühwein*, my favourite! Thank you, Grandmother Mohll.'

'You'll need something to warm you up, my girl,' his mother said. 'Just look at your bright red nose and cheeks. This is what comes of your mother being so fair.'

Katrin's mouth tightened at this taunt. Hermann knew being fair had always been one of her pleasures, but she said nothing.

He took off his coat and spread it out to dry before taking Liesl's and doing likewise. His mother ladled out cups of hot wine and passed one each to him and Liesl. He was glad of its warmth, though it would take more than wine to sweeten his mother and stop her being so quarrelsome.

Liesl grinned. 'Thank you, Grandmother Mohll, this is delicious.'

He took a cup of wine over to his wife and sat down.

'See how your mother's eyes glint with pleasure at stealing my daughter's love?' She took the stocking off the darning egg and folded it before stretching the next one over it. 'If only the crone had stayed in Germany. In fact, I would have preferred a life of poverty in Solingen in my own home, rather than being stuck here with your mother.'

'Don't worry, *Liebe*.' He rubbed her neck and whispered in her ear. 'Perhaps she'll die soon ...' Although he sincerely doubted it. His mother was fond of saying creaking carts go far, and she was the creakiest of all carts. For all her seeming frailty, she'd no doubt outlive them all, out of spite if nothing else.

Liesl hefted the sack onto the table and tapped Katrin on the arm. 'Mother. You're not listening to me.'

'What?' asked Katrin. 'Sorry, Liesl.'

'Grandmother Mohll was asking why there's so little mistletoe but you weren't listening. You were too busy smiling.'

'Was I? Who knows?' Katrin began sorting the sack's contents into piles. 'We have enough for our wreath and that's all that matters.'

His mother scraped her chair over to the table and sat down. 'Wonderful. Now, this year, I want to show you how my mother made a wreath.'

Hermann wondered whether she could recall her mother's wreath-making since she remembered nothing before the night her town burnt. She was spared the ordeal of failing to remember when Katrin pulled some wire from the shelf behind her and breathed sharply. 'We'll make the wreath as we've always made it, thank you, Anna. It will be a Solingen wreath.'

A flicker crossed the old woman's eyes. She might be a Lutheran and she might be Hermann's mother but she wasn't a Solingener and never would be.

Hermann joined them at the table. 'How about some carols while you work?' Who could argue while singing?

'Perfect.' His mother clapped her hands. 'How about we start with something by Luther himself?'

Katrin smiled. 'Or even better, one of our traditional Köln songs.'

Liesl sighed, picked up some holly and began singing loudly about an angel coming to earth.

Hermann grinned behind his moustaches. His daughter was an angel herself and was in no danger of finding a switch under her pillow on St Nicklaus' Day.

⌐

Christmas Eve went slowly, with no meals to give shape to the day, but as the sun began to set, Liesl was allowed to light the fourth candle on the Advent wreath and they made their way to the chapel. Snow fell, silent layer upon silent layer. His daughter paused to gaze up into the night to let flakes as large and round as communion wafers drift from the sky and melt onto her upturned face.

In the quiet of the church, its walls were plain and there was nothing to distract the worshippers from their duty. There were no bright colours or dizzying patterns to awe the eye or confuse the mind and no seat pads or cushions to bring comfort to old knees. The church, plain as the inside of a lamb's skull, was a clean space in which to commune with God. Hard-working men and women, plainly dressed, hands clasped before them, their words spoken simply, offering humble thanks to the Lord. Hermann prayed it would soon be over.

Oligh delivered a lesson, not one designed to lift the heart above its proper station or to give false hope, but to remind them that work was necessary and work was proper. To earn, to prosper, all was good. The service lasted an eternity and Hermann's knees ached. Even Liesl constantly shifted position. His stomach rumbled and he fidgeted, earning sharp looks from his wife, so he tried to think of the coming feast to take his mind off his knees. A rustle caught his attention and he turned in time to catch his mother taking snuff. In God's house. Katrin would have a fit if she saw her. The old crone met his eye and continued snorting. She'd never change.

Every year on their anniversary, Father had complained about her taking snuff during their wedding, and she'd always rejoindered by saying she'd needed something to stave off the boredom. Father used to say no man should have to put up with such a woman. His poor, mad mother who'd once seen a neighbour smash an infant's head against a wall to spare him a more terrible end. Mother always claimed she'd never screamed once, not then and not since, but Hermann knew differently. She'd grown up amidst the sound of steel on steel, of steel on flesh. Holy wars. Nothing in her belly. Nothing in the larder.

Nothing in the fields. Those wars had finally ceased but only because gallons of blood had been signed away on proclamations of peace. Now the Lutherans were tucked inside these edicts, wrapped in words and supposedly given safety, but his mother always warned him never to trust the Catholics. It was hard to believe so much blood could be spilt over a few words written differently. Mother had cuffed him many times over the years, claiming he was nearly a heathen. He turned, ready to cast a kindly look at her, just as she snorted another pinch of snuff and winked at him. His father may have had a point.

When Oligh stopped speaking, Liesl took her place with Pieter Schimmelbusch. Together, they gently placed the wooden infant into a cradle and rocked it while the congregation sang 'Beside Thy Manger, Here I Stand'. Oligh ended by thanking God for their daily bread and for the strength He gave them to go on making it. The congregation gave thanks for the birth of the Christ child and Oligh ended the service by lighting a large candle, which would be left burning long after they'd gone home.

When they stumbled into the night, the snow had stopped falling and the village was still and white. The river was frozen solid so it laughed no more and the street felt empty without its eternal rushing. The families gathered and began singing 'The Morning Star is Risen'. Afterwards, they gazed up at the night sky, watching for Venus to appear and herald the start of their feast, waiting in silence, with only the sound of stamping feet for company. Liesl pointed to the newly risen star first and was allowed to make a wish. Hermann watched his daughter, eyes tightly closed, and wondered what she would wish for. He smiled. If he knew Liesl, she would wish for sweetmeats.

Before long, tiny specks of silver began dotting the sky. Flasks appeared from pockets and were passed freely amongst the congregation, who drank cheerily, mist trailing from their warm mouths as they gave greetings to their neighbours before making their way home through the deep snow.

Once the door closed behind them and their cold outer clothes were steaming before the fire, the plain fare of everyday was forgotten for this one night. Candles were lit in the dark room and the fire was stoked high. The family carried dishes to the table until there was no table visible. First came prayers. While Hermann gave grace, Katrin twice stopped him from reaching out to snatch something as if he were a boy. Eventually, platters were passed about and piled high. There was little conversation as food was savoured and eyes were closed in pleasure. Spiced sausages, fat duck, honeyed ham, saged rabbit, succulent pork, apple stuffing, red cabbage, nut-laced cheese and bread dumplings in browned butter sauce. Golden *Pfefferkuchen* twisted slowly on scarlet threads hanging from the mantel, and the scent of ginger and cinnamon infused the air.

After the family was replete with meat, sweet spice, beer and wine, they gave thanks to God for giving food to all flesh. The two women washed the pots, Liesl sorted the remains into crocks, Hermann stacked more logs and Griselda gnawed on a ham knuckle. When they sat around the blazing fire to share their gifts, Liesl opened her stocking to find a cake of marchpane. There was also an orange, brought all the way from Spain, its strange colour standing out against all the red and green in the room. Hermann had carved and painted a wooden angel playing a lute and Katrin had knitted a pair of white stockings. With a wink, his mother gave the girl a battered old ring, telling her to put the gold away for her husband to make into a wedding ring in case he was English and couldn't afford gold of his own.

Liesl glanced from her grandmother to her mother. 'Thank you, Grandmother Mohll, it's very kind of you.' She picked up her marchpane. 'As I won't need to use your present for a long time, I might eat this one now. Besides, I'm sure Pieter will have lots of gold to make me a ring. I've told him to make me one just like Mother's.'

Hermann put his hand over his mouth to smother a laugh.

'Don't be in too much of a hurry to choose, little bride. You might prefer Joseph and he certainly doesn't have any gold.'

Liesl grinned and shook her head. 'No, I won't marry Joseph,' she said. 'He's English so Herr Oligh says he'll have to find an English wife.'

Hermann raised his brows. 'Herr Oligh says so, does he?' Really, the man went too far at times with his dislike of the English.

'Yes, he does, but I won't marry Pieter just because he's German. I like him because he's handsome.'

Katrin smiled. 'A good choice, Liesl, I chose your father because he's so handsome and look how happy we've been.' She held out her hand. 'Come, you mustn't eat any more before bed or bad genies will visit your dreams. Keep that marchpane for tomorrow, eh?'

Liesl sighed and tucked the sweetmeat back into her stocking.

Hermann passed a small bundle of wool scraps to Katrin and she opened it carefully to reveal a silver cuff, rounded, sparkling and perfectly smooth, as true as a wedding ring. It was solid and heavy, containing all his love for her. She smiled up at him and made a goose bill of her left hand to slip on the cuff.

'And now, another gift for my favourite daughter must surely be hiding in the bottom of her stocking …'

'Oh, Father, there are no more gifts in my stocking. It's empty, apart from my marchpane, see.'

'Are you certain, Liesl? Why not check the toe again? It's best to be sure.'

Her face lit up. 'Oh, this must be my wish coming true!' she said. 'Is it a hammer of my very own?'

Hermann scratched his head. 'What on earth would you want with a hammer?' he asked. 'Never mind. Please look in your stocking again.'

Liesl put her hand into the bottom of her stocking and pulled out a small circle of silver.

'Oh, it's a cuff.' She slipped it onto her wrist and held it up against her mother's. 'See, we're the same. Thank you, Father, it's … very well made.'

Very well made? Perhaps the girl had been serious about wanting a hammer. Whatever was he to do with her? Katrin hugged her daughter and Hermann passed his mother a parcel. He expected his mother to complain that her gift wasn't gold, but instead, glee lit her eyes when she took the third cuff and shoved it onto her bony wrist. Katrin stiffened at the sight. Too late, he realised his error. With this act, he'd sucked the joy out of the gift to his wife.

Katrin held up her arm. 'Hermann, so much silver and so pure. How have you hidden it all this time without my knowing?'

His eyes danced. 'The silver encircling your wrist comes from up the road, *Liebe*, from the mine up past Healeyfield–'

'So, it's not some fine silver from home?' A scowl marred his wife's beautiful face. 'I would rather lead from Germany than silver from England and I'm sure we can't afford this.' She lowered her voice. 'What about the steel bill? I know Herr Hayford has written again.'

She made to tug the cuff from her arm but he grasped her hands in his. 'Katrin, we can afford it, I promise.' In truth, Farmer Johnson had helped him strike a deal with the mine owner, and he'd traded some blades for silver, fervently hoping neither the company men nor the cathedral men would ever hear of it. He preferred not to think about the steel bill right now. 'The local silver is perfectly fine. The cathedral mint takes its supplies from that mine and if it's good enough for God …'

His mother cackled. 'Katrin Gerner thinks herself mightier than God, does she not?'

Sometimes, he wished his mother could bite her tongue but

she'd never learnt the art. Hermann saw a fissure open in his marriage, only a small one, but he hoped his wife wouldn't hand his mother the means to widen it. Fortunately, Katrin swallowed and forced a smile.

'Well, if it's good enough for God, of course it's good enough for me. It's beautifully worked, Hermann, thank you.' She leant up on tiptoe and kissed the corner of his mouth, making him smile.

Liesl looked from her mother to her grandmother and then to Hermann. 'Oh, Father, you've made all three of us the same.'

His daughter's eyes were as bright as her soul, and just as innocent, but his mother smirked and Hermann rued his clumsy gift-giving, knowing that even Liesl's shining face wouldn't undo the tarnishing of the gift in Katrin's eyes.

Good as Gold

Morpeth Gaol, 1703

The Mole got a reply to his letter today when the man it was sent to turned up carrying a parcel. Decent of the man to come all this way in winter. Big and broad-shouldered, this Oligh, with not much to say for himself. I tried prying some details out of him about the smuggled swords to see if he would let slip any clue. This man would be part of it, along with all their neighbours in Shotley. Oligh was having none of it and peered down his long nose at me as if at shit on his shoe. Lucky for him he's only visiting.

Roasting Jack took to him, or at least to his parcel, and I had a job pulling the dog off him. Anyone would think the little lad had never been fed in his life. We interrupted the Mole warming his hands by an imaginary fire. His visitor greeted him in his own tongue but the Mole is well trained and told him to speak English, telling me his dear friend was just asking after his health. The Mole grasped Oligh's shoulders and the dear friend did well not to pull back and clap a hand over his nose.

Mohll spread a hand around his cell, 'Life's not too bad here but the cooking isn't quite up to Katrin's standards.' He laughed at himself but it was a brittle laugh and Oligh's face was tragical. All well and good the Mole being so cheery but treason's no laughing matter. The visitor told the prisoner his family were bearing up but the grim line of his mouth gave lie to his words. He mentioned some English lad doing the heavy work around the forge. Aye and doubtless helping around the house and all. The Mole's a good right to look worried. No good comes of leaving womenfolk to their own devices.

The Mole knelt to untie his parcel, the master swordmaker all fingers and thumbs. Oligh crouched down to help and lifted out stockings, mittens, a hat and a scarf, all in forest green. Then he reeled off what foodstuff was in the parcel: 'Chicken pie, a hock of ham, a wheel of cheese, a ring of sausage, four loaves of black bread, six iced gingerbread hearts and two flagons of ale. I've paid Herr Tipstaff to make sure you get to eat some of it.' Who does this Oligh think he is? As if I wasn't well-enough fed by my own hand. The Mole pulled on all the woollen goods. Someone must love him. Lucky so-and-so.

The Mole patted Oligh's arm with his newly mittened hand and asked him not to describe his true state to his family. Begged him to paint a prettier picture and say the gaoler would allow no women to visit. If he hopes to spare his womenfolk, he might as well save his breath. I know women and they won't rest till they've been in. The Mole asked his friend to pass on a message to his wife, 'You're in my thoughts every morning when the sun rises and every night when the moon rises.' Funny that, since he's no window to see the sun or moon, so how can he know when they rise or set? Must be something they say to each other in Germany.

I thumped the door and said visiting time was up. Good as gold this Oligh, not so much as a harsh glance, but did say goodbye to his friend in his own tongue: '*Auf wiedersehen*, Hermann.' The big man gave me a hard stare as he said it but I let it pass without remark. He'd soon sing a different song if he was my prisoner and not just a visitor.

When Oligh left, the Mole ran his eyes over his parcel, plucked a wheel of smoked cheese, a loaf and a cask of ale then shoved the rest at me, 'Share this with Sergeant Ross and Burke, the Scot. Give some to the watermen, Davison and Surinam. Be sure the men off the ship get some as well because they have nothing and no one. Don't forget Walter. He's not well.' Doesn't miss much, does he, the Mole? Lucky to have an honest gaoler since there's naught to stop me helping myself except my good conscience. Mind, that sausage and cheese do smell good. Not a patch on the mutton dinner I'll make myself and Roasting Jack later but still tempting. I took his provisions and put them in my larder to keep the rats off.

HOT METAL

Shotley Bridge, 1692

The bottle of schnapps slipped through Hermann's fingers, fell to the floor and smashed.

'*Verdammt.*'

Griselda yelped and ran to Joseph.

Hermann toed the shards with his boot. 'Don't stand there petting the hound, lad, get it picked up. No! Not with your bare hands. Show some sense. Afterwards, you can go and fetch me a new bottle.' That was one of the last from home. He was surprised they'd lasted so long – nearly five years through careful supplementing with English spirit. Now, he'd have to make do with English spirit on its own, which didn't taste half as good.

Joseph began sweeping, eyeing his master all the while.

'Sir, do you think you might have had enough already? What with being at work and all?'

By way of reply, Hermann aimed a hammer so it skimmed past the lad's ear but Joseph ducked and continued sweeping.

Hermann would have to find his own bottle. There had to be one in here somewhere. He dragged toolboxes from under the long bench until he found what he was seeking. 'Aha! One more from the old country.'

He took a swig and wiped his brow, waving his hand in front

of his face. It was scarcely spring but the forge was already filled with horseflies, their grey bodies landing too lightly to notice until they bit. There was a sharp pain in his arm and he swiped, too late, as the horsefly drank its fill and fled on dusty wings. These nasty creatures were the bane of his life. They loved the sweat and the hellish heat of the forge. Joseph swatted at his arm but he was too late and a rivulet of blood trickled from the bite.

'Stop fussing, lad. It's a smith's fate to be covered in bites, burns and blisters.'

'I've plenty of those from gripping the tongs.' Joseph held up his left hand.

Hermann couldn't see a single mark. 'Your hands will soon harden and you'll not feel anything. Right, if that fire's hot enough, find yourself a blade blank and shove it in.'

Joseph raised his brows, mouth open. 'I'm to work a blade today?'

'Not if you let the fire burn down while you stand there catching flies.'

By now, the lad should be reading the fire and keeping it fed. He showed Joseph how to find the heart of the fire where it burnt hottest. The lad was making hard work of gripping the tongs and turning the blank at the same time. The fire always fell in on itself so he showed him how to keep building it back up. It was a lot to remember, but Joseph was doing alright, although he kept taking his eye off the fire and opening his mouth to ask questions. Even after all this time spent making nails, the lad was still awkward with the tongs and it was an effort not to step in and take over.

'Now, Joseph, keep heating the blade and when you've brought it up to orange, you can start hammering. First, you must draw out the tang as I've shown you. Griselda, you come here out of the way.' Hermann turned his back to check his stores and heard the clear ring of a two-pound hammer hitting cool metal. 'It's not nearly hot enough yet, Joseph. Get it right up to orange.'

'But how did you–?'

'Eyes in the back of my head, like all masters.' He turned to see Joseph putting the blade into the fire but still staring at him. 'Eyes on the blade at all times, lad. You'll learn to use your ears in time. The metal has a duller ring when it's hot enough but for now use your eyes.'

It took a while, but the lad managed to draw out a decent enough tang. When Hermann had checked it, he told him to put the blank back into the fire.

'Take care with that tang. It's the smallest, thinnest bit of metal and if it burns and falls off, the blade is lost.'

Joseph twisted his wrist away from the fire, grappling with the tongs to move the tang out of the fierce flame. 'Is there nothing to be done in that case?'

'Something can be done,' Hermann said, 'but it'll cost you valuable hours drawing out the steel again. You can meld it back together but it's a clumsy solution and we're not clumsy. Better for it never to happen. Use your senses. There! That fizzing noise. Smell the acrid burning? Get the blade out. Now!' The boy was flustered and couldn't manage his tongs well enough. 'Too late! Look at the state of the tang. All you've got now is molten metal.'

The boy's face fell as the tang melted from the shoulders of the blade. 'Begging your pardon, Herr Mohll, sir.'

Hermann took his own tongs, snatched the tang from the fire and held out the stub of metal.

'See how it's burnt? How the steel is blistered now? Always remember that fizzing noise and the change in smell. Don't hesitate to wonder about it. Just get the blade out. Clear?'

The lad's cheeks flamed. This was a hard lesson, but a vital one, and if he learnt it now it would save waste later.

'But the blade …' said Joseph.

'There'll be no waste this time,' Hermann said. 'You can draw out a new tang and make your child's sword. Always keep your mind on the metal and all will be well.' But first, he needed to correct that hammer swing or the boy would be exhausted in a minute and him being lanky with the build of a reed didn't help. He grabbed the lad's wrist and raised his hand to shoulder height. 'That's it. Now, let the weight carry it down. Let it drop. Yes, you hear that ring? Now up again. Let the hammer have its way on the downward arc, none of these pit-pat strikes, you're not working a nail now.'

The boy turned crimson again but redoubled his efforts.

'Like this?'

'Better. Remember that the metal is always hit twice, once by the hammer and once by the anvil, but the under-blow from the anvil is softer so you must turn the blade always. Turn it to keep it even.'

'My arms ache, especially from gripping the tongs,' said Joseph. 'When might I use the water hammer?'

'All in good time. First, you must master the hammer and learn to ache because you weren't born to the work.' Had Joseph been Hermann's son, he'd have been forging from the crib. As it was, he'd had to teach him from the beginning.

'That means I'll never be a master swordmaker as I wasn't born to it.'

'You'll soon get the knack,' said Hermann. 'Here, already your right arm is bigger than your left.'

The boy gave a rueful smile and started hammering under his master's watchful eye.

Hermann wanted to be kinder to this lad with no father and no mother but the world was hard in its ways and he must already know this. Joseph was industrious enough, and keen, so he'd learn the Mohll skills before too long and have himself a living. Although he might be better steered into other work since bladesmithing must soon reach its natural end. If they'd only had the foresight, the signs were there in Solingen: too many swordmakers and not enough orders. Instead of seeing the dying days of the sword, his brother blademakers imagined them as the glory days. Men's inventive minds were always busy building new machines to end lives and the gun was fast becoming the favoured weapon. One man with a musket could shoot a dozen armed with swords and all from a distance. Strength and youth were no longer needed for war, just a good eye and a steady hand. In truth, there was more money to be made from ornamental swords. A certain class of man felt himself improperly dressed if he had no sword and scabbard dangling from his belt, but one such sword would last a man a lifetime, so not many orders would come from that quarter.

This problem had presented itself in Solingen but instead of seeing it for what it was, the beginning of the end of the big wars and the end of their industry, they'd merely tried to outrun it. Now, instead of being at home with their family for comfort and the guild for protection, they were hidden in a remote dale. Still, he mustn't let these thoughts eat into his soul. He took a pull from his flask. Hard work was its own reward. It was important to go on working so he could put bread on the table while keeping one eye open to the future for new ideas.

The river clanged with hammers striking metal, a cathedral of sound, until Joseph's false note spoilt the symphony and Griselda whined. Hermann corrected him once more. While Joseph hammered, Hermann flexed his hands. They were becoming clawed from a lifetime of gripping the hammer and the tongs. His face and torso were roasted by thousands of forge fires and the grit dust must have cured his lungs like Katrin's bacon. At the thought of bacon, his gut rumbled, but it wasn't time for his stomach yet and he pulled his thoughts from his gut to his hands. Once the blade was cooling, they'd fill their bellies.

Joseph interrupted his thoughts with a polite cough. 'Here, sir.

I've finished. Will you check it please?'

Hermann examined the worked blade. 'Good. Almost time to quench it and make it hard enough to hold an edge. Bring the metal back up to a dull cherry red and then get it straight into the quenching vat.'

'Are you sure, sir?'

'Yes, you seem to have the knack now,' Hermann said. 'There's a small risk of wasting the steel but doing is the best path to learning. Besides, you've no beard to singe.' If he didn't trust in a future that needed more blademakers, he'd find it hard to rouse himself from bed in the morning. 'It's the way I learnt. Go on, get on with it. Place it back in the fire,' said Hermann. 'Come, you know what to do. You've seen me do it a thousand times.'

The lad slid the blade back into the fire while Hermann shovelled on more charcoal and raked it over the blade. He warmed an old poker on the side of the fire. 'No, don't look at me. Keep your eyes on the blade.' How many times would he have to be told? Hermann kept a close watch on the lad, tapping him on the wrist, reminding him to keep the blade turning. 'When it's time to go, sing out "hot metal" in case of unwary passers-by, whether you can see any or not.' Hermann walked to the vat of grease and slid in the poker to warm it up. 'Then plunge the blade into the vat, straight and fast. Keep your head well back.'

'Why, sir?'

'Too many men's whiskers catch fire when quenching. Sometimes you get a fireball, most times not, but there's no way of telling. So always expect one. You've no beard to singe yet but you will one day so get into the habit now.' The blade had almost reached the right shade of red so Hermann touched it with a large magnet kept for the purpose. The fire had swallowed the blade's magnetic force and it was ready for quenching 'That's it, lad. Go. Go now and mind the hound.'

Joseph gripped the tang of the blade with the long tongs, held it out vertically before him and scurried to the quenching vat, calling 'hot metal' as he went. He lowered the blade into the vat, keeping his head well back. No flames emerged and nothing cracked. Hermann stopped holding his breath. Quenching was always the point of make or mar. As an apprentice, he'd cringed whenever he heard the crack of metal breaking in the vat.

'All that remains is to see whether it's warped when you retrieve it. Come, lift it out now. Keep it straight. Head back!'

Joseph did as instructed and lifted the blade clear.

'Well done. Now hold it out before you, tang to nose, and look along the length of it. Quick, what do you see?'

'It's lost its lovely silver shine?'

'To be expected,' Hermann said. 'Notice how dull, black and sticky it is? It means the blade's taken the soot from the grease and that's all to the good as it'll make for a harder sword. But what of the blade itself?'

'It seems straight enough to me,' replied Joseph.

'Close one eye at a time and look again, lad. Now what do you see?'

'Ah, when the blade jumps from side to side I can see the slightest of bends as it moves.'

'Good. Good.' Hermann had seen the fault from afar but it was better to teach the lad to seek out his own faults and mend them. That's how masters were made. 'How will you put it right?'

'Heat the blade and hammer it straight again, sir?'

'The blade is hardened now and you must be gentle or you'll shatter it like glass.' In his youth, another apprentice had shattered a blade, along with his hopes of becoming a master swordmaker, but he wouldn't frighten Joseph with that tale today. 'When it's cool enough, the kiss of the glasscloth will be enough to take out the belly.' It was cruel to refer to the slight rise as a belly but the lad had to learn. 'Fasten the tang into the vice and let it hang until it cools and we'll fill *our* bellies while we wait. Come, Griselda.' As if either hound or lad needed telling.

When they'd eaten and returned to the forge, Hermann lifted the cooled blade from the vice. 'Here, run your fingers over the blade. Close your eyes if it helps and hold your breath so you can listen with your fingers.'

Joseph moved his fingers backwards and forwards across the steel. His face was blank and Hermann knew he'd not felt the tiny unevenness.

'No matter if you can't feel it yet, just keep practising,' Hermann said. 'Even beneath calluses, the flesh is alive. Always touch and smell wood and steel until your fingers and nose tell you what your eyes can't in a darkened forge.'

The forge light would steal the lad's sight one day so it was as well to train his sense of touch now. Long before Hermann had ever touched a piece of metal, his father had given him cubes carved from different types of wood so he learnt the wood by grain and smell, and only then had he been given iron and steel. Nowadays, he could close his eyes, press the metal and know how much soot was in it. He could tell the hard wood from the soft, the oak from the larch. He could tell silver from gold without ever resorting to the gross act of biting the metal. When he was a lad himself, raking out the ashes and learning at his father's knee, he'd never realised his father was doing him a great kindness as well as a great cruelty, for he was preparing him for a life where his sight would be poor, where he would one day live in semi-darkness behind the white caps coating his eyes. Now Hermann would do the same to Joseph and make him one of a band of men, stretching back thousands of years. Should he tell the lad and let him make the choice? But what choice did a lad like Joseph have? No mother or father and not a hope in life. This way, he'd at least have a trade, although who knew for how long.

The lad coughed. 'Sorry, sir. Is it alright? The blade?'

Hermann took the blade and weighed it in his hand. 'It should be a pound.' He adjusted his grasp. 'This one is slightly over but don't be despondent. When I say slightly, I mean a tenth of an ounce over.'

The boy's shoulders relaxed. 'So it's alright?'

'It'll do but you can take out the excess when you're polishing and we'll temper it to give it some spring.' Hermann stood at the doorway and held the blade up to the sun so it gleamed. 'A decent blade and one with not too many hammer marks on it.' He raised it on three fingers. 'And well balanced. It'll do. You'll do.' He could say more, should say more, but too much praise was like too much honey and could lead to indolence.

The boy grinned, accepting his master's words as high praise. 'So, its owner will be pleased?'

'As proud to carry it as you are to have made it.' Or would be, once engraved with the Mohll mark. 'Next time, you can make a hunting hanger.'

Joseph turned back to the fire but Hermann stopped him.

'Not now. No more today.' The lad was giddy to begin with. Hermann had been the same, although a lot younger, when he'd forged his first blade. 'Come, you've worked well today, so you can try some of Katrin's special beer and some schnapps, but stick to half measures until you've grown a beard. Come, Griselda.'

⌒

Joseph rubbed Griselda's breast with one hand, raised his tankard with the other and smiled coyly at Liesl. 'This beer is good,' he said. 'Your mother should run the inn.'

'Listen to the little apron-hunter,' Hermann's mother scoffed. 'If my daughter-in-law's beer was served at the inn, there'd be no work done in the village and the men would spend their days fighting.'

A flush crept up Joseph's neck and he put his head down.

'Grandmother!' said Liesl. 'Joseph isn't an apron-hunter. What a terrible name to call him when he was just being kind about Mother's beer.' She turned to Joseph. 'I'll tell Mother when she gets back from church. She'll be pleased you like her beer so much.'

Hermann dismissed his mother with a flap of his hand.

'Take no notice of the old woman, Joseph. Still, she's not wrong about Katrin's beer. The English cannot stomach their beer and it travels straight to their fists, if Blenkinsop's tales hold any weight.'

'Not with me, sir. I'm not the fighting sort.'

Hermann's mother swiped the table with her apron and set down some pies. 'Not many are until they have a skinful. My husband was a god-fearing man, but like all swordmakers, he had the thirst and would fly into drunken rages—'

'Give over, Mother. Joseph looks like he's trying to shrink into the chair.' Hermann put down his tankard. ' Now that you can make a decent sword, what will you do with yourself, lad?'

'I'd hoped to stay with you, sir,' replied Joseph.

Hermann looked from Joseph to his mother. 'Well, Mother, what do you say?'

She clipped Joseph's ear and laughed when he jumped. 'He's terrified of his own shadow, is what I say. It's doubtful he's up to the Mohll name.'

Liesl clicked her tongue. 'Grandmother Mohll, please don't be unkind to Joseph. Father, tell her.'

'Mother stop teasing the lad. Joseph, of course you'll serve your time with me.' He raised his tankard. 'To the newest swordmaker of Shotley Bridge.'

An Unknowing Cuckold

Morpeth Gaol, 1703

*C*aused a right to-do in here today when the Mole's womenfolk arrived, weighed down with baskets. The big Oligh
fellow fetched them on a cart. Once the women got down, he
drove his horses away. Must be putting up at the inn. The nags
looked half-dead and no wonder in this weather. Nothing must
stop these women.

Freezing cold outside, but no matter to them, being decked
out from head to toe in heavy cloaks, fur-trimmed boots, mittens
and hats. When they took their hands out of their mittens,
they all wore silver cuffs. Must be plenty of money to be had
in swordmaking. Haughty-looking, all three of them, even the
tiny beldam. She was more shrew than mole. Ancient and thin
as wire but sharp with it. Having herself a green old age. The
daughter, a fair-haired lass, blue-eyed, nose and cheeks pink. The
spit and fetch of her mother but longer-nosed and lankier. No
wonder Sergeant Ross was so smitten with her. Judging by the
lass, mind, it looks to me as though friend Oligh is not so much
of a friend after all. The Mole must have no clue by the looks
of things. No man more deserving of pity than an unknowing
cuckold.

I tried telling them the Mole could have no visitors but when will women ever learn to take a telling? A waste of good breath. The lass stooped to fondle Roasting Jack's ears but he was more interested in her basket. Overflowing, it was. Cured meats, smoked cheese, preserved fruit, seeded cakes and winter ale. Enough to last the Mole a month. If he survived that long. The lass held out an armful of woollen goods, 'For the men. From us.' They were old and worn but the men would be glad, with it being Christmas and all. I tried chasing the women away one more time but the lass held out a small cushion with a family of deer embroidered on it. Being soft-hearted, I gave way. It would make a fine pillow to support my gouty foot.

Not one bit squeamish, these three women. Didn't stop to sniff the air or look where they put their dainty boots. Charged straight into the cell and flurried around the Mole, who looked in danger of happy suffocation. All four exclaimed in their sibilant tongue. I insisted on the Queen's English but the Mole begged me to let them speak German, 'My family can't speak any English, except for my daughter, and she has no more than a dozen words. Please let them speak in German and I'll translate their words for you.' No choice then but said I'd oust them at the first sign of artfulness. Fancy being loved by such a family. And him tied to go to the gallows, if not worse. The Mole embraced each woman in turn and held on to his wife. Cannot say I blame him. What a wife she must be. Much smaller than me and a lot younger than me. Lovely and rounded, deep of breast, fair of face and hair. It must pain the Mole to wonder what will become of her when he's executed.

What will become of her? A young widow and perhaps another man's wife soon. That must hurt him more than anything I can do to him. Still, he'd want her to be looked after. The girl as well. Mebbes less so the beldam. It might do to keep in with the Mole. He'd want someone gentle and not stupid. Although how stupid must the Mole be, risking his neck for a fight in which he has no dog? It might pay to have a word with this Oligh. He'll be the one helping the family when the Mole's time comes. See if he can help me squeeze the wax on a settlement, unless he has hopes in that direction himself.

It seems Christmas Eve is when my German guest celebrates the Saviour's birth instead of on Christmas Day. What queer ideas they have. But I thought to give the Mole a festive treat. It took a bit of enticing but I got the lass and the beldam away for a time and left Roasting Jack on guard. I took the two women to the kitchen. Made them take everything out of the basket and put it all back. Put on quite a show of testing every morsel. Spent a good half-hour testing the provisions. The lass didn't suspect a thing, but the beldam knew what was afoot, judging by her thin lips. Still, what mothers want for their sons and what sons want for themselves are often two very different things.

Just doing my duty. Part and parcel of the keeper's duties to test everything that comes through the gate. There's been plenty of strange goods fetched in over the years. Mostly strong liquor poorly disguised as wine. As if I cannot tell the difference. There's always the odd blockhead trying to bring in a flagon full of gunpowder. It's no mind to me, though, as all confiscated goods become property of the gaoler and the turnkey. The odd flagon of rotgut is a welcome warmer and more so when it's not lightened my own pocket. Have to shake the flagons these days since some visiting idiot hid a nail in a flagon of ale last year. Poor turnkey nearly choked to death. What would a prisoner do with a nail anyway? He'd have to be daft or desperate trying to escape in this weather. A man would soon founder and be found cold and still within a day. Nowhere to go and no one to help. This is a lonely enough place to work, let alone live.

WOLF LIGHT

Shotley Bridge, 1693

Winter was more bitter than Hermann could remember, and in the early days of the year, the hills surrounding their adopted valley must have caught every flake of snow that ever fell. In the morning, a mist had settled and it floated over the frozen silver path that was once the river. But underneath, the icy water still coursed, a swift current that flowed into the Tyne and on to the German Sea. Little work could be done in the forges when the river was frozen. Whenever this happened back home, the time was often spent drinking and fighting, which sometimes spilled over from the tavern into the home. Katrin had patched up Hermann many a winter in Solingen but life was different here. There weren't as many men for the fighting to get out of control and the men here mostly got along well. Apart from Blenkinsop, Johnson, Maddison and Wilson, there were no Englishmen to speak of, let alone fight with, and Wilson had never once set foot in the inn.

As if Maddison wasn't more trouble than a hundred men put together. After Christmas, he'd become even more belligerent and the swordmakers had started leaving the inn if he was there, which made the innkeeper cross. But Maddison was bad enough sober, let alone with drink on him, and it was only a matter of time before there was trouble. If Blenkinsop wanted the Germans' money, he'd have to bar Maddison from the inn, though the innkeeper would no doubt bring down the madman's wrath on his own head by doing that.

Hermann was busy sharpening Liesl's skating blades while she drew on her scarlet coat and cap.

'Hurry up, Father, please,' she said. 'Pieter and the others are out there already and I want to get out.'

'Here, they're sharp enough now.' He held up the blades. 'Be careful not to cut any holes in the ice.'

Liesl laughed and dug him in the ribs. 'You say that every year!' She opened the door and leaned out. 'Father, why is Herr Oligh up a ladder scrubbing at his lintel when it's freezing out there?'

'I've no idea but close the door before your mother catches you. Get your skates tied while I go and find out.'

Hermann glanced at the heavy pewter sky. The low sun was struggling to permeate the fog so it was almost as dark as night. He shivered and walked to his neighbour's house, put his foot on the bottom rung of the ladder and sniffed.

'Horseshit?' asked Hermann.

Oligh swabbed at the stone for a while. 'From a grey mare, I'll warrant.'

'Maddison?'

Oligh climbed down and rinsed his cloth in a bucket before replying. 'Who else would dare pour horseshit on the word of God?'

'Who else, indeed,' said Hermann, 'but what's to be done about the man? The constables don't seem troubled by him. Perhaps …'

'No "perhaps", Mohll. We're on foreign soil. The judges might turn a blind eye when it comes to rich Englishmen but you can be sure they'd notice us taking the law into our own hands.' Oligh paused while he climbed back up the ladder. 'Even so, sleep with your pillow sword at the ready.'

Oligh was probably right but who knew where it would all end? Aside from the swordmakers themselves, there was scarcely a handful of Englishmen nearby and they wouldn't stand up to Maddison. Who could blame them when he'd got away with murder already?

Liesl tottered over on her blades, wrinkling her nose.

'What's wrong with your lintel, Herr Oligh?'

'Good morning, Liesl,' Oligh called down from his perch. 'You know me, I'm so proud of our lintel that I want it to be perfect for God. It's very cold this morning. Are you wrapped up warmly enough?'

'Yes, Herr Oligh.' She grinned at Hermann, stamped her feet and looked up again. 'Don't you think it's much colder here than it ever was at home?'

'You might be right,' said Oligh. 'It's certainly wild up on the hills. They say Healeyfield is the snowiest place in all of England.'

She watched Oligh scrubbing then wriggled her wrist until her silver cuff appeared between sleeve and mitten and showed it to Hermann. 'Is that why the silver's so fine, eh, Father?'

Hermann laughed. 'Don't let your mother hear you saying such things. Only German silver is good enough for her and don't let her catch you wearing your cuff for skating.'

'Oh, I know Mother wants me to keep it for best but what's the point of having a lovely present if you can't admire it all the time?' She held up her arm and even the silver was dull in this queer light.

'Liesl, your mother's right,' Hermann said, 'why don't you keep it for best?' He tugged her sleeve down to cover the offending cuff and looked towards Joseph, who was wearing an old coat of Hermann's that Katrin had cut down to size. 'See, he barely has clothes to cover his back.'

'Oh, Father. I never thought of that. Will you hold it for me?'

'A good idea,' he said. 'Give it to me for safekeeping.'

Liesl took off her mitten, wriggled free of the silver cuff and passed it to Hermann, who put it in his pocket.

She peered up at the sky, smiling. 'Isn't it a strange sky today? The trees look enormous and I feel so small it's like being in a fairy-tale forest.'

'It's just the fog loom, girl,' he said. 'A trick of the eyes.' She was right though and even the little rowan trees appeared to be gnarled and mighty oaks.

The low winter sun began to break through the mist, making the Germans' skate-blades gleam. Joseph had no skates but skidded over on his boots.

'Good morning, Joseph,' said Liesl. 'Still no blades, I see.'

'No need for them.' The boy raised his boot, revealing a worn and patched sole hammered with segs. 'Perfect for sliding on the ice and faster than blades. You'll see.'

'Even so, lad, you should have some blades,' Hermann said with a sharp glance at his daughter. 'There's plenty of odds and ends of metal in the forge that you can use to make some.'

The boy blushed. 'No need, Herr Mohll, please.'

'Don't worry. It's not a gift. You can do some extra forge work in return.'

Joseph grinned. 'Alright, sir, but you'll see I'm faster than anyone,' he said. 'Are you coming, Liesl?'

It was pleasing that the orphaned lad was so cheerful, although he was just putting on a brave face. Hermann glanced up and down the river. The mist troubled him. He knew the Wupper – its twists and turns, its currents, its moods, its weather, and it was an old friend – but this Derwent was still something of a stranger in many ways. He'd been walking it for years now but that didn't mean he fully knew it yet.

He put a hand on his daughter's shoulder. 'I'm not so sure you should, Liesl. I don't like the look of that mist.' Laughing water, Carnforth called it. Sparkling water. It certainly sparkled under the sun now, like diamonds, but only fool's diamonds because ice was no more than water in a changed state.

'Oh, Father, you're not saying I can't go on the ice, I hope? Everyone else is playing–' she paused to wave. 'There's Pieter. Ho, Pieter!'

Hermann opened his mouth to speak but Liesl skated away before he could stop her and was soon deep in a knot of boys and girls, their arms threshing the air to stay upright, stamping feet and clapping hands to keep warm, clouds of vapour boiling from their mouths and floating away to join the mist above their heads. As their confidence grew, they began skating in ever-widening loops.

A screeching noise overhead made Hermann look up. Above him, a skein of swans flew out of the mist, soaring in a line, their slender necks straight and their great wings outstretched. They began landing, crashing onto the frozen Derwent, and sliding along, one behind the other. The strange birds must have lost their way.

At the bend in the river, where it was deep and wide, with dark trees hanging overhead through the mist, there was a grand rink and the merriment grew with shouts and jokes as the skating became wilder. Some of the German boys were jeering at Joseph and pointing at his humble boots but he didn't get angry with them. Instead, he grinned and began skating in fast figures-of-eight, weaving in and out of the German boys so quickly they had no time to catch him. Pieter Schimmelbusch skated like a clumsy deer and Liesl took his arm to steady him. Joseph's smile fell only a fraction but it might as well have been a mile if his slumped shoulders were anything to judge by. He soon picked up his smile and skated on as if nothing had touched him but his eyes never left Liesl, and when she skated off with Pieter, Joseph's eyes burnt into their backs.

A thunderous clapping from above set Griselda off barking. A monstrous swan flew low, wingspan the length of two men, its brain likely addled by the fog. Griselda's barks must have startled it, and just shy of the stone terrace, the swan gained height and rose over it. Hermann stared hard. *Schwan.* The lost bird was more dragon than swan in this wolf light. Even when the fog swallowed it, he could hear the beating of its wings. So busy was Hermann thinking about the swan that he hadn't noticed how far away Pieter had led his daughter.

Now, they'd raced along the frozen path and were long past the bend, where the river ran deep and fast, and Hermann could no longer hear the scratching of their blades. Their laughs and shouts had faded away and without the rushing river, the woods were strangely silent. He ran along the riverbank but he was surrounded by fog. It was thicker now, making it harder to see. He ran faster, panting, until he could just make out the children's shapes.

'Liesl, Liesl. You've gone too far. Be careful.'

But she continued skating on serenely through the muffling mist.

His heart hammered. This mist was wrong. The ice wasn't right, either. It was too wet. Then, as if pulled from a dream, he heard a great crack and, in the distance, screaming. His gut lurched and he sprinted along the bank, slipping and losing his footing, grabbing at shrubs to keep his feet and avoid falling onto the ice.

'Get off!' he shouted. 'Get off the ice.' A black crack was travelling along the river towards his daughter and she stood stock still. Had she not seen it in the mist? Or was she frozen in fear? His body strained to run onto the ice and snatch her but he knew he'd go through it and lose her instantly. 'Liesl, get off the ice. Turn around. Come back. Pieter. Pieter!'

Helpless, he watched as Pieter let go of his daughter's arm, skated away, dived for a branch and scrambled up the far riverbank before being swallowed by the mist. Only his distant voice suggested he was still there.

'I made it, Liesl, I made it!' Pieter shouted. 'I'm safe. Come this way, come to me.'

'No, Liesl! Don't follow Pieter. He'll have weakened the ice. Come to me. Come to your father now, *Liebchen*. Turn around. Come to your father, please.'

The ice was so thin around his daughter that he could see dark shapes flowing beneath. Fish. Her feet had taken root and she blinked, panic in her eyes. He must stay calm, for her sake.

'Liesl, Liesl. Come to me.' Hermann knelt at the river edge. 'I'm going to lie on the ice. You lie down as well, very carefully, and roll towards me.'

He lay on the ice and began edging towards her, but there was another sickening cracking noise. He groaned. 'Liesl, I can't stay on the ice without breaking it. I'm too heavy. Please come to me, *Liebchen*. Don't be afraid.'

She vanished back into the mist and he heard her sob. He was startled when Joseph flashed past, skilfully avoiding the thin ice, grasping branches and swinging over melted pools. But why had he stopped short of Liesl? Could he not see her? Was the ice too thin to go any further? The mist swirled around her. When she raised a foot to take a step forwards, Hermann found himself praying under his breath. As she lowered her foot, a soft sound came. Not a cracking but a giving way. The ice opened and the black maw swallowed his daughter. Liesl opened her mouth to scream but the ice-cold water must have stolen her breath as nothing came out. She clawed at the edge of the ice only for it to come away in her hands. The current beneath must be pulling her, as if frantic to take her to the sea. She clutched the ice, scrabbling to crawl back to the surface but either her clothes were too sodden and heavy now or the cold had frozen her limbs. The river took her under, her red coat visible beneath the thin skin of the ice.

Hermann raced back along the river, heart hammering in his ears till he feared his head would burst. His whole body was numb, apart from his lungs and his legs, which burnt. He would run to the next weak spot in the ice and plunge in to pull her out. He had one chance. By now her lungs would be screaming at her to breathe, to give in, to draw in the icy water. Then it would be over and she'd sleep.

Ahead of him, he spotted Joseph, lying on a sheet of ice before a pool of dark water, arms and legs spread out. Liesl surfaced at the hole, gasping for breath, choking and struggling to take in air. She floundered, reaching out for something to grab but her hands came up empty, clutching at air until Joseph's hands locked onto her wrists.

'Liesl! Liesl!' yelled Joseph. 'I've got you.'

Joseph had her! All she had to do now was keep breathing. She was shivering so hard, Hermann felt it through his own bones but this was a good sign. He prayed, eyes open, as he lay down on the riverbank, stretching his arms across the thin and cracking ice towards Joseph's feet.

'Hold on, Liesl, I'm going to pull Joseph's feet and that will haul you from the river. Hold on tight, *Liebchen*.' Her eyes closed. Hermann dug his toes into some tree roots, grasped the boy's ankles and gave a huge wrench. He watched his daughter's hands slipping from Joseph's but the lad grabbed her coat-sleeves and hauled her until she was lying on the ice and being dragged across it so quickly that she'd burn her lovely face. Hermann pulled Joseph onto the riverbank and gathered his daughter into his arms while she coughed and choked with the effort of breathing.

Katrin appeared with Oligh and Wupper's wives either side of her, their arms filled with blankets. 'Oh, Liesl, thank God. Thank God for His mercy.'

'Thank God for your stitching, Katrin,' Hermann turned to nod at Joseph, 'and for brave English boys.'

'Come, Hermann,' said Katrin, 'put her down and get out of our way. We need to strip her. She's not out of the woods yet.'

The three women cloaked Liesl with their bodies, stripped her sopping clothes and wrapped her in a thick quilt. Liesl wept against her mother, shaking violently.

Hermann took a spare rug from Frau Oligh's arms and wrapped it around Joseph's shoulders. He rested a hand on the lad's shoulder and felt him shivering. 'God bless you, Son.'

The boy was modest and dropped his eyes. He tried to reply but his teeth were chattering.

'Come, let's get you both home and in front of a fire.' Hermann scooped Liesl from her mother's arms and stalked along the riverbank. They passed Pieter Schimmelsbusch, whose mother was clucking over him. The boy wasn't even wet. That his own daughter could show such poor taste was quite beyond Hermann. He eyed the unreliable river. No more skating. It wasn't fair on Liesl but she'd have to stay close to home from now on. Tomorrow, Joseph could heat up her skate-blades and forge them into something useful for her bottom drawer. Some sugar scoops or pastry cutters to keep her safe in the kitchen and away from the dangers of nature.

⌐

They sat around the fire and Katrin simmered chocolate and cinnamon. The smell of burning sugar caught Hermann's nose and he breathed in the sweetness of home. Here was his daughter, safe and sound, in a house of stone, with the door locked and the fire high. Saved from a watery grave. In the room, her saviour, Joseph, who blushed whenever the girl looked at him. Before the hearth, Griselda, who worked on the ham knuckle she'd been labouring on since Christmas. Upstairs, his mother was mercifully asleep. In Liesl's hands, a bowl of sweet cocoa. In her mouth, fragrant *Pfefferkuchen*. She was safe. They were all safe.

Hermann's heart swelled with joy.

He took a flask of schnapps from his pocket and poured a measure into his chocolate and a smaller one into Joseph's. 'Here's to you, Son,' he said. 'The hero of the hour, who saved our daughter, our one child. You're a good lad. Drink up.'

When Hermann raised his bowl and took a draught, Joseph did the same, only to begin choking and turning purple in the face.

Katrin was on her feet immediately. 'Hermann. You've ruined his cocoa. Here, take this one from him and I'll make another without schnapps to spoil it.'

But Joseph grinned and took another swallow, coughing all the while.

'There,' said Hermann, 'a lad after my own heart. He'll get used to it if he tries hard enough. It'll keep his chest warm.'

Katrin shook her head. 'Another one lost to the bottle.'

Liesl, swathed in quilts, her feet perched on an embroidered footstool, clutched her steaming bowl. 'Father, I wonder how poor Pieter is. Will you please go and ask after him?'

A muscle tightened in the lad's brow but Joseph said nothing, put down his bowl, removed the rug from his lap and stood up.

'I'd best be on me way so I'll go and check on Pieter. Danke,' he said, smiling at Katrin.

Hermann pressed him back into his seat. 'You're not going anywhere, Son. You gave us our daughter back from the ice so I'll go and see how young Schimmelbusch fares. You stay here and get yourself warm.'

The lad protested and Katrin gave Hermann a look but he shook it away and put on his coat.

'The cold night air will be harsh on your lungs, Hermann.' Katrin wound a muffler around his mouth and nose and tucked it into his collar. 'Is there any need to see how he fares? The boy was barely wet.'

'Exactly. I'll say my piece to this "poor Pieter" and hopefully that will be an end to Liesl's interest in the pup.'

The hound buried her bone under the mat and got up but Hermann shook his head.

'Stay, Griselda, keep warm.'

For Liesl's sake, he'd go and check on young Schimmelbusch. In all honesty, he couldn't blame Pieter for not risking his neck. The lad was all that stood between his family and starvation.

SAVIOUR'S DAY

Morpeth Gaol, 1703

Not such a good day for the men today, with nothing to mark the Saviour's birth for most of them. Walter's in a bad way and could barely raise his ghastly face this morning. Gaol fever more than likely. Burke is not so canny these days. His gout is playing him up. Must be all the fine gaol fare.

I tried to lead the men in a bit of a song but it's not the same anymore. Not like the good old days when the men could be trusted to play with muskets and set tar barrels burning. We've had some grand festive times in the past, lighting up the windows, but Queen Anne's coronation last year put paid to all that. It was a fine idea drinking the new queen's health but it took a while to put the fire out and the chaplain refused to set foot in the place again. Still without a chaplain now. I lead the men in prayers once a week so they're not entirely godless but my heart's not in it. Hard to believe in any God that would snatch so much away from a man and yet force him to go on breathing.

It was a bitter day and one best spent close to a crackling fire. The turnkey got to stay at home with his family. Lucky him to have one. The harsh conditions didn't stop the Mole's wife, though. She certainly has spirit, you have to give her some due for that. The lass and the beldam must have stayed snug at the inn. Oligh fetched the wife in his wagon, bound head to foot in rugs, which took some unwrapping. Bit of a special Christmas box for Oligh, the lucky devil. I'll wager it's not the first time he's unwrapped that particular parcel. A plump little pigeon like her, plenty of men would fancy their chances. After his enjoyable task, Oligh wouldn't come in for love nor money and stayed outside in the freezing cold, tending the horses.

She'd fetched another basket, much like before, but with almond paste and a brace of oranges. I'd like to get my hands on those if a deal could be struck. The good Frau didn't mess about but dropped her basket on the mucky floor and ran straight into the Mole's arms. Didn't blanch and was happy to be pressed against him, filth or none. What it must be to have such a woman.

The Mole held her to him and didn't speak, content to breathe her in. She clung so tight, it looked like she was trying to press him into her in the hope of carrying him away home. When she stopped weeping, the Mole held her at arm's length and took a long look at his wife. She started crying afresh so he pulled her back to him. Must be hard for her to look at the Mole now. Not been here two minutes but very thin already. His inner fire must burn high. Men like that cannot hold a scrap of weight on them. Not a problem for me. I've always been a good keeper, in more ways than one.

I coughed and held up a finger, 'One hour.' Long enough for them to make feet for bairns' stockings and long enough for me to walk Roasting Jack. The Mole looked over his wife's shoulder and gave me a grateful look. Those oranges were as good as mine. It's all well and good the powers that be saying who might and might not join giblets but they're not the ones lumbered with enforcing their daft rules.

At the finish, the dog's walk didn't take long and I called down to Oligh, who tipped his hat. The horses were stamping and champing, poor beasts. Plumes of steam coming off them.

Easy enough to put them out of their misery by sending their passenger on her way. I took a slow walk back to the Mole's cell. His hour wasn't up, but that couldn't be helped. I caught him and his good lady in a delicate state, but that couldn't be helped either.

Enough of Hounds

Shotley Bridge, 1693

*H*ermann stepped outside of the forge, glad of the tall trees surrounding him. Sapphire dragonflies danced in the air and as soon as Joseph followed, he told him to shut the door so they wouldn't frizzle their wings on the fire. Sunlight filtered pleasingly through the green leaves, making a dappled glade. He took a draught from his flask, coughed and rubbed at his eyes. The English had a lot to learn when it came to spirit.

Joseph picked up a flat stone and skimmed it at the river.

Hermann raised a brow. 'Seven skips. Not bad.' He took a few steps through the carpet of bluebells and the wild garlic flowers and eased himself onto a flat rock. While Joseph continued skimming stones, Hermann kicked off his clogs and slipped his feet into the cool water. It was a hot day but still cooler than inside the forge. The savoury smell of garlic was irresistible so he picked a long leaf to chew on while he waited.

Liesl soon arrived, Griselda at her side, with the hound's grey snout snuffling at the basket. His daughter carefully placed two flagons of beer in the river, securing them behind a small rock. When she opened the basket to share out the food, Hermann was pleased to see his favourite sausage, a hunk of cheese, a loaf and some cherries. The hound feasted on cheese rind, bread crust and the heel of the sausage. When they were done, Hermann fished a flagon out of the river. As they passed round the beer, Griselda loped to the river and stood chest-deep, lapping water. A dragonfly circled the hound's head but she didn't notice the pretty creature until it almost landed on her nose. When she snapped, it soared off but her eyes didn't follow the insect and Hermann realised she was relying on hearing and smell, rather than sight. She wasn't so old but her eyes were already getting milky from the forge light. He'd need to do something, and soon.

'Liesl, you stay outside and clear up. Joseph and Griselda, come with me.'

Back in the forge, with Liesl safely outside, Hermann placed the flat of his hand on the shoulder-height grinding wheel. He turned it, examining it from top to bottom, checking for any cracks, though it was impossible to see what lay beneath the surface of the stone. Satisfied, he wriggled onto his belly in the wooden cradle in front of the wheel. Without being called, the hound came and lay across the back of his knees and the dampness seeping through his breeches from her wet fur was welcome in the heat of the forge. Joseph took the brake off the grinding wheel so it began to spin. The dog gave a soft whine and Hermann braced himself for the grating of steel against stone. It must be a hundred times worse for the feeble-eyed hound, whose solitary ear could detect a hare a mile away. Finally, he picked up the blade, held it before him with both hands and touched it to the wheel, closing his mouth and eyes against the grinding dust. The vibrations passed through the steel and into his hands, along his arms, down his spine and legs and on into his hound. She trembled against him as the vibrations rattled her bones. After a while, he lifted the sword from the grinding wheel, blew on the blade and examined the newly ground edge before turning it over and pressing the other side to the wheel.

Griselda was truly a swordmaker's hound and every grinder

who valued his life owned such an animal. Her senses were sharper than the blades being ground and she knew when the stone wheel was set to crack. If she jumped off, it was time to leave the forge. Too many men and boys had suffered bloody deaths through these stones breaking without warning. As an apprentice, he'd witnessed a grinder being carried out of the forge and the bloody mass of that corpse haunted him still. Hermann owed his life to this hound and to all those who'd come before her.

Finally, he lifted the last blade from the spinning stone and told Joseph to apply the brake.

'Good girl, Griselda, your work here is done for now. You too, Joseph. Let's get some cool air and a drink.'

The hound slid off Hermann and he got to his feet, stiff after lying for so long on his front with arms outstretched and a heavy weight draped over the back of his legs. 'Time to find a smaller hound, eh, Griselda? My old bones aren't up to the task of holding one of your weight.'

Liesl rushed into the forge and petted the hound. 'Father, how can you talk of getting another hound, let alone a smaller one? Griselda's feelings have been hurt. See how sad you've made her. Come with me, *Hündchen*.' The girl led the hound to the edge of the river with Joseph close behind.

'Settle down, Liesl,' said Hermann. 'Griselda's not going anywhere yet but she'll not be here forever. Look at how milky her eyes are becoming. We can't leave her like that.' There were tears in his girl's eyes. This hound was nursemaid, playmate and guard to his daughter. 'She'll be here for some years but it'll soon be time to train up a pup to take over her forge work.'

'And what will Griselda do then? You can't get rid of her, Father. She's not that old.'

'Griselda will become a house-hound for the rest of her days, useful only for soaking up the heat from the hearth and tripping unwary feet in the night. You can set yourself the task of finding us a pup.'

Liesl looked unconvinced and inspected the hound's eyes closely. 'Father, don't force Griselda to stay at home, or she'll feel useless and unwanted. You can take the couching needle to her eyes, can't you? You did it for old Herr Schaffe, didn't you, and for Herr Voes?'

Hermann plucked the second beer flagon from the rocks at the river edge and took a long draught before passing it to Joseph. 'It's one thing to save the sight of a man but it's a lot of pain to cause a hound who can't understand what's happening to her. She'll get by well enough using her nose and her ear.'

But his girl wasn't giving up easily. 'Herr Schaffe was barely more sensible than a hound and you saved his sight for him.'

'Don't speak of Schaffe in that way, my girl. I won't be drawn further on this. Now, there are many hounds in the street so you and Griselda can enjoy inspecting each pup born until you find the right one. Griselda's eyes will do for that.' He held out his hand to Joseph for the flask and passed it to Liesl, who declined. Hermann shrugged and drained the remaining beer. 'Enough of hounds. Joseph, it's time to show you how to engrave the running wolf. Maybe when you've mastered that, it'll be time for the crown and crossed swords. Unless my haughty daughter would prefer a small portrait of her father surrounded by bluebells and garlic flowers? Liesl?'

But she wouldn't be teased from her ill humour and buried her face in Griselda's fur. 'A crown and crossed swords will do.'

Hermann returned to the forge, followed by Joseph, a sullen Liesl and the hound. He'd show Joseph how to strike the running wolf mark. His hands knew the pattern so well he could engrave it with his eyes shut. One day, he might have to do that or he might even have to resort to a stamp. In truth, his own eyes were failing and he no longer dared to use the couching needle, even on a hound. Swordmakers and their hounds shared that in common: milky eyes that were the unwanted gift of the forge fire. In time, Joseph would have to take over the fine work. Even if Hermann could do the job with his eyes shut, his hands wouldn't be steady for too much longer. What the forge flames would do for his eyes, the miasma rising from the steel would do for his hands. Once the shaking palsy set in, he'd be unable to engrave or write. Joseph could be trained to nick his eye with the couching needle and push back the ruined lens, which would give his eyes more time, but once the tremors set in fully, they'd finish him. He sighed. These were dark thoughts about a day that was still far off in the future and so he put them from his mind.

'Here, Joseph, I'll show you how to strike the running wolf. Come closer and watch me make the sign.'

The lad leaned over, ready to observe. Hermann quickly struck the seven lines of the Solingen mark. He blew the blade and held it up.

'Now, memorise that image and practise drawing it, lad. Get a stick and draw it in the earth or scratch it on a slate with a nail. Keep doing it until you can do it with your eyes closed.'

Joseph fumbled in his pocket, pulling out his key of Hubertus. 'Will I do it with this nail?'

'No, never with that one,' Hermann said. 'Keep that one safe and find an old nail but in your own time. Now, it's time to earn your bread. There's your blade to harden.'

Joseph put his blade into the flames, and once the metal came up to a dull cherry red, touched the magnet to it. Hearing the repeated clinking of the magnet, Liesl looked up. Hermann winked but the girl was still in a sulk and ignored him.

'When you're ready, Joseph, you may go ahead with the quenching. Keep your head well back.'

Joseph dashed forwards, calling out 'hot metal' as he went, before plunging the blade into a vat of grease, which burst into flames. Joseph pulled his head back until the flames abated.

'Quickly now, hold it steady so it doesn't warp. Good, Joseph, very good.' Hermann glanced at Liesl and turned back to the lad. 'One day, depending how you get on, I'll show you how to make the Mohll family mark, eh?'

Joseph put his head down, his ears and nape the same colour as the blade before he'd quenched it. Liesl wouldn't meet his eye, busying herself by pressing the magnet to the finished blades that were ready to send to London.

Eventually, Liesl had complained of boredom and returned home, leaving Griselda behind her. Joseph wiped the cooled blade dry and rubbed it with glasscloth until it lost its soot and scale. Finally, he handed the gleaming blade to Hermann, who skimmed it with his practised eye. Was the lad holding his breath while he waited?

'It's a good blade, Son, and true,' said Hermann.

Joseph flushed and grinned. 'Thank you, sir, thank you. Do you think you'll manage to make a master swordmaker of me?'

Hermann thought for a while and nodded once. 'If you keep working hard, you'll be a master one day, but the journey is long.' He didn't add that there might not be any work at the end of the journey. The lad would be a skilled smith and there was always plenty of work making horseshoes and nails, so no need to disappoint him yet. Hermann looked at the lad, earnest green eyes peering up at him. This lanky, red-headed lad with such a ready smile was easy to like. Joseph was a son any father would be proud of. He was growing and he'd soon be taller than Hermann. The boy overtaking the man.

'Sir, what shall we do next?' asked Joseph, interrupting his master's thoughts.

'Next, we temper the blade,' said Hermann, going on to explain that while a sword needed a sharp edge for battle, it also had to have some spring to stop it breaking, which meant softening the spine of the blade by tempering it and quenching it in the river. There was no magnet test to indicate when the metal was ripe for tempering so the lad would have to learn the shade of blue that decreed it was time to pull the blade from the flame. The ephemeral shade that bloomed in steel ready for tempering existed nowhere else exactly, except in the hue of his daughter's eyes. Hermann often wondered whether she was born with that colour or whether her eyes had taken it from the turning steel but he knew himself fanciful.

'You need to watch out for a certain shade of blue and that will tell you when the steel is ready to temper,' said Hermann. 'I have my own names for the colours but you'll want to make up your own.'

He showed Joseph how to hold the blade by the tang and turn it above the flames. Holding the steel at arm's length would help the lad steady his eye at the right distance so he could take a true sight on the colour. The tang remained grey in Joseph's bare hand, even though the spine of the blade was growing hotter, turning from silver to gold and from gold to bronze to brown to purple.

'Get ready, lad, here comes the blue,' Hermann said. 'See, the flash on the wing of a magpie. The glaze on a newborn pup's eye. Then mountainside cornflowers. Now an August sky.' Hermann continued watching the metal, waiting for the moment when the blue of his daughter's eyes would find its match in the steel. Just as the blade was almost the right colour, Griselda's hackles rose and she began growling. Joseph blinked and took the blade away from the flame. Hermann watched the blue fade from the steel, put one hand on his sword and held back the growling hound with the other. The hound was never bothered by the swordmakers and their families so who could this be? Maddison?

He'd never ventured near their forges before when Hermann was working but there was always a first time.

The door opened and a beam of bright sunlight bore in a man dressed in travelling attire, his boots and gloves covered in the dust that only a long journey could bring on such a fine day. Not Maddison but almost as bad. Den Hayford, the devil who sold them their steel at increasingly punitive prices. Hermann feared no man and would fight with his bare hands until his final gasp if necessary but now his stomach turned. He owed this man money and must be humble because he couldn't presently pay the bill. Although it didn't fall due for another month, unless the heavens rained gold pieces or the Widow Benson paid what she owed, there was no way of paying this steel bill in full. Hayford, a young man who spent his time travelling the country at his father's behest to gossip and spy on other men's work, must know this. Still, it was unusual for such a man to travel to the far reaches of Shotley Bridge. Were the Hayfords so short of funds that they sent their scion to chase what amounted to a small debt? He must have another motive for this visit.

Hermann jerked his head at Joseph to leave the forge and to take Griselda with him. His apprentice frowned and dragged his feet, as well he might at leaving a blade half-worked, but Hermann didn't waver and he left. Under the visitor's gaze, Hermann moved around the forge, attending to well-ordered tools and materials that didn't need his attention. He'd not be the first to speak, supposing his life depended on it.

'Mohll. You know why I am here.' There was no question in Hayford's demeanour or his words.

Hermann eyed him. Yes, he knew why this youth was here. To remind him of his shameful debt. To put him in his place. To take his livelihood and also his manhood. These English. He said nothing. From outside came the rush of the river, the clank of the waterwheels and the chirrup of birdsong. At this time of day, the forges along the river usually resonated with metal being hammered. To silence a forge cost money that no man could afford and certainly not these days. His countrymen must have seen Hayford's horse. By now, they'd certainly have noticed Joseph outside, cooling himself under the willows instead of working. Hermann shifted his weight, silently willing his neighbours to continue their work. There were orders to fulfil and they mustn't waste the steel bought so dearly.

Hayford took off one travel-stained glove and moved carefully around the confines of the forge, fingering blades and running his eyes over the machinery. His hand hovered over the new blade. The metal was silver once more but it was still hot. Hayford knew steel well enough but how well did he know forges? It was tempting to find out.

'Let me move that blade out of harm's way,' Hermann said, deciding it was bad enough dealing with a creditor, let alone an injured one.

Hayford withdrew his hand while Hermann removed the hot blade. 'I say again, Mohll, you know why I am here.'

Again, Hermann eyed him. This game could be played all day, should the unwelcome visitor wish it. Through the open door, he glimpsed the steel man's horse tied to a tree. There was no sign of any cart so he wasn't about to grab the steel and take it away.

Hayford trailed the back of his hand across the grinding wheel. 'Gritstone. Cut from the riverbank. A bounty from God, no doubt. You know, wherever you go in the world you will find three things: a Scot, a rat and a Newcastle grindstone.'

'We have licences for each and every grinding wheel cut from the rock since we arrived here.' Hating himself for doing it, Hermann reached for his metal lock box and withdrew a sheaf of papers. 'See, all bearing the seal of the Moot Hale. We pay God's bills.'

The steel man took the licences, held them up to the light

coming through the door and read each one. 'It seems God is a more fortunate creditor than my father.' The youth's gaze swept the forge, taking stock of the machinery and tools. 'All leased to you, Mohll, I imagine? Like the forge, your home and your church. Sorry, I forget English is not your native tongue. "Leased" means owned by other men.'

'I know the meaning of the word, and no, the forge—' Hermann wished he could take back his words but it was too late and his hot head had made him stumble unseeing into the waiting trap.

'So, the forge and house are your own,' said Hayford. 'The greedy little Germans have decided to buy a piece of England. Much benefit may it bring you. Yet, it may bring my family some benefit. Your capital means you can pay us.' Hayford withdrew a small book from his pouch and leafed through it. 'I doubt you need reminding but you owe us the sum of £49 10s and 5d. One way or another.'

Hermann was thankful his daughter wasn't present, not so much to spare the girl from seeing her father humiliated, but because the Englishman would no doubt size up his girl to place a value on her and there was only so much anger his body could contain before it found its way into his fists. This youth must be both brave and foolish, throwing out sharp words in a forge hung with the sharpest of blades, but an Englishman's blood wasn't worth a German's neck.

'You may leave now, Hayford. You'll have your money. There's no need to remind me. We'll pay this bill in full and on time, just as we paid your last bill in full and on time.'

Hayford flicked through the pages of his book. 'Ah, yes. Here we are … the sum of £375 4s 10d in October past.'

Hermann ignored the book. The figures were firmly held in his mind. He said nothing.

'Clearly, you're purchasing much smaller quantities of steel these days, which tells me your sword orders have fallen,' Hayford said as he turned and appraised a half-full sword chest. 'Or, you and your countrymen have fallen into difficult financial straits. There can be no profit in pretending otherwise.'

'This latest bill doesn't fall due for one month yet,' Hermann said. 'You'll get your money, as you always get your money. I'm sorry for your wasted journey.'

The Englishman closed his book and stowed it back in his pouch. 'Oh, my journey wasn't wasted at all, believe you me. One month, Mohll, and that generosity is solely because you work in the service of King William and Queen Mary.'

Hermann inclined his head enough to avoid any accusation of treason but not enough to show any deference to Hayford. Oligh had cautioned him again and again to be humbler when dealing with creditors but it was a skill beyond him. Let Oligh be humble. Good manners made Hermann see Hayford out of his forge – good manners and the desire to prevent the man from addressing his neighbours or his apprentice. Hayford walked to the tree where he'd bound his horse. After untying it, instead of mounting it, he led it to the river. A decent man would have done that first. Hermann noted the damp wooden bucket placed beside the tree where the horse had been.

He caught Joseph's eye and winked. 'Come, lad, no more lingering for there's still work to do.' He raised a hand to Oligh, who stood outside his own forge.

His friend said nothing but his expression was grim and his fists were clenched at his sides. No doubt he'd pay a visit that evening.

⌒

Hermann picked up the meagre square of paper and wondered how he could fit all that needed to be said onto this page. How had he been brought so low in life that he was forced to write a dunning letter to an Englishman? Were his father alive, the shame would kill him. Still, were his father alive, this letter would go to him and at least that way the shame would remain within the family, leaving only his father to face. He smoothed the paper with one hand. It was pointless dreaming the dreams of a proud man when he no longer possessed the luxury of pride. Steel needed to be bought and paid for, even though English hands were emptying his coffers on two fronts: the likes of the Widow Benson, who wouldn't pay her blade bill and Den Hayford, who wouldn't wait for his steel bill to be paid. The English cutlers were protected by the London guild and the English steel importers were protected by their debtors' assets. If Hermann didn't pay his steel bill, that sly youth would take the forge, the machinery and every blade in it. A swordmaker without a forge would be a sorry sight. So, here he sat, close to the window, using the last of the daylight, not for grinding blades or designing new ones, but on debasing himself before an Englishman who owned much of the land in the north-east of England and no doubt the souls of many of the men who lived there. Now Hermann's proud German soul would join them.

He squeezed the day's events onto this square of paper. Of necessity, his thoughts were crammed into a tiny, slanting hand. As he wrote, he calculated how much time it would take for his missive to reach the company men. Even then, how long would it take them to respond? Might it be better to travel and make his suit in person? A waste of a day though, if the company men weren't there or refused to grant him audience. Briefly, he allowed himself to consider what would happen if the answer was no but he closed his eyes against that thought. He melted some wax onto the folded paper and pressed his seal to it. Before going to find Joseph at the forge, he filled his pipe and lit it.

The boy must have eaten as he seemed in good humour. If he was bitter at losing a night's sleep, he never said so and set off down the river path without complaint. Hermann watched the sky turning. The last of the light was fading so Joseph would have to walk in darkness to deliver the letter by morning.

He tapped the hound lightly on her rump. 'Go, Griselda, be a good girl and keep the lad company.'

The hound sniffed the air and trotted after Joseph. She'd walk at his heels and keep him safe against most of the ills abroad in the night.

He smoked awhile, considering the day's events while he walked home along the riverbank. As the sky reddened and turned to black, the moon rose and silvered the river before him. It brought to mind all the times spent watching its reflection in the water at home in Solingen. Here, the Derwent ran into the Tyne, which ran into the German Sea. At home, the Wupper ran into the Rhine, which ran into the German Sea. Liesl had been right all those years ago. Water connected people as surely as blood and all eyes gazed upon the same moon at night, whether English or German. He drew on his pipe and wondered whether the folk of Solingen were gazing on the moon right now.

Oligh finally emerged from his own cottage, his face in shadow. 'So, Mohll? What to do about Hayford?'

Hermann raised his chin to the north. 'I've sent the lad with a letter to the company men asking for help or that insolent fellow will ride on our shoulders as long as we live.'

'Well, with any luck, that request should resolve the steel bill, for now.'

'We can only hope.' Hermann held out his tobacco pouch. 'But to be called a greedy little German is a sharp insult.'

Oligh shook his head and held up his own pipe, already lit. 'So, we flee our land for the sake of profit? What does it matter? Let Hayford think whatever he pleases. Poverty is the wolf that stalks everyone's door, sooner or later.' He placed a big hand on Hermann's shoulder. 'Telling our tales of woe would serve no purpose. Do you think hearing our troubles might tug at Widow Benson's conscience and make her pay for her blades on time? Or that it might temper Hayford's heart and make him charge us fairly in future?'

'So, we say nothing and let these English think it was greed and not need that led us across the German Sea?' asked Hermann. 'Should we battle on here, no matter how hard life becomes?'

'Yes. Our hearts know the truth. We can't go back. The time for going back was after the Solingen notice,' Oligh said. 'There are worse problems than lost pride. You know that.'

'I know it all too well. The worst problem is the English.' Hermann took a long draw from his pipe and blew out the fragrant smoke. Lost pride he could live with but poverty and the English were another matter.

IN FINE FETTLE

Morpeth Gaol, 1703

The watermen and the mariners were over the moon with the woollens fetched in by the German women. Like bairns at Christmas, the lot of them. Walter looked past caring but the Mole wrapped a muffler round his neck. Burke had watery eyes watching over them. Kept saying, 'Bless you. Bless you.' Must think himself a man of the cloth. Thanks to the Mole, all the men have fared a bit better belly-wise. The German women left such a store of goodness that the Mole's better provisioned than me this Yuletide. And what looks good in the basket tastes better on the tongue. Those women must know some secrets. Sausages spiced enough to warm a body for hours. Cheese like cream. Hoppy beer, bitter and dark. They can keep their flat black bread, though. Still, I suppose they cannot be good at everything.

The Mole was in fine fettle this morning and looked a foot taller, or mebbes it was me feeling a foot smaller. Astounding what half an hour with a beautiful woman will do for a man. What it must be to be loved. He relished his meat, chewing every mouthful for all it was worth, grinding every bit of goodness out of it. Determined to stay alive, the Mole, but he's only sparing himself for the noose, or worse. It'll soon wear off, this happiness. Every man in gaol goes through the same mill when it comes to visiting time. First off, they're giddy to see their loved ones. Carrying on as if they were snug in their own parlour and not behind these walls. But it sharp changes once the visitors have gone. The men shrink inside and shut their eyes tight. Not sleeping, mind, but trying to remember what their loved ones look like. All memories fade in the end, as I know to my cost, then there's just the long days and nights ahead of them. That's when they go downhill, and fast. Might be better all-round if no visitors were allowed. A visit buoys the men for a short time but the sinking after makes it more trouble than it's worth. Left to me to shore the men up again.

For now, the Mole was full of goodwill and happy to hand over the almond paste and oranges. In truth, fruits were never a friend to me as they set off the old trouble and so I found a good home for them. The local lads haven't had much, poor souls, as their families don't have a pot to piss in. It weighed on me, them having nothing. Goodwill must be catching so I decided to share my bounty with them: the oranges and half the almond paste. None had seen an orange before and the Alnwick clod complained the colour made his eyes ache. I ask you. When I drew my eating knife through the centre of the fruit and opened it out, a sharp scent cut through the gaol stench. Little Jimmy with the bad leg sat next to me and closed his eyes, breathing it all in, the greedy get. The smell made water well up in my mouth. Just now, talking about it, water rose around my tongue again. What a trick! I cut the orange again and again, giving each lad a chunk to suck before busying myself making balls from the almond paste. These lads, made bitter by harsh living, their eyes shone with gratitude, and I had to leave before I fetched the turnkey and set them all loose. No good having a keeper with a soft heart.

When I was back in my quarters with Roasting Jack asleep across my feet and snoring his little heart out, I toasted the lads with a glass of buttered rum. The thought of them and their suffering set me off. It put the wind up the dog, who got off my feet and stared at me with baleful eyes. Yuletide always opens the old wounds. The one time I let myself think of what I've lost. Dina and our bairns: Tom, Jack, Jim and baby Peggie. Our last Christmas was filled with song, a warm hearth, roast goose and figgy pudding. And all of us were filled with great cheer. But not anymore. All gone now, thanks to the fever. I was lucky to survive it. That's what they say. Strange kind of luck, if you ask me.

ON GUARD

Shotley Bridge, 1694

*I*t was long after dark when the hound began growling, and someone started hammering on the door. Hermann took Griselda with him and told his family to stay back. He opened the door a crack to find Joseph holding a shovel. Behind him, the innkeeper was pacing back and forth, with a halberd in his hand.

'Herr Blenkinsop? What's wrong?' asked Hermann.

'I've to set up the hue and cry for the madman in Hole House,' the innkeeper explained. 'He's murdered another man.'

Liesl squeezed past, her eyes wide. 'Murdered! Who?'

'This isn't for your ears, girl. Joseph, get inside and lock the door behind me,' said Hermann. 'Keep the hound close and beware of fire.'

Joseph opened his mouth to protest but Hermann shoved him through the door.

'Griselda, on guard.' He took up the long axe from the hook.

Katrin ran to the door, her face pale. 'Please be careful, Hermann.'

He inclined his head slightly. 'As careful as I can be, *Liebe*,' he said and pulled the door shut.

Blenkinsop pointed at the axe. 'That's a fitting weapon for a swordmaker.'

'I wouldn't blunt a fine blade on Maddison's thick hide,' Hermann said. 'This'll do. Who did he kill?'

'Gent by the name of Atkinson. Laird of Cannyside Wood, away up in the hills,' replied Blenkinsop. 'You'd better rouse your countrymen. All hands are needed. I'll go and ready the cell for when you bring him in.'

The swordmakers gathered and Oligh pointed over the river to Hole House. 'He's likely gone to ground there, in hiding with his wife and daughter.'

'Do you think,' asked Hermann, 'that the desperate man might slaughter himself and his womenfolk with him?'

'Yes, I do,' said Oligh, 'so we need to get into the house and arrest him without any further bloodshed or at least without any innocent blood being shed. That includes yours, do you mark me? Mohll?'

Hermann nodded and looked at his neighbours, scarves fastened around their faces and clutching snatched-up weapons: axes, spades, picks and a few pillow swords here and there. They could have done with the innkeeper's halberd, to say nothing of the innkeeper himself. Why had he made himself scarce? He didn't strike Hermann as a coward but it was impossible to judge a man until the worst happened.

'On my command,' said Oligh, 'we spread out and circle Hole House in silence.'

His neighbours made for the bridge but Hermann scrambled into the river, the cold water seizing the breath in his chest. As he waded, he held the axe above his head, trying to keep his feet against the rushing water. Hole House stood silent, shining white under the moon, a dozen daughter moons rippling in the dark water around him.

As Hermann reached the far riverbank, there was no sound

apart from a lone owl, either crying out for his mate or telling her there was danger afoot. Hermann slipped in the mud and had to use his axe to haul himself up, clenching the vegetation with his free hand.

He crept towards the house. Maddison's mastiff would be the first to sound the alarm if it was tied at its usual station. A scraping sound startled him. Was that a latch being moved? He looked up and glimpsed a face at the window. Not the madman's face but that of a young woman. The daughter? The moon revealed the whites of her eyes. Had she seen him? Heard him most likely. Why did she tarry so? Did she have a message? He willed her to move away. If Maddison were drawn to the window, he'd notice the Germans surrounding his house and would take it badly.

Hermann put his head down and stopped moving. His heart raced. What was he afraid of? Not much would happen if he kept his wits about him. What lay inside the house? The daughter was alive, but what of Maddison's wife? The madman had already killed one son-in-law, maimed another and shot a magistrate. And now he'd killed a laird. Even in the fog of his mind, Maddison must know his neck was the price. Still, he'd killed before and lived to tell the tale so the man evidently held no fear of the justice and his nooseman.

The owl hooted again and Hermann jumped. He closed his eyes until his heart slowed down again. He was thinking like a man ruled by logic, whereas Maddison must be ruled by a more unruly master or mistress, most likely the moon, which now shone as fiercely as a silver sun. How might the balance of his mind tip? Hermann's family was alone, as were the other men's families. There was no saying where Maddison was. Were they risking their own women and children to spare two Englishwomen? Griselda would fight to the death to protect her charges, but would that be enough?

A volley of barking jolted him from his thoughts. Maddison

had released his dog. The beast was almost madder than its master and driven more so by the moon. Here it came now, thundering towards him. When it lunged for his throat, he swiped at it with the shank of the long axe. The dog latched onto the shank and he kicked it off but the dog only leapt up again, teeth flashing in the moonlight. Hermann swung the blunt poll of the axe down and cracked the dog's skull. The beast fell to earth, its face stupid in death, all threat removed. It pained him to kill a dog, whose single fault lay in loyalty to a wicked master, but there was no time for regret. He heard a whistle and lay down, inching forwards, the earth cold against his wet belly.

A gruff voice called out, 'Rex. Rex.'

When the dog didn't return, Maddison would know something was amiss. Hermann feigned a whimper and held his breath. Would a mastiff whimper?

'Rex?' A question this time.

Another whimper from Hermann.

A scuffle of footsteps, running.

One more whimper and Maddison was before him, eyes bulging at the sight of the dog's corpse. A great sob broke from him. While the man grieved, Hermann swept his legs from under him with the shank of the axe and Maddison fell. Immediately, Hermann was on him, knee in the small of the back, pinning his arms. Hermann was strong but his opponent was a giant, pulsing with rage, so he wouldn't be able to hold him much longer.

'Over here,' yelled Hermann. 'Help!'

Hermann's sinews strained as the wildman bucked and writhed beneath him. He couldn't hold him down much longer. Why hadn't he put the axe to Maddison's head when he'd had the chance? Who would complain?

'Help!' he yelled again. 'Hurry!'

Running feet clattered over the bridge and a lamp shone down. Oligh and Wupper. Not before time. His friends seized

Maddison, and between them, they held him fast. The madman's hair stood on end, his face filthy and streaked with his dog's blood as he howled for his mother.

⌒

The three men dragged Maddison to the Bridge End where the innkeeper, true to his word, had the cell open.

'From here, Maddison will go to gaol in the morning and on to meet his maker,' said Blenkinsop. 'At least he will if there's any justice in the world.'

While the prisoner did battle with his restraints, Hermann examined the steel door and checked the bolts, wondering whether even stone and metal would contain this raging man.

Blenkinsop shoved Maddison forwards into the cell with so much force he stumbled and fell in the corner.

'Never fear.' The innkeeper slammed the door shut. 'The door will hold him but he's a big bugger. When he's in this state, he'll need a double watch kept on him. Will you do it, Mohll?' he asked. 'You know if he breaks out … what it will mean?'

Kill or be killed. And all that followed. The moon was full, Maddison's blood was up and all the demons in his head had been given full rein. Oligh had gone home to check on the families and would send Joseph to fetch the constables. Hermann didn't envy them the task of getting Maddison away from the valley to face sentence in Durham. Hopefully, they'd bring many men. Soldiers might be better placed. Manic laughter came from the lonely cell, followed by sobbing. A dull thudding suggested bone against stone. Was the man dashing his own brains out?

Hermann turned to Blenkinsop. 'Should we—?'

The innkeeper shook his head. 'Drunks and moss-troopers, we can reason with, but a man who would slaughter so readily? Best left to the constables.'

'The man's sick in the head,' said Hermann. 'Could something not be done to help such a man? Leech his blood when it was too high or take an augur to his skull and cut out the offending part of his brain?'

The innkeeper scoffed. 'Save your pity for the man's victims.'

His companion was right. Maddison had killed, not once but twice. With no money to buy his way out of gaol this time, Maddison would swing, sick in the head or not.

'What of his wife and daughter?' asked Hermann. 'I suppose they'll be relieved now they've been delivered from Maddison?'

'I doubt it, Mohll. Come morning, they'll be knocking on my door, fetching hot pies and begging mercy for him.'

Hermann raised his brows, 'I sincerely doubt that.'

'Oh, aye,' said Blenkinsop. 'Always the way. It's a strange business, love.'

Hermann scratched a callus at the base of his thumb. 'It cannot be called love if it exists only in fists and feet and harsh words.'

The innkeeper gave a barking laugh, 'Well, mebbes it needs another name but something keeps them locked together.'

'Need or fear,' said Hermann.

The innkeeper gave him a scornful glance. 'Aye, call it what you will.'

Much of this misery must result from Maddison putting too much money in the innkeeper's pocket. The madman had a curious way with ale: drinking as if it was his last day on earth, as if no more would ever be made, finally reeling out of the inn, drunk and belligerent. In the main, Hermann enjoyed his beer as he enjoyed his food: enough to nourish, satisfy and bring cheer, taking his last drop at that cliff edge of merriment, when hearts swelled in song and loving words. Stopping though, for the next drop brought tears, insult and anger. Hermann was no angel though, and many's the time he'd ground swords with grazed knuckles and a black eye. Still, he'd never killed a man. Blaming the innkeeper was like blaming the moon. Ralph Maddison had killed. He'd kill again if not stopped. Hermann supposed the justice's rope would stop him.

⌒

Although the sky was blue and the sun was warm, it was frosty this morning. After the hot summer, the trees were still mainly green, at least the oaks were, but the high winds had stripped the birches before they'd had much of a chance to turn colour.

Hermann stirred his cocoa, scraping the spoon round and round. 'Today, Ralph Maddison is hanged at Durham.'

His wife leant over and took the spoon. 'You can't possibly mourn him, Hermann. He was a killer.'

A sip of cocoa. Too bitter. Katrin wasn't with Maddison at the end, though. She didn't hear the way he wept for his dog or the way he cried out for his mother. 'Something inside him was a killer,' he said. 'You could see it in his eyes – something or someone he had no control over.'

'Even so, two men have lost their lives at his hands,' she said. 'You can't have a man like that at liberty.'

'So, they should have taken his liberty,' he said. 'Taken him somewhere to be healed.'

'Men like him can't be healed. God set him that way in his mother's womb.' Katrin removed a strudel from the oven. 'You've looked too long into the madman's eyes and he's affected you.'

Hermann stretched out a hand for strudel but it was swiftly moved out of his reach. Why wasn't Katrin wearing her silver cuff? Had she even worn it after the Christmas before last? 'That wasn't a man there. A man's body but with a sick boy alive inside.' He drank his cocoa and stared at the strudel.

'Are you forgetting he nearly killed your mother?'

'No, but she's alive and well,' Hermann said, looking at the ceiling to where she slept above. 'And of that, I am glad.'

Eventually, Katrin relented and cut him a slice of strudel. She placed the knife too near the edge and he wriggled his eyebrows until she laughed and moved the knife along to make a bigger slice. He took the platter, breathing in the golden fruit of autumn and the soft spices that had travelled more of the world than he had. Sugar sparkled on top. Tiny diamonds from distant shores. That he should sit, five-hundred miles from home, eating English apples sweetened with spices from thousands of miles away.

'Hermann, you have that look in your eye.'

He took a bite. It wouldn't do to start talking of home. Instead, he opened his mouth and fanned away the heat of the apples.

'You couldn't wait, could you?' said Katrin, but she said it softly with kind eyes and pressed her hand to his face.

He wanted to say it wasn't so bad here but the dark shadow of the sea that lay between England and home was something best not mentioned. Katrin had Liesl, her kitchen and him. Surely that could be all she needed. But this was wishful thinking. He'd watched her laughing often enough with her mother, her sisters and their children. Sewing with her mother and Liesl, three heads bent over the task of quilting. He'd watched her walking through Solingen, a busy place with hundreds of families, all known to one another, where she could walk out of the house, basket over her arm, and stroll to the market with throngs of friends, all laughing and chattering.

What did she have here? A handful of neighbours and the nearest market a trudge away. 'A perfect strudel, *Liebe*.'

'I doubt it,' she said.

He smiled. Of course, she'd consider the English apples wormy, their flour coarse and the butter thin, but this was life now. Not perfect, yet good enough.

'Do you think his wife will attend?' asked Katrin.

Hermann paused from eating. 'What?'

'The hanging,' she said. 'Do you think Maddison's wife will attend?'

'Hard to say.' He pondered awhile. 'Would you attend, if it were my hanging?'

'That could never happen.' She paused to cut herself some strudel. 'But if it did … yes, I would come to your hanging so you'd leave this life knowing you were loved.'

'I already know that.' Hermann took another spoonful and blew on it. 'I wouldn't have you, Liesl or my mother witness such a terrible spectacle.'

'Perhaps it would be a relief for his wife and daughter,' she said. 'Who knows what they might have endured in that house?'

Hermann wished Katrin would move on. It made him uncomfortable when she spoke of what women endured at home. His own wife endured nothing but others weren't so fortunate. It pained him to hear tales of men – good men – and what their wives suffered at their hands. He couldn't match the two halves of these men in his mind. The man he knew was a hard worker, a kind master, who was fair in trade, who was genial company, who paid his way in the inn. Yet, the same man's wife wore bruises beneath her frock, according to his own wife.

'Frau Maddison and her daughter may well attend to make sure he's gone.' He sighed. 'And if Maddison's hurt them in the past, then he can hurt them no more.'

He looked at the old clock, still ticking away in the corner, keeping time from their old country. Katrin poured some more cocoa, and in the morning light, he noticed the black smudges shadowing her worried eyes.

'Have you heard back from Newcastle about the steel bill, Hermann?'

He shook his head. 'Not yet. They helped us last time,' he said. 'I'm not sure they will again.'

'So how will you pay the bill this time?' she asked. 'And how can you get more steel? Why don't you ask your mother to sell her gold?'

'I couldn't do that,' he said. 'It's all she has. Besides, Oligh has a plan to pay the bills and get the forges going at full strength again.'

'Oh, so Adam has a plan, does he? And will this plan work?'

He brushed the side of his hand across the table, sweeping crumbs and grains of sugar into his free hand, opened the door and threw the crumbs out for the birds before slamming it shut again.

'It has to work.' He kissed the top of her head. 'We have no guild backing us.'

He glanced at the clock again and took a long breath. Eight o'clock. It was all over for Maddison. He was in God's hands now.

THE PRICE OF BLADES

Morpeth Gaol, 1703

*R*oasting Jack howled through the small hours when Walter passed in the night. It's funny how dogs know these things when they have no souls. Since we're still short of a chaplain there was no one to pray over him so Burke said a few words. Not much of a Noel for old Walter and not for me either. No fees to keeper or turnkey when a prisoner's released into the arms of the Lord. A lucky escape for Walter. His passing knocked the men back a bit. Always does when we lose a prisoner. Not much chance of getting the crowner out in this weather so we cannot get the poor man decently buried. I set the men away digging the grave anyway. Something to take their minds off the grief.

For such a large group of working men, they made heavy weather of the work. Soldart complained about the ground being like iron beneath the snow. As if he expected me to do something about it. Little Surinam didn't look too grand. Kept standing still and staring at the wall. Like a lost lamb till Davison pulled him back to the job, flashing defiant eyes at me. Wants to watch his step, that one. Sergeant Ross had a quiet word in Davison's ear and he settled himself down.

Every time I went out for another look, they'd barely got down another couple of inches. Still, they kept at it and now the ground's ready for Walter once he's been declared. When the weather clears, I'll get the vicar to come and bless him. Best to get it over and done with so Walter doesn't prey on the men's minds. The Mole took it to heart more than most. Stayed outside long after the others had gone back in. He stood over the empty grave, eyes closed and head bowed. The freezing fog must have done his chest no favours judging by his shivering and wheezing. He'll have no need to worry about his sentence if he faces the same fate as Walter.

When a messenger came with a letter from Newcastle, I went outside to tell the Mole. His blades have been shifted from Tynemouth Castle. Gone to one of Her Majesty's warehouses in Newcastle. Getting them ready for the exchequer's surveyor to value them. They must be worth a pretty penny but it was hard work getting the Mole to put a price on them. Refused to be drawn on what he'd paid for them over in Germany. Did tell me that once over, he'd have been paid thirty bob for a dozen swords. Nowadays, he'd be lucky to get half that. Struck me as odd the price going down when there's so much war but what do I know? Mebbes he was talking down the price to keep any fine low. Even if his hard-luck story is true, he'd have sold his blades for the best part of a hundred pounds. A safe bet though, that the surveyor will value them at the higher price when he comes to work out the duty and the fine. If he doesn't swing for treason, this is going to break the Mole. Still, Colonel Villiers has done alright out of it. Did well to get away with paying five shillings for a score of swords.

The Mole pressed me for news of his trial but there was nothing of use to tell him. No sign of any quarter sessions list yet. A lot hangs on which justice is in charge of the trial. Not that it'll make much matter with this case, mind. Not with Dismal so interested. Never known the like of it, the queen's own secretary of state taking such a keen interest in a trial. When I shoved the

Mole back to his cell, he trudged along as if wearing lead boots. Should have left him out there to freeze to death. Might be a mercy. Certainly better than what's coming his way.

CANDLE AUCTION

London, 1699

*G*oing anywhere in England evidently meant shaking loose the nuts and bolts holding together the body. The rutted roads were barely more than jumble-gut lanes, which were bad enough for men but worse for the horses, foundering and whipped for slowness or throwing a shoe.

This journey to London was a grim prospect and it would have made more sense to sail alongside their blades. At this rate, Hermann would be gone for weeks and he wasn't keen on leaving Katrin at his mother's mercy for so long. The old woman's mind was slipping of late and she was becoming harder work than usual. Still, Liesl was a sensible young woman and would help keep her grandmother out of mischief. At least Maddison was no longer a worry with him being dead coming up five years. Hermann traced the shape of the running wolf in the grime on the coach window, revealing the greyness outside.

Oligh nudged him, 'What's wrong?'

'You know me,' Hermann said, 'I can't stand sitting still at the best of times, let alone in a confined space.' A stout man opposite scowled. Did he not like them speaking in their own tongue or was he cross at the tracing on the window? 'I'm a bad traveller.'

'Rich,' said Oligh, 'from a man who sailed five-hundred miles without blinking.'

'Oh, I blinked alright but got on with it anyway.'

'To think, this journey to London and back, we could go to Solingen …'

At this, Hermann cocked a brow at him. 'Hankering after the old country?'

'A touch of *Heimweh*, that's all.' Oligh clapped his fist over his heart. 'It never leaves you, this sickness for home.'

'You and my wife both,' said Hermann.

Hermann wasn't made for cramped quarters, wedged between other men, knees touching those opposite, breathing air made fetid with the crush of bodies. He drummed his fingers until he felt the glare of both the stout man and Oligh fixed on him.

'By God, I'm bored, Oligh. You should have fetched Wupper. He'd sit still.'

'I might yet put you out so you can run alongside the horses with the wind in your hair.'

'I might well prefer it,' said Hermann.

'You're like a phial filled with quicksilver at the best of times,' Oligh said. 'Try to sleep, eh?'

Hermann couldn't sleep. As soon as his eyes opened at dawn, he was awake until the night claimed him once more. He envied the stout man who, despite his irritation, had now escaped the tedium by nodding off. As wide as he was high, he'd slumped backwards, snoring, his neck wobbling with the motion of the coach, his belly tender and exposed, as trusting as an infant. Even now, the man might be dining in a fine palace on roast swan stuffed with quail, flying over the desert on a tasselled carpet, swimming with sharks in a turquoise ocean or wrestling with whores in a London stew. Hermann envied his sleep. The imp in him yawned and stretched out a leg, jolting the man from his slumber. When the stout man sat up, rubbing his eyes, Hermann feigned innocence by looking out of the window.

It wouldn't do to ask if they were nearly there, because although Oligh had a long fuse, travelling made him irritable and this journey would irk him more than most, with only the humiliation of a candle sale at the end of it. The English might be poor blademakers but they were certainly skilled when it came to sapping the soul. This measly island gave no quarter for men to breathe or stretch and its paucity of air must cut off some vital portion of the brain. Still, at least he had his flask with him for comfort and could sup from it whenever Oligh was looking the other way.

At the warehouse under the sign of the five bells, chests of swords were being loaded onto wagons. Hermann's head throbbed in time with the clank of the blades and he took a sip from his flask, wincing as he did so. Once the horses had left, Oligh nudged him and they set off up Fetter Lane. A great screeching and cawing rose above the clattering carts and traders hawking their wares but this was immediately drowned out by a guttural roar. As they turned into Shoe Lane, the source of the racket became clear. A throng of gentlemen mixed with working men, all waving fists and hurling coins, all cursing and spitting, all reddened with rage or glee. Hermann dashed forwards. At last, something to relieve the monotony! In the centre was a pit where two gamecocks slashed at one another, silver spurs glittering in the sunlight. He felt in his pocket for coins until Oligh gripped his arm.

'No time for squalid sporting now, Mohll. You can wager to your heart's content when the auction's over.'

Hermann closed his pocket and followed Oligh, muttering and scuffing his boots on the cobbles as he went, the hot sun making his eyes ache. As they neared Cloak Lane, an overpowering stench arose from the running sewer and he rued the mutton pie he'd forced down earlier. Eventually, the street grew darker with the tall buildings looming over his head providing merciful shade.

'*Kerzenauktion!*' Hermann exclaimed. 'That it should come to this. Forced to sell our stock in a candle sale.' He stopped to lean his forehead against a cold stone wall. 'The shame of it, my fine blades going for a song.'

'Come, Mohll, we can't be late.' Oligh turned and walked back to him.

'It makes my heart bleed,' said Hermann.

'And mine,' said Oligh, 'but what choice do we have?'

'Choice?' asked Hermann. 'It's hardly a choice when we're caught between the hammer and the anvil.'

'It's the only way, Mohll, and they might fetch more than a song. Fair blades might fetch a fair price.'

The notices had been placed in the *London Gazette* at rather more than a fair price. The venue was set for Cutlers' Hall on Cloak Lane, where Hermann and Oligh were to oversee the proceedings, as if their presence would make a ha'porth of difference. Of all Oligh's plans to pay their steel bills over the years, this was by far the most hare-brained.

Ahead of them was a great white building, its arched windows glazed with many square panes and set off by a massive arch curving around the door. The crest showed three pairs of crossed swords beneath an elephant bearing a castle on its back. While he scrutinised it, Hermann took out his pipe, ready to fill. '*Pour parvenir a bonne foy*: to succeed through good faith.' Considering the last guild hall was devoured by the Great Fire not three months after completion, he was amazed the guild had any faith at all. Hopefully, this new building would fare better. He cupped one hand over his brow so he could see through the window. Chests of swords were arranged down the middle of a resplendent hall. There was a long table along one wall and low benches ran around the other walls. In the far corner, Carnforth was talking to a small man with steel-grey hair while two stocky men were busy hefting a long chest. Hermann hammered on the window. The small man jumped and the men carrying the chest scowled.

Carnforth left the room and emerged through the archway.

'Mohll, you nearly put the glass out and the auctioneer's heart all but stopped – he's no longer a young man. There's a perfectly decent knocker on the door that you might have used. Oh, never mind, we can't stand here all day yapping. Come, you need to get a move on before the buyers start arriving. Put your pipe away. There's no smoking allowed in the new building, for obvious reasons.'

'It's not obvious to me when there'll be candles smoking.' Hermann wished heartily that he'd stayed at home. An evening with no pipe was not a promising one at the best of times, let alone when he had a pounding head. They followed Carnforth inside and he introduced the auctioneer, who eyed the swordmakers carefully before asking his lackey to show them the candles, which weren't so big – no more than stumps – and all different shapes and sizes.

Hermann picked one up and examined it. 'I see no nail, so how will the auction work?'

The auctioneer gave a prim sniff. 'We don't use horse nails in the City of London,' he said. 'Using no more than an inch or two of candle gives everyone a fighting chance.'

'Except the swordmakers,' muttered Hermann to the auctioneer's back as he walked away.

Oligh dug Hermann in the ribs. 'If you can't trust your mouth to say the right thing, keep it shut.'

'You should have brought Wupper,' Hermann said. 'I'll never master the art of pressing words into pretty shapes to please Englishmen.'

'Just try to think before you speak,' Oligh said, 'and keep that flask in your pocket.'

The auction room started to fill with richly dressed men and women, who immediately began circling the chests of blades. For a moment, Hermann regretted his working clothes but his boots shone, his breeches and jerkin were clean and his whiskers were neat. He had no need of shiny buckles, snowy stockings or jewel-coloured coats, whereas the London guild members were dressed up like gentry. Carnforth greeted each new arrival and whispered their names to Hermann and Oligh. Buyers would have to pay for their blades straight after the auction so they must all be carrying large sums of money about their person. How much gold was in the room? Enough to buy and sell their forges many times over, no doubt. The English armourers picked up blades, weighed them in their hands, held them at arm's length and rubbed their thumbs over the edges. They wore the same expressions as the crows he'd chased off a dying rabbit when he was a boy.

'See how the English carrion birds are here to peck out the sick Germans' eyes.'

Carnforth leaned forwards. 'A little louder, Mohll, if you please?' He nodded in the direction of a portly woman, whose black skirts swept the floor as she entered. 'They say the Widow Benson is hard of hearing and you don't want her to miss the insult.'

So, this was Widow Benson, author of the venom-inked letter that had rattled him so. Wife of the bill-dodging London cutler, Henry Benson. He turned to Oligh. 'If that old purloiner looks set to gain at our loss, I'll bid for my own swords and take them home again.'

'Dreaming again, Mohll,' said Oligh. 'Empty coffers mean we can't afford pride.'

Den Hayford slid into the room and sneered in Hermann's direction.

'That sly youth's not here to buy blades,' said Hermann, 'he's only here to collect what's owed to him, as if we're men without honour.'

Oligh placed a restraining hand on his arm. 'Settle yourself, Mohll, I should have left you at the cockpit after all.'

'Have you seen all these gawkers? People with no wish to buy blades, with no need to collect debts, who just want to watch us being humbled.' Hermann raised his chin. He wasn't here through shoddy workmanship but because he'd been squeezed by the people in this room. The likes of the Bensons, who'd driven down blade prices, and the Hayfords, who'd driven up the cost of steel. 'How short-sighted are the English? Their greed, hatred of men from distant shores or envy of our skill has killed the goose that laid the golden egg.' This candle sale would be the finish of him. He wouldn't buy another ounce of overpriced steel from Hayford and he'd never sell another blade to the Widow Benson and her ilk. 'Let them buy inferior English blades and send their men into battle.'

'Hide your teeth, Mohll, and keep that flask in your pocket. I've told you once as it is.'

Carnforth shot them a warning glance. 'Shh, the pair of you. Stop bickering. You're going at it like a pair of old hens. The proceedings are about to begin.'

At long last, the auctioneer cleared his throat and pointed to the first lot. 'One chest of hollow blades, made from the finest Swedish steel, forged and ground in Shotley Bridge by master swordmakers from Solingen in High Germany. All marked with the sign of the running wolf.'

The auctioneer's lackey moved to the door and began stuffing the keyhole and the gap under the door with rags before stationing himself before it. The other lit a taper, held it to the base of the candle stump, planted it on the table and paused, awaiting instruction from his master. The auctioneer held up his hand for silence, eyeing all interested parties to ensure he had their attention. When he tapped his gavel, the lackey lit the candle.

The flame had barely taken hold of the wick when Widow Benson called out, 'A tanner the lot, and that's generous, given their parlous workmanship.'

The candle flickered and a cold hand squeezed Hermann's heart.

'Twelve pounds, the lot.' This from a deep-chested man by the name of Henry Slipper. His voice carried across the room on a big breath and the flame bent before righting itself, which was a shame as this was a decent-enough price. Hermann wondered how far his own breath might carry if he sighed. If only the door would open now … not that there was much chance of that with the auctioneer's man stood sentinel before it. Much safer to use a horse-nail in the candle so the clatter of iron would signal the winning bid instead of the flame going out but the Londoners were a headstrong lot. In the darkened room, the flickering candlelight showed the avarice shining in the buyers' eyes. Their cheeks and necks were flushed. The hunt was on and a bargain might be made this night at his expense.

'Thirteen pounds the lot,' said Sarah Quillon.

Hermann smiled at her. This widow was a fair woman and a regular customer, as had been her husband before her. This was a sensible price and he hoped the candle might falter for her.

'Alright, you've forced my hand,' called Widow Benson. 'Two shillings, the lot. I'm nothing if not generous.'

Her jibe provoked such hearty laughter that the flame bent over and Hermann feared the candle would be blown out. He held his breath, but the flame rallied and with it, his spirits.

'Ten pounds, the lot.' This from Benjamin Fox. Not a man well known to Hermann but Carnforth seemed to know him.

Hermann watched Sarah Quillon as she watched the candle

intently. The flame flared slightly and she called out again, 'Thirteen pounds.'

When Widow Benson opened her mouth, Hermann was ready to bid himself but the flame doused itself as the wick burnt away and a spire of white smoke rose.

'Thirteen pounds to Widow Quillon,' declared the auctioneer, with a tap of his gavel.

Hermann beckoned to Carnforth. 'We can't have the Benson woman behaving like this. She's making a mockery of us. Can't we do something?'

'Aye, mebbes.' Carnforth glanced at the widow. 'If she doesn't button her lip, she'll be up before the Master of the Worshipful Company for behaviour unbecoming.' Hermann made to move but Carnforth got in front of him. 'Leave this one to me, Mohll or your tongue will get us all slung out.'

Carnforth crossed the room to address the widow, who flung bitter glances at Hermann. The Newcastle man's words must have done the trick, though, as the auction wore on with no further ludicrous bids. The candle let them down a few times, but overall, most of the winning bids were reasonable.

Oligh raised a hand to acknowledge the auctioneer. 'That wasn't so bad, was it?' He wagged his head from side to side as he totted up. 'We've come out at slightly under half a crown per sword. Not too bad. The English must hold a little sympathy in their hearts for us after all.'

'Less than half a crown per sword,' Hermann snorted. 'They stand to gain a small fortune at our cost.'

'Still, we can pay our debts,' said Oligh, 'and that's what matters most.'

'Here comes the steel devil now to collect his takings,' said Hermann. 'The gold hasn't even left English hands before being returned to them. God forbid the Germans should make a profit from their sweated labour.'

At a nod from Carnforth, Oligh led Hermann outside and walked him quickly up Cloak Lane. 'Come, Carnforth can take care of matters from here. Let's get you to a tavern. There's a decent one near the warehouse and a walk in the air might revive you.'

His friend's long strides were hard to match and Hermann panted trying to keep pace.

'I know what you're about, Oligh, don't let the hot-head upset the English.'

'They're still our customers and we need them for future orders. Once you're settled, I'll go back to show my face.'

'They'll never have another blade ground by me if I can help it.'

'That's right, Mohll, get it out of your system here. Your words bounce off me, whereas if heard by the English, they might lodge in their tender hearts and cause all kinds of resentment.'

They turned into a Fleet Street alley and Oligh pointed to a gloomy tavern. 'Here, this'll do. Get yourself a space at the table, Mohll, and I'll see you when this business is over.'

Hermann wandered through a maze of dim rooms lit by fires, where the heat was suffocating, even by forge standards. Eventually, he found the chop room and sat at a long table. The wench fetched him a platter of boiled beef, carrots and potatoes. Despite the poor fare, he was pressed in on either side by other travellers and there was barely room to move his elbows to saw through the beef. He should have stayed with Oligh. No doubt the merchants would be dining at Cutlers' Hall, and on finer victuals than this, but he couldn't stomach breaking bread with the likes of Widow Benson or Den Hayford. It had sickened him seeing the London armourers clustered in that dark room, greed slicked across their faces as they slavered over the blades. Had Widow Benson succeeded in gaining a chest of cut-price swords, who knows what might have happened.

He took a draught of weak ale and pulled a face. They were

held fast in a vice of English design. There was nothing here for Hermann anymore and bile rose in him each time he thought of the English. He wouldn't be responsible for his actions if he remained here much longer. While he chewed, an idea began to form. The Swedish king was offering a bounty to metalworkers and their bar steel was decent, not like the mucky stuff from Shotley Bridge. The bad half of him was sorely tempted to travel to Sweden if only to sully Hayford's name so no more good metal would go his way. He smiled grimly. It wasn't like him to be spiteful. The poison of the English was starting to infect his character. Moving to Sweden wasn't his best idea though, as his family wouldn't take to it. His mother wouldn't take kindly to another move, Liesl wouldn't be pleased to be taken away from her sweetheart and Katrin hated anywhere that wasn't Solingen. Ach, it was no good thinking bitter thoughts.

'Mohll, why so gloomy?' asked Oligh, clapping him on the back.

Hermann started as if his thoughts had been read but recovered himself. 'No reason. Just thinking.'

Oligh signalled to the serving wench before squeezing in opposite Hermann.

'You're back soon,' said Hermann. 'I thought you'd still be at Cutlers' Hall, with your new friends, feasting on venison.'

'I've left all that to Carnforth, who enjoys that side of things.' Oligh turned to accept a jug of ale and a bowl of beef from the wench.

'So, old friend, how would you feel about buying my forge?' asked Hermann.

'Is this the schnapps talking?' Oligh pointed to the pocket where Hermann hid his flask.

Hermann touched his pocket and grinned. 'I might go to Sweden.'

'Sweden?' asked Oligh, with a lift of his brows. 'You would

take Liesl and Katrin away from Shotley Bridge?' He took a long draught of ale and wiped his mouth with the back of his hand. 'If you're serious, you'll need to go through the motions and place a notice in the *Gazette*, for form's sake. It will all take time ...'

'Ach, the English and their form.' Hermann took out his flask and offered it to Oligh, who shook his head. 'More German gold into London men's pockets.'

'There's no other way. You'll get a fair price from me.' Oligh swabbed his bowl with a hunk of bread and swallowed the sopping mass whole. 'If you get a better offer for your forge, take it.'

'I will,' Hermann said, even though it would surely trouble Oligh having an Englishman working nearby. He wouldn't sell it to Hayford though. That man had plans. If Hayford gained a foothold, who knew what would happen to steel prices? He'd undercut the Germans and sweep up all the forges.

'I'd not sell it to Hayford,' said Hermann, 'or the Benson widow.'

'Are you still letting that woman bother you?' Oligh laughed and swigged some more ale. 'It's the old viper's way of trying to lower the price. Typical merchant tack and no need to take it to heart.'

'Yes, but who knows where she sprays her venom?' Hermann pushed away his platter. 'Was life in Solingen so bad that we've subjected ourselves to this?'

'It seemed so at the time,' said Oligh. 'Aren't you eating that beef?'

'Not likely. Even *my* knife won't go through it and I ground the edge on it myself.'

Hermann handed his platter to his voracious friend, who set about the meat.

'Mind your teeth, Oligh,' he said. 'If the English had soldiers as tough as their beef, they'd be unbeatable at war.'

A DAY OF FASTING

Morpeth Gaol, 1704

*R*oss's mother came in today with a basket of game pies, mutton chops and fresh loaves. Not such tasty fare as the Mole's women fetched in but not bad at all. Pity she had a wasted trip since the queen saw fit to order a day of fasting in memory of those lost in the Great Tempest. The crowner finally landed to see to Walter and he fetched a letter and a parcel. The parcel contained Burke's book and his papers, along with word from Dismal ordering me to set the great lump free. Seems Burke's friends in Scotland have vouchsafed him so he's of no further interest. He's to have his precious book and papers back as well.

That little book has journeyed more in a month than I have in a lifetime. I'm a homebird and always have been. I told Burke he should follow suit but he just shrugged, shoved the peruke back on his fat head, kissed the little book and stowed it in his pocket along with the papers. What wouldn't I give to know what they said? But the big Scot didn't want to waste time talking to me once freedom beckoned so the turnkey put him out. A cold day and not the best one for walking. Lucky Burke has plenty of beef on him, although it's still a fair hike to Scotland for a man with gout.

The letter listed the trials and justices for the Christmas

Sessions. Not before time. At least the men will have their hearing date and know something's going to happen, one way or another. All those involved in the carry-on with the swords are to be tried together under the gimlet eye of Colonel Villiers. Not a surprise, since he's in charge of what goes in and out of port. A fine man that stands for no nonsense so it might not go too well for the Mole. It was Villiers' men who stopped the Mole and his band of smugglers. It'll be satisfying for the Colonel to see it through to the finish. Mebbes he pushed for the case. Almost makes me sorry for the Mole.

Mind, he's an odd one, my German guest. When I gave him the news about the sessions list, he smiled like a saint and started whistling. What's he got to be so cheery about? He's up for bail in a few days so he's chanced to be getting his hopes up and thinking of going home to that that wife of his. Clearly, my prisoner doesn't know Colonel Villiers. He'll sharp change his tune when he finds himself back in my company.

When the crowner had seen to Walter and pronounced him dead of gaol fever, he took a buttered rum with me. Full of gossip from Newcastle and well worth the price of a drop. Told me there was news from Rotterdam. Turns out it was Soldart's own brother who'd made the shipping arrangements for the blades. The Dutch man hadn't been shy when it came to telling about it, neither. You should have seen the good captain's face when he heard that. Wouldn't fancy being in the brother's shoes when Soldart gets home. If he ever does get home.

Travelling Papers

Shotley Bridge, 1703

*H*ermann yawned. It was bad of him to be late to the meeting but he'd been up all night with Mother and had fallen asleep in his dinner. She'd aged a good deal in the last few years and she'd never really been the same since he came back from that first candle sale in London nearly five years ago, which had put paid to any plans of moving to Sweden. Now that the iron encasing her mind was softening, she'd begun screaming in her sleep, and no wonder. Her heart must be clogged with horror and who'd want to take that to their maker? It had to come out of her somehow. So when sleep came, the stopper came out of the small flask that was his mother, and bit by bit, the poison leached from her soul. The racket was no good though and it was setting Griselda off in the night so no one could sleep. He'd have to put Mother in the garret. She'd grumble about her knees and the stairs but what else could he do? Liesl wouldn't mind swapping, and in any case, she was bound to marry before too long.

When he entered the inn, Oligh gave him a pointed look and Hermann shrugged by way of apology. What could he do? The innkeeper's face was even more florid than usual from the exertion of serving so many customers in one sitting. Farmer Johnson and Witch Wilson tipped their hats by way of greeting and the innkeeper made a drinking motion. Hermann nodded to Blenkinsop, though he'd need more than English ale to get him through this night. The inn was filled with Solingen men sat in small knots. Carnforth was waiting, impatience written all over his face. Only the innkeeper looked happy and Hermann could almost see his ears wagging, though he was pretending to be deep in conversation with Johnson and Wilson. It was a bad idea having the meeting here. They should have held it in the church but Oligh had quailed at the idea. Hermann was sure God wouldn't have minded them using His house to improve their industry but Oligh was not to be swayed, arguing there was nothing to stop them holding the meeting in their own tongue now that Herr Maddison was no longer with them. Given the parlous state of their finances, Hermann thanked God the Englishmen couldn't understand their tongue, beyond a few mumbled attempts at their names and wishing them good day or good night, but it wouldn't be too difficult for the locals to work out what was going on.

'Right, let's get on with it.' Carnforth opened his satchel and unfolded a document.

So, Carnforth had finally got the new contract from the company men. The men who could never be seen but for half an hour on a Sunday, so busy were they grasping after trade. The war was raging on the continent over the Spanish succession, so the company men wanted more swords for less gold, only they hadn't the foresight to help the swordmakers buy steel more cheaply. The company men wouldn't care too much if they had to buy inferior English swords for half the price and look the other way when their young men were slaughtered in their thousands. The war looked set to go on for years. War would bring the Germans work but it might also take their sons. Oligh had said more than once that Hermann was fortunate to have a daughter but there was also Joseph to worry about. If Hermann didn't start selling more swords, he wouldn't be able to keep the lad on and he'd be almost bound to join up.

The sun shone through the grease-smeared window and the parchment breathed its rich hues into the inn while the Newcastle man searched in vain for a dry surface to stow the contract.

Hermann gave him an irritable glance. 'Give it here. I'll hold it up.'

Carnforth seemed troubled by this but handed it over and Hermann held it out in front of him with both hands so everyone could see it.

'You have an agreement with the company.' Carnforth glanced around the inn. All eyes were on him, including those of the three Englishmen. 'And you aren't meeting its terms.'

Hermann concentrated on keeping his hands still and his mouth shut as he'd promised Oligh to hold both tongue and temper. Best to let others speak.

Carnforth continued, his smile failing to blunt the edges of his words. 'You're not making enough swords,' he said, 'so what are we to make of that?'

Hermann said nothing and continued holding out the document, rocking back and forth on the balls of his feet. Their best hope was Oligh. His friend was reserved at the best of times but must realise that silence now would create a vacuum, one that Hermann couldn't resist filling. He eyed the tankard of ale waiting for him, thought of the flask in his pocket and regretted volunteering himself for such a thankless task.

'We can't meet the terms, Carnforth,' Hermann said. His chin was jutting out but he couldn't help himself. 'There's no way we can make blades quickly or cheaply enough to fulfil this contract at this cost. My brothers should never have signed it.'

Oligh looked as if he'd like to strangle Hermann and Tiergarten was clenching his fists but Carnforth ignored them and pointed to the document. 'Your names.' The Newcastle man tapped each name and pointed at each swordmaker in turn – Wupper the Younger, Wupper the Elder, Tiergarten, Oligh, Schaffe – as if making certain every man knew the burden of duty weighing on his shoulders.

'See. You put your names to it and now you won't fulfil your obligations.'

Hermann's name wasn't on this document so it was easier for him to speak his mind. Even so, he avoided Oligh's eye. 'It's not that we won't fulfil our obligations, Carnforth,' he said. 'It's more that we can't when your countrymen have us trapped in the middle.' Carnforth was in the same boat, really. Hermann knew the Newcastle man wasn't cut out for this kind of hard-headedness and must have been put up to it.

'Keep out of it, Mohll,' Tiergarten said. 'Your name isn't on the contract so it's not your concern.'

But Voes cut him down. 'My name's not on there either, Tiergarten,' he said, 'but I still consider it my concern. It affects us all. Let Mohll be.'

Carnforth coughed. 'If you've quite finished, gentlemen,' he said, 'that won't wear well with the company men.' He looked from Hermann to Oligh. 'Besides, you're surrounded by iron ore and woodland, so you can make your own steel, can you not?'

'Out of the local ore? When it's so mucky with sulphur?' Hermann hated to whinge but it was hard to be silent. 'The simple truth is that the English have sold us a pig in a poke and now the forges stand idle. No money to buy steel. No steel to make swords. No swords to sell. No money to buy steel.' He stirred his finger in the air, ignoring Tiergarten's purpling face and Oligh's desperate signal to stop talking. Plentiful iron made for cheap steel but the iron hereabouts needed lengthy processing to make steel pure enough for blademaking.

'What would you have us do?' asked Hermann. 'Spend our

days making blades? Or spend our days making steel? Because it can't be both.'

Wupper sat shaking his head slowly at him but Hermann ignored him. His neighbours shouldn't allow him to attend meetings, let alone speak at them.

Carnforth studied Hermann before speaking again. 'Are you telling me that you're not capable of fettling the steel prices yourself?'

The thrust of this invisible blade found its mark in Hermann's sensitive pride and he stayed silent.

'Listen, you must meet the requirements of this contract or—' Carnforth stepped away from Hermann and rubbed the flat of his hand backwards and forwards on his forehead.

Hermann almost felt sorry for the man, being sent here to do the dirty work for the company men. He must realise they were not only exploiting the Germans' labour but they were also failing to help them meet their obligations.

Carnforth righted himself and began again. 'Listen, you must meet the requirements of this contract or you'll be in breach. I'm sorry to all of you, but if you won't work with me, I cannot help you.'

Hermann nodded slowly. 'Leave it to us,' he said, 'we'll meet the terms of the contract. One way or another.'

He waited while Carnforth put on his coat and saw him to the door. It wasn't fair expecting the Newcastle man to control the company men simply because they shared the same country of birth. Carnforth was a swordmaker like himself and hadn't the stomach for this sort of business. None of them did. Not even Oligh, judging by his grim face.

⌒

Hermann waved his hand over the contract. 'A hundred pounds per breach, Oligh?' he asked. 'To say nothing of the measly prices and the monopoly on our work. What on earth were you thinking when you signed this and why did nobody consult me first?'

'Because,' Oligh replied, 'you're impossible to reason with half the time, that's why.' He rubbed his face and took a drink of ale. 'There'll be no breach, Mohll, so there'll be no fine. That's why we were happy to sign it. We're industrious and honest men so God will take care of us.'

Hermann closed his eyes at this announcement. Oligh was an upstanding man and an excellent swordmaker but he had to question his friend's sense and his sanity at times. What on earth had made Oligh and the others sign up to such a punitive contract when war was raging across Europe and every sword was needed? To pay their mounting steel bills, they needed a lot of money from somewhere. To get that, they'd need other customers, so they couldn't allow the company men to monopolise them in this way. Since Oligh was his oldest friend, Hermann would do his best not to insult him but fines of this size would finish them off. How had none of them seen it? How could so many men, clever men, allow the English to hoodwink them like this? Someone had to rescue them from their mess. They needed more swords, and quickly, before the forges ground to a complete halt.

Hermann stood before Oligh's house. The lintel hadn't weathered well and already the lettering was in bad condition. He looked west through the trees to the hills that gave England its backbone and in plentiful years sent water crashing down from a great height into the valley to power their forges. The azure sky was untroubled by clouds and there wasn't a drop of water to be seen. They'd had a wet spring but from midsummer there'd been no rain for weeks, if not months. The trees drew water from deep underground but those with shallow roots did badly and the silver birches drooped. The mud paths were bone-dry. The river was low and rocks normally covered by water were bare, revealing holes where grindstones had been cut free years ago. Even with the mill races in place, the water was a slow trickle, which wasn't enough to power their water hammers or bellows so the forges were all but silent. Slow water wasn't their sole problem but it certainly wasn't helping their cause. The dry spell must end soon. He was hot and sticky and even the bees were lethargic from the heavy air, so the sky was holding water, but when would it let go and rain?

'Come, Griselda, old girl.' Hermann waited until the hound caught up before entering the forge. He filled a pipe and lit it from a glowing charcoal, his eyes roving over the bundles of swords. There were many but not nearly enough. They were almost out of steel and with the little that was left, there was no chance of filling orders if no rain came. Hayford wouldn't extend any more credit and the company men were no help. There, in the dim light of the forge, he considered their problems. Not enough water to power the hammers and bellows. Not enough steel to make all the swords they had to make. Not enough money to buy more steel. Sword prices forced down. Steel prices gone up. They'd never find the gold to pay a hundred-pound fine. Even one fine would be ruinous, let alone more. What on earth had compelled the others to sign such a contract? They were good workers, but too proud. Only a man proud of his work would be willing to wager on himself against such high odds.

The numbers, regardless how many times Hermann restacked them, refused to work themselves out. This wasn't something they'd reckoned on. At home, the guild took care of everything – whether rules, prices or ill-feeling – but here, there was no greater authority than himself and Oligh. Sometimes, it was a heavy weight to bear. Perhaps he'd been too hasty moving to England. All he'd achieved was to condemn his family to a life in poverty. So much for following English gold.

They'd sold their secrets cheaply and for what? He drank from his flask and laughed at himself. What did he expect? The English owed the swordmakers nothing. Even so, a sour taste came to his mouth thinking about it. Ach, there was no point being bitter when no one had forced his hand but he had to fix this. Carnforth was a decent man at heart and he would help him get travelling papers. Griselda yapped and wagged her tail, stirring him from his thoughts as Oligh put his head round the door.

'Mohll, how are you getting on?'

Hermann left off from his worries to tell Oligh that no matter how many times he moved the numbers about, they wouldn't add up. There was no way to meet the English orders, even if they had enough steel and they worked in their sleep. He picked up a blade and ran his finger along the lines of the running wolf. Not a solid creature but one made of air and energy. It didn't belong locked into the steel but looked ready to run off the edge and into the fray.

He'd have to tell Oligh about his solution, which wasn't ideal but would help fulfil their obligations and put meat in their families' bellies.

Oligh opened a chest of blades to inspect them. 'We should talk to the English first to see if we can reason with them.'

'The English are in no mood for talking,' said Hermann.

'Then what do you propose, friend?'

Hermann put down the blade and rubbed his hands on his breeches. 'I'm going back to Solingen to fetch enough blades to meet the contract so we can pay our steel bills and avoid being fined.'

'Back to Solingen?' asked Oligh. 'Are you mad? The *Burgomeister* will have your neck. What about the Solingen notice? You must remember what it said.'

'Hah!' said Hermann. 'You know as well as I do that indictment had fewer teeth than my mother. It's been fifteen years. Not a single one of us went back and what did they do? Nothing.'

He let Oligh ponder this awhile and picked up a blade to polish. The notice was posted for form's sake, to serve as a warning for others not to follow suit. The Solingen authorities needn't have bothered with threats when they could have contented themselves with posting the price of decent iron in England, along with the falling sword prices and punishing contracts. That would be enough to deter anyone else from absconding. The notice was no more than an idle threat. It had taken the court more than a year to put pen to paper, so how long for them to draw blood? Twenty years? Thirty? There was no real risk from Solingen and Oligh would realise it made sense. Solingen's steel was won from hard bargaining by the guild so it would be cheaper to buy their blades ready-made. With any luck, Solingen might be glad of some English silver.

Finally, Oligh spoke. 'Even supposing Solingen does let you out with your hide intact, the English will flay it from you on return. The cost of the voyage, the blades and the duties will be more than you stand to gain.'

'No need for duties.' Hermann paused, wondering how to break the news to his God-fearing friend. 'I'll bring the blades in under the table.'

His friend barely blinked, which was a sure sign of how bad times were.

'Under the nose of the customs men?' asked Oligh. 'So your plan is to turn pirate and let the English have your neck?'

'Not pirate. Smuggler. I won't be stealing anything other than taxes from Queen Anne's coffers and she owes us far more than we owe her. Besides, how could I get caught when I lead such a charmed life?'

'Mohll, be serious. There's a strong chance you could be caught. And if so, what then? You'd go to gaol and lose your left hand, to say nothing of your good name.'

Easy for Oligh to say with all his sons but the Mohll name looked set to end with Hermann. 'Or I succeed and become a legend.' He grinned but Oligh wasn't going to indulge him so he became more serious. 'Once we fulfil this contract, we could all go home.'

'There's no need to go home,' Oligh said. 'It's not so bad here.'

'Providing we fulfil our obligations, which is seemingly impossible on some days.' Hermann grunted at the thought of the turn their lives had taken. No wonder Oligh didn't find it so bad here. He'd finally melted like tin and taken on the shape of this country and was possibly the happier for it. But they owed England and that meant England owned them. Hermann had no desire to be owned by anyone, least of all the English.

Oligh took up a blade and examined it along its length, running his thumb down the edge.

'Have you stopped to consider, Mohll, what if our old friends in the guild refuse to help you – us?'

'They'll do what I ask because they'll be glad of the money. More importantly, they'll enjoy having to save us.' Hermann retrieved the blade from his neighbour and put it in a chest. 'It'll give them something to gloat about for a few years.'

'It'll give them even more to gloat about if you wind up in gaol,' said Oligh.

'It won't be a problem.'

'I pray you're right, for all our sakes.' Oligh examined another blade and held it out. 'This is a bit heavy. One of Joseph's?' He picked up some glasscloth and began rubbing the blade. 'I keep telling you the English aren't cut out for swordmaking.'

'One of my own,' said Hermann. 'My eyes aren't so clear of late.' It *was* one of Joseph's but he wouldn't give his friend the satisfaction of knowing that. 'Here, give me that blade, you've taken the edge off it.'

'You'll soon put it back on.' Oligh passed over the newly blunted blade. 'Well, Mohll, I wish you luck informing your womenfolk of this venture.'

Hermann had already considered this. Katrin would be deeply unhappy about being involved with breaking the law, and even unhappier about Liesl being involved, but she'd relish the chance to visit her mother and that would win the day. His own mother wouldn't come, though, as she mightn't have another sea voyage in her, let alone two. The old hound certainly didn't have a sea voyage in her. She'd always been grey but now Griselda was grizzled and her eyes were opaque. Her mouth was almost bare of teeth and she'd barely the energy to thump her tail anymore. The hound might not last until they got back and Liesl might refuse to leave her side but he couldn't leave the girl with only his mother to keep an eye on her.

BASTARDY

Morpeth Gaol, 1704

Nine prisoners to the Christmas Sessions this morning and three back with me. First was a new prisoner, George Michaelson, labourer. It's the old, old story with him: bastardy. I've no sympathy for the bedswerver if he's not willing to keep the woman and her bairn. Mind, she's lucky to escape a whipping at the reformation post. Even more lucky that Michaelson didn't do away with her for there's a solution commonly found. Beyond me why some men would sooner go to gaol than pay for their own bairn when others would give all they had for a family. Not Gorgeous George, who reckoned someone better might be down the road, 'You cannot expect me to stay put with that old hatchet-face.'

I told him he should be ashamed of saying such things about the mother of his child but Gorgeous George burst out laughing. He'll laugh on the other side of his face before long. A shearer, this George, ranging up and down the county, taking his pick while the farmer's back is turned. He'll fleece no more now he's ruined a lass. All for the want of a strip of gold. What chance will her poor mite have? He'll soon see sense once he's under my roof. I'll sharp prick his conscience and find out if there's a soft spot for his innocent bairn.

Gorgeous has a nasty curl to his lip but I wager that sneer doesn't see the light of day till it's too late, till the lass comes chasing after him, pale with sickness, only to find herself licking the hare's foot. Well, handsome is as handsome does and good looks soon fade. If he's an ounce of sense, he'll borrow the surety and marry the lass. Bonny lads don't stay bonny for long in my gaol.

My two other prisoners were none too impressed with George. Daresay they'd have looked the other way while I gave him a good flogging. But you never can tell which way they'll go, soldiers and foreigners.

Villiers bailed Soldart and his mariners, Anders of Surinam and little Tommy Davison, so they're all away back to the Tyne. The Mole was pleased for them and nodded as they left but he's morose now and I cannot blame him. His hearing went badly. A few of his countrymen were there, and between them, they offered to put up surety. Even so, Villiers wouldn't let the Mole go for love nor money. Out of his hands, of course. A man can be bailed for smuggling but not for high treason. Not looking too clever for the Mole and he knows it. Going back to gaol, he just stared across the snow-covered fields.

Ross took it to heart. Went white as a sheet when he learnt he wasn't getting bail. His blessed mother started keening into her pinny but it was all for show. She's not daft and knows her lad's better off in my keeping than over the sea in Marlborough's hands. At this rate, Ross's furlough will be up and he'll have spent the whole time in gaol. He'll be back in Holland with no time to find himself a wife or toast his toes on the hearth. All without recruiting a single soldier. That's if he gets back to Holland. Looks like he might find himself meeting the same fate as the Mole.

THE JUNIPER TREE

Solingen, 1703

*H*ouses with steeply pitched roofs nestled behind black trees and brown meadows, with white windmills scattered in the distance. The whole town sheltered in the shadow of the church on the hill, which overlooked the market, making sure no one mis-sold, cheated or took what was not his.

Hermann, Katrin and Liesl travelled by wagon through the heart of the night into Solingen, and as they neared the crossroads, Hermann recalled his mother's tales of the werewolves that haunted them and smiled to himself. There was no way a man could turn into a wolf. Such magic wasn't possible. He knew that now. Yet, the moon itself should not be possible – its shining face growing and then hiding away. It was strange to imagine the moon controlling the tides of sea and man alike. Some men were of a watery disposition and so they must feel a greater pull on their inner tide. He thought back to Maddison, the hanged man. They hanged men at crossroads. He shivered.

The horse picked its way downhill and Hermann glanced at his sleeping wife and daughter, wrapped in thick rugs and snuggled together in the back of the wagon. There was a little way to go yet and the rest would do them good.

When they finally arrived at their bend in the Wupper,

Hermann could barely make out the familiar black and white lines of home in the scant moonlight. Their house was still closed up, its shutters tight against the world. How would they ever leave it again? He climbed down from the wagon. A remnant of paper fluttered on the door. It was too dark to read, and no doubt the ink had been faded by the sun and rain so it would be barely legible anyway but he knew its contents well enough. He slipped the note off its nail, folded it once and put it in the pocket nearest his heart. The waterwheel was still and weeds had taken over, half strangling the garden, except for the juniper tree, which had fruited, its dark purple berries gently silvered under the moon. They would please his mother and he'd take some back to her.

The wagon-driver loosened the straps from the wagon and began unloading their trunks. Hermann found the key to their door but paused when bells pealed from the night sky, cutting through the silence. He leaned against the black oak timbers of their home. All Souls, when the bells pealed to remember those who'd passed through the veil. He thought of his father, who had gone so long ago and left him on this side with his mother. Ach, his mother. An ocean in mid-storm, all contained in the waif-like wrappings of womanhood, carrying her rage and love about her in equal measure. He plucked a berry from the juniper tree and squashed it between finger and thumb, its bitter perfume making his mouth water.

Mother said that before the Great Fire came the great marauding. Soldiers speared new-borns on their swords. They roasted the naked infants over fires until their eyeballs burst before devouring their tender flesh. *Devouring*. She'd never spared him a detail if she could help it, even when he was a boy. Her brother had ended this way and she'd watched as the soldier wiped the fat from his chin – baby fat, made sweet by mother's milk. The soldier stomped on her brother's skull and belched, unbuckling himself. After the soldier had finished with her, Mother had stolen forwards and wept on the infant's remains before gathering his bones in her kerchief. She'd carried them to the edge of the Elbe, but the river was filled with corpses, their eyes and hands raised to heaven, begging God to save them, so she got away from her town and carried the bones with her to Solingen. She came here because it was known for its swords, and what better refuge could there be than the town which forged the swords that had slaughtered her people? She came to pray over the blades in the hope they might one day bring vengeance for her dead brother. She'd boiled his bones clean, wrapped them once more and stowed the red silk kerchief in her bottom drawer until she became a bride. On the first day after her wedding, she'd begged her new husband for some juniper berries, dug a hole large enough for the boy her brother would have become and planted his bones beneath the berries. Though her tears, she'd sworn to live and die a Lutheran, to raise a hundred sons, all proud to proclaim their faith so her brother wouldn't have died in vain. That was her stand against the barbarous Catholics.

The juniper was stunted and leant the way the wind pushed it. No bird had ever visited this tree. His mother said it was because the birds knew the berries belonged to her. From them, she distilled mother's tears, an oily spirit for women brought low by soldiers. He knelt under the tree and ran his hands over the roots, over the infant laid to rest, and wondered whether the child's bones would still be there. The oily spirit wasn't just for women brought low by soldiers. His mother dosed herself liberally with the bitter liquid each night. It was a miracle Hermann had been born at all, but who could blame her?

As the sun began to come up, the church bells ceased their joyless pealing. He found the key in his pocket and unlocked the door. There would be time enough for maudlin thoughts. For now, his place was with the living.

The driver finished unloading, coughed and climbed back onto his wagon. Hermann paid him, woke his slumbering family and helped them down so the wagon-driver could get away. He pushed the door open and shepherded his wife and daughter inside, still bleary-eyed with sleep. Their home smelt empty and cold but was otherwise the way they'd left it, even after all these years. Katrin ran her hand over the kitchen table, made by Hermann, but too big to carry with them.

When they climbed the stairs, their bed looked exactly the same as when they'd left, but in Liesl's room, the bed was rumpled.

Liesl walked around her old room. 'I can hardly remember this room anymore.' She pointed at the bed and laughed.

'How did I ever fit into such a tiny bed? My feet would hang over the edge now.'

Katrin touched the mattress. 'Not cold or damp. Someone's been sleeping in Liesl's bed. No one but my mother has a key.' She put her hand to her throat. 'Do you think my poor mother's been sleeping here?' She knelt and pressed her nose to the mattress. 'Goose-grease and lavender. My mother's liniment. Has she missed her grandchild so much that she's taken to sleeping in her bed?'

Hermann thought of the plump and cheery old woman soaking up the essence of her lost granddaughter. He took his wife by the shoulders and turned her to face him. The smudges under her eyes had darkened, fine lines had etched themselves at each side of her mouth and the first strands of silver were appearing in her blonde hair. What had it cost his wife to go to England? And what had it cost the family she'd left behind?

'We'll go and visit your mother now,' he said. 'Would you like that?'

Katrin's eyes glistened and she nodded.

The three of them walked along the Wupper until they reached the Gerner family home. Smoke puffed unevenly from the chimney and there were shingles missing from the roof. The old woman would be up, ready to go to church and pray. Hermann knocked gently on the door and pushed it open, letting his wife and daughter enter before him. A waft of warm bread rose to greet them and his mother-in-law dropped the loaf tin with a great clatter when she saw them.

'Baking before church again?' asked Katrin. 'Sorry, Mother. I should have sent word.'

Frau Gerner opened her trembling arms to her daughter and granddaughter. Hermann was shocked by how frail the old woman had become when she'd always been so vital. She wept for a while before peeling herself away from Katrin and Liesl, wiping her eyes.

'I thought never to see you again in this life, Katrin,' Frau Gerner said. 'Are you come home?'

'For a while,' Katrin replied. She swallowed and dabbed at her eyes. 'Not for ever but for a while …'

'So let's not waste any more time,' his mother-in-law said. 'Liesl, look at you, you're a woman and just look at how tall you are. I'll have to stand on a stool to talk to you now. Oh, I've missed you so much, so very much.'

Liesl blinked rapidly. 'I've missed you too, Grandmother Gerner, and I've brought you some presents from England. See, some wool, some lace and here are some seeds that will grow into lovely pink roses to remind you of me.'

Liesl held out her packages and Frau Gerner took them, patting each one to her heart, weeping all the while. His mother-in-law looked as though she didn't have another winter in her. Perhaps they should all come home, at least for a year or two. Once this contract was fulfilled, there was nothing to hold them in England, apart from his own pride, and not so much that he couldn't swallow it.

His mother-in-law pressed her fingers along the hem of his coat. 'It's a wonder you can stand under the weight of so much silver, Hermann. You'll be in need of sustenance after such a journey. Let me get you some sausage and we'll salvage this bread.'

Hermann put a hand over Frau Gerner's. 'No, we'll break our fast after church. Come, we'll go with you.' He was ravenous and his gut rumbled but it would mean a lot to his mother-in-law. Anyway, he might make peace with God and the guild at the same time.

Her face creased with pleasure and she patted his hand before turning to Liesl. 'Come here, my lovely girl.' She opened a tin hand-painted with field mice and lifted out a slice of cake. 'My best walnut. You're allowed to break your fast, as you're still growing.' She winked. 'Now you sit there and eat that. God will wait. He's ever patient and it's early yet.'

As they walked the streets, the cobbles felt harder under Hermann's feet than English ones. This was whimsy, though, since no foot clad in decent leather could tell what stone it walked on. Yet, his own land felt more ungiving and less welcoming as he walked towards the church, passing many empty houses with tattered papers fluttering on their doors.

The church was still when they entered, and empty. No one had voiced it but arriving first meant attracting less excitement and comment than entering a filled church. Hopefully, breaking bread and supping wine with the guild men might ease Hermann's path.

After the service, many men waited for him outside the church. Some wore pinched expressions that spoke of hurt and suspicion but many clapped him on the shoulder, welcoming him back to the fold. Hermann's neighbours in England had filled his pockets with gifts and his ears with messages and these he duly delivered. The men of Solingen hung on his every word, heads shaking to and fro at news of the English tricks that had been played on their old friends. His townsmen were only too glad to help in his time of need, disloyal though he'd been, and Hermann was invited to present himself at the guild the following night.

⌒

Back at his mother-in-law's home, he said grace, and once he broke his fast and started eating, he feared he might never stop. The table wobbled as Frau Gerner placed food on it.

'Hermann, you don't need to eat Solingen in one bite. You can take some of it … home with you.'

She took very little for herself: a morsel of rye bread, a sliver of cheese and a slice of sausage. Poverty? Old age? Heartbreak? Sickness?

'Don't stare at me so, Hermann. My bellows are small and I scarcely need to eat. I have so little work to do. I feed the pig and the goat, fuss over my hens and pick at the vegetable garden. There's a bit of mending I take in to pass the time. After that, apart from going to the market and church every day, my time is my own.'

Katrin hugged her mother. 'As dogged and busy as ever, Mother. At least let us help you while we're here.'

'There's nothing I need, my girl. Your father left me well provided for, and your sisters and their husbands visit every so often. Now, we need to decide what'll happen to my home when the time comes–'

Frau Gerner took a deep breath that was overtaken by a hacking cough. No wonder the old woman was coughing when there was so much soot in the air from the fire. Those sisters and their husbands weren't caring for her too well.

'Frau Gerner,' he said. 'That won't be for years yet.' He winked at the old lady. 'You know the bad always die late.'

Her eyes twinkled but she shook her head. 'We mustn't lie to ourselves about such matters. I've been living on borrowed time as it is. And now I've seen my daughter and my granddaughter, the Lord will call me soon enough.' She closed her eyes, showing transparent violet lids. 'Thank you, Hermann, for bringing them home to me. I know it's not for ever but it's enough to see them once more.'

He swallowed, his appetite lost. Taking them away a second time would break Frau Gerner's heart all over again.

'Refusing to talk about it won't thwart God's will,' the old woman said. 'Katrin, your father's forge and all the equipment will stay with your sisters' husbands, which is only right as they've worked it for so long, but this house will go to you and Hermann.'

Katrin pushed her platter away. 'Unless the authorities lay claim to it, as they must when …'

Frau Gerner swatted her daughter's words away with a hand. 'It won't be taken,' she said. 'No home has been touched in your absence. Now, the house will be no help to you in England so I'll bequeath it to you but arrange for it to be sold–'

'Mother,' said Katrin, 'arrange nothing. It's too morbid. I should never have left you.'

A draught came through the window with a slight whistle. Frau Gerner followed Hermann's gaze and smiled.

'I like the air,' she said, 'but if it'll make you happy, Son, you may fix it. Katrin, you may take Liesl to visit your sisters.'

When his wife and daughter had gone, Frau Gerner turned to Hermann. 'Now, you'll go to the guild tomorrow. They're good men and they'll help but for today, you're mine, and when you leave, you'll take as much sausage, cheese and cake as you can carry. I can't believe the English soil would make produce as nourishing as here.' She pushed a glass towards him. 'And maybe I can find you a bottle or two of decent schnapps.'

Hermann accepted it readily. He'd do whatever jobs needed doing and before they left, he'd arrange for a lad from the guild to come once a month and do any necessary repairs.

'Now, Frau Gerner,' he said, 'let me find Herr Gerner's tools or have my brothers-in-law taken those as well?'

The guild was full and it warmed Hermann's heart to see so many familiar faces. Age had worn them a little since he'd left. The apprentices were now journeymen and the little boys had grown up to become apprentices. He stood before the roaring fire, its mantel way above his head, and explained his predicament.

Henckels responded first. 'So, you require twenty-five-hundred blades from us, at cost?'

'Yes,' said Hermann. 'If you'll do it.'

In the ensuing silence, Hermann tried his best not to fidget while Henckels ruminated.

'We'll do it,' said Henckels. 'Not at cost, but not too much more, and not because you were once one of us but because you're a paying customer and we never turn those away, especially not these days.'

This knife found its target in Hermann's heart but he couldn't blame the man.

'Considering tariffs, though,' said Henckels, 'it must be cheaper to make blades over there in England, even with inflated steel prices?'

'True enough, but I've no plans to pay any tariffs.' Hermann scratched his neck. 'It's best you don't know about those plans.'

Smiles broke out. Taxes went not to the needy but to furnish palaces and government buildings and to fund wars. Many swordmakers had suffered from high taxation over the years. No man here was a friend of the tariff and they'd enjoy besting the tax collector.

THE CONDEMNED MAN

Morpeth Gaol, 1704

The Mole must have had a good night of it as he looked well this morning. Clear-eyed and not huddled in his corner. Gaol bravado at work again. Convincing himself he'll be a free man. Something's seized in his brain to stop him seeing what's ahead. He's on trial in the morning and he's bound to be condemned to death. I offered him his supper. Mebbes his last, though he still softened a bite for Roasting Jack. Swallowed down the rest of his bread and cheese in two gulps then swilled it down with ale.

The Mole will soon know his fate and I warned him it might not be a kind one but he laughed in my face, 'For smuggling? It's England's favourite pastime and no judge will hang me for it, you can bet your rum money on that.' He had me there, mind. Barely a smuggler gaoled for many a moon, let alone sent to the gallows. There's plenty like the Mole who delight in cheating the customs men, even those with pockets already weighted down to their knees. Not my place to criticise the law but the exchequer has got too greedy, trying to fill its war coffers. It's bad enough paying duty on rum. Nowadays, even the price of tea's enough to make anyone's eyes water. The duty costs more than the tea. No wonder smuggling's seen as fair game. Plenty of money to be had that way.

I told the Mole straight it's not smuggling that concerns the justices but the other small matter of sailing with Scots and Irish soldiers. That could be seen as plotting against the queen's fair person, which is a treasonable offence and high treason at that. The Mole didn't turn so much as a hair and grinned at me through his whiskers, telling me 'Hanging's not so bad if it's quick.'

It's my own fault for filling his belly so now he's full of his old huff and puff. Had to knock the wind out of his sails for his own good. Stop him building up any false hope. A visit from the chaplain would have soon fettled him. It's a shame we're still short of one. But I did my best to prepare the Mole for the worst. Told him hanging wasn't always a quick death – that some men danced awhile. Still, he jested, 'There are many worse deaths than hanging.' When I told him traitors get hanged, drawn and quartered, fear flickered in his eyes, but he laughed again. Bit of a forced laugh, though. 'Drawn and quartered after I'm hanged?' he asked. 'That doesn't worry me. They can do what they like with me when I'm hanged. Now, if you'll excuse me, I need to sleep.' He drained his tankard, belched and banged it down.

He's so innocent of our ways that I had to put him right. 'You'll be drawn through the streets first,' I said, 'and hanged till not quite dead.' Mimed the noose being pulled tight. 'Taken down,' I said and rubbed my neck. 'Gelded.' Cupped my balls. 'Eviscerated.' Showed him how they'd pull out his guts like sausages. 'Quartered.' Carved him into four with my right hand, as if delivering a blessing on him. 'And all while you're still breathing.'

But these warnings fell on deaf ears and the Mole shrugged off my words, 'First, Herr Tipstaff, they must find me guilty.'

Within minutes, he'd turned his back on me and started snoring. He's got some hard neck on him. Most men stay awake on their last night on earth to fend off the eternal darkness as long as they can, but the darkness always comes, and for the Mole it will come all too soon.

THE WOODEN FISH

Rotterdam, 1703

*H*ermann stood on the deck of the *Eufro Angelique* while his wife and daughter slept below after being awake for so long on the wagon and then waiting around at the port. They'd been held up by a pompous Englishman who'd tried to take over their ship, pointing at hordes of people and horses. After a visit from the captain's brother, the Englishman went to look elsewhere for passage. Just as they were about to depart, the captain furled his sails, saying there was a bad storm at play. Days went by before they finally set sail – in a warship of all vessels. Fortunately, Katrin had barely noticed their vessel, let alone complained about it, because she was grief-stricken about leaving her mother again. It had been hard leaving Solingen, even though they'd barely been there a month. Mother Gerner had seen them off from their old home, dabbing at her eyes with a large flowered kerchief, supported on each side by a grim-faced daughter. Depending on how his entry back into England went, this was probably the last time Liesl, Katrin and Mother Gerner would meet on this earth. His wife and daughter had clutched one another and wept almost all the way to Rotterdam. Hermann was sorry for bringing them home and causing the agony of parting again. Katrin wouldn't hear a word of it, though, and through her tears, promised him it was enough. She'd seen her mother once again and now she would return to England in peace.

He peered at the leaden sky. If he was any judge of the weather, Mother Gerner might outlive them. Surely the ship's master wouldn't put to sea if another storm was brewing. Next to him, a fidgety young man in a red coat laughed too loud and talked too fast. His beard was sparse and his face was still so tight that it shone. Hermann knew the callow lad would be restless the whole voyage and irritate him. For every breath sucked in, the gibbering youth immediately spewed one out again in news of his parents, his siblings, his dislike of fish, his hopes regarding women. Hermann suspected he'd taken a shine to Liesl as he blushed every time he looked her way and Hermann was glad she was now safely below deck with her mother. Such a talkative man might be quite repellent to his daughter, who, after all, could do enough talking to fill everyone's ears and would certainly resent a man taking up any of her valuable gossiping time. Besides, she was almost certainly spoken for.

As the last remnant of Rotterdam receded from sight, all Hermann could see was water foaming as the wind whipped it into peaks. Their tiny vessel was entirely at the mercy of the mighty elements. They weren't fish and had no business being on the waves. His mother was right, after all. He wished the young man well and walked nearer to the bow, hoping he wouldn't follow.

⌒

Hermann tried not to think of the fathomless depths beneath him and concentrated on floating, breathing deeply and keeping his lungs full so that he might help the ship remain buoyant. Now wasn't the time for heaviness and clogged lungs. If only he'd not chosen to sail in winter.

The sound of the sea was foreign to his ears. Of course, he was used to the sound of rushing water, having lived and worked on the river all his life, but why had he placed his trust in this strange vessel, which was no more than a few trees sawn down and forced together against their will with nails – iron nails at that, which hated water? Not that sinking in a storm was the worst that might happen to them when the sea was awash with warships.

Getting out of England and into Solingen hadn't been straightforward but all he'd been carrying home was money. Now, as the ship lurched over the German Sea, he began to consider the real risks of getting back into England while carrying so many blades. His palms began to sweat and he rubbed them dry on his breeches. The swords were concealed in barrels of food and there were plans in place for when he disembarked, which would be a little before any of the other passengers, including Katrin and Liesl. He tried not to think too hard about the man of high standing who'd signed his travelling papers and the number of swords he'd have to give him to make sure the customs men turned a blind eye. Still, it was a price worth paying if it meant not getting caught.

Hermann paced around the *Eufro Angelique*, wondering whether the wooden fish was seaworthy enough to get them back to England, and passed the time of day with five more soldiers. Each wore the red coat of Queen Anne's army but as for how well the scarlet cloth covered what their hearts held, it was hard to tell. Two of them were papists haling from Scotland and Ireland. So much for the barbarous Catholics of his childhood nightmares. Were they truly like those who'd sacked his mother's town? Something must have given way in Magdeburg that night because those soldiers can't have been men but monsters. What had turned them? Hunger? Rage? The pull of the moon? The soldiers with him now were disciplined men and seemed decent. Ach, there wasn't so much difference between Catholics and

Lutherans, and God was God. If only men the world over could accept there was a single Creator but many ways of praising Him, the world might be a happier place and mankind might stop tearing itself apart.

The voyage was proceeding well and no one paid Hermann any heed until Soldart, the ship's master, took an interest in his casks, which had been laded by the crew and the brother of the ship's master. Most of the casks were filled with smoked cheese, sausages and dried fish but some had false bottoms. These were filled with hundreds of blades, covered with a layer of fish that was thin but enough to cause a stench and hopefully deter too much probing. Getting the weight right had been hard and the casks were still bottom-heavy. The English customs men at Tynemouth would normally take a close interest in what a foreign swordmaker might carry in with him but they'd been bought off and it was Soldart he was most worried about at present. The ship's master eyed him. He was a big Dutch man without a tooth in his head.

'You don't have the look of a merchant, Herr Mohll. What's in your casks?' Soldart asked.

Hermann took a long breath. 'You have a keen eye, Master Soldart,' he said. 'Provisions from the homeland to take back for my friends and neighbours.' He rubbed his belly. 'Nothing tastes the same once you cross the sea to a new land.'

'Aye, you're not wrong there.' Soldart snapped his fingers at his men. 'Still, you'll not mind if I take a peek, Herr Mohll. Come, down to the hold with you.'

Hermann followed Soldart, with two of his men close behind, his heart speeding up with every step. In his haste, he bumped his knee against a crate of chickens and set them off squawking. Two matelots cracked open the casks and the aroma of smoked cheese wafted from the first barrel. Soldart raised a round of cheese and sniffed it.

'Please, take one.' Hermann was sweating. Soldart's brother had promised faithfully that the ship's master was practised at turning a blind eye. 'My mother-in-law's finest cheese. The finest in the whole of Solingen. Please. Take one for each of you.'

Soldart passed out the cheese and pointed at the second barrel. 'And in there?'

'Sausage,' said Hermann.

'Also from your mother-in-law?'

Hermann nodded. His armpits prickled so he folded his arms and tucked his fists there to soothe them.

'I suppose she makes the finest sausage in the whole of Solingen?'

'If not Germany. The very best.' Hermann's left eye twitched and he forced himself not to rub it, pressing his fists deeper into his armpits. 'She slaughters the pigs herself and drains the blood for puddings.'

Soldart slammed his great hand down on the cask. 'Open it.'

Hermann flinched. The matelots did as ordered and the smell of salted meat, garlic and pepper made his mouth water. He removed three rings of sausage and shared them out.

'There are four crew.' Soldart pointed his chin towards two men lurking in the shadows. 'Five of us in all.'

Hermann took out two more rings of sausage, his hands shaking. It was hard to hold his temper when these men were taxing him almost as much as the English government.

Soldart sniffed the sausage and lobbed a ring to each of the two lurkers. 'And in these casks?'

A bead of sweat emerged at the top of Hermann's spine and trickled down. He prayed his forehead wouldn't sweat – not in this frigid winter air. He mustn't mop his brow. He must keep his voice steady, and his hands.

'Dried fish,' he croaked. It was getting harder to breathe out and he tried hard not to gasp.

Soldart stepped back. 'Fish?' he asked.

'Yes,' said Hermann. 'The best in the whole world, and the most pungent.'

'Leave it.' Soldart put out his hand to stay the matelots. 'We've no need of fish and the reek of it will sicken me for the rest of the week. Bad enough in here as it is.'

Hermann knew he was a dreadful liar and it was as well he had a faceful of whiskers to hide his relief.

Soldart poked him in the chest with a thick finger. 'Still,' he said, 'I wouldn't be doing my job if I didn't check all my cargo thoroughly.'

Hermann smiled, or at least his lips did, turning up sharply at each side, his eyes never wavering from the master's face.

'Then you must check, Master Soldart. Duty must come before a preference for breathing through the nose, eh?' Hermann stood back, convinced his heart was thumping so much that Soldart must hear it. Had he not been so warmly swaddled, the captain might well have seen it, too.

An almighty crash from the corner startled all six men. The crate of chickens had been upended and the creatures began a furious squawking and flapping. Was that a glimpse of flaxen hair he spied behind the cage? Ah, his clever girl.

'These damned hens, they'll have each other's eyes out if I leave them.' Soldart pointed to the corner where Liesl hid. 'Your girl can catch them. Unless you want to watch her being whipped?'

Before Hermann could reply, the ship's master turned, clamped a big hand on his shoulder and squeezed until his bones ached.

Soldart grinned his toothless smile. 'Your dried fish can wait for another day,' he said, 'and please don't worry, because your bundles of swords are quite safe beneath them.' He laughed. 'Look at your face. You think my dear brother wouldn't tell me what I was carrying in the belly of my own ship?'

Dealing with Katrin after Liesl's adventure with the chickens was surely worse than any harm Soldart could do to him. Liesl promised faithfully to stay by her mother's side until they alighted at Jarrow Keys and were safely back in Shotley Bridge, which seemed to mollify his wife. Liesl had found it a great adventure but Katrin was not pleased about his plans to begin with and she was even less happy at having Liesl embroiled in them. Still, it would all be worth it when they had enough money to pay their bills. Even Katrin accepted that and had made her peace with God, if not with Hermann.

Now they'd survived the sea crossing, the only perilous moment remaining was the passage into the Port of Tyne. Germany might not care too much if its finest blades left under cover of fish but the English customs officers would care very much – as much as if the missing duty were bread taken from their own children's mouths. Hermann would have to put his trust in the man who'd promised the officers would turn a blind eye. There was no other choice now. He kissed his wife and daughter farewell in readiness for their forthcoming separation and tried not to notice Liesl and Katrin's pale faces. He promised them all would be well and that he'd be home soon. Finally, he went down into the hold to ready himself and his wares.

It was starting to get dark when the boat neared the mouth of the Tyne. He prised open a porthole and peered out, hoping to see the promised wherry pulling alongside. As the vessel finally approached, there came shouts and jeers from above. Curse those damned redcoats! Did they want the customs men to get wind of what he was up to? He opened the casks and scraped the reeking fish aside in readiness. Through the porthole, he was just able to see the outline of a wherryman straining on the oars, trying to hold his wherry steady against the tide while a small, wiry man stood up, arms outstretched before him. Hermann put on his leather gauntlets and began hauling bundles of swords out of the barrel, fish oil making the paper slippery. Eighty-odd bundles of swords. It was taking too long. The bundles were splitting open, scattering paper, string and straw all over. The wrappings would give him away. This was a terrible plan. His heart was racing and sweat was pouring off him. It was dark and hard to gauge the distance to the boat. He slipped the first bundle onto the sill and lowered it down into the waiting man's arms. The wiry man leaned nearer to the porthole, almost overbalancing, yelling at Hermann to tie the bundles with his belt and lower them. Moving as quickly as he dared, Hermann followed the order and lowered bundle after bundle into the wherry.

He had four bundles left to go when he heard heavy boots and English voices overhead. Was this the English redcoats marching to and fro? It seemed unlikely. His heart lurched and it was hard for him to breathe out. He pressed a hand to his chest. What if the customs men had come aboard? He'd have felt them boarding, surely. Were they even allowed to board a vessel at sea? Would they search the casks? He had to get the rest of his swords out but the wherryman must have got wind of the company and started rowing off into the night.

The muffled sounds that beat through the hold weren't the sounds that had accompanied him over the German Sea so far. He'd become used to the slapping of the sea, her thunderous heartbeat soothing in its regularity, but these new sounds were erratic. They sounded like footsteps hurrying above him. No one on this ship hurried. They worked and walked at the pace of the sea. These were urgent steps. Heavy dragging sounds came from overhead. They *had* been boarded. Definitely the customs men. Searching the ship. Hermann's heart took up residence in his throat, its beat echoed in the cavern of his mouth and seemed to amplify in the hold around him.

He was hidden in the hold with four bundles of Solingen swords on board a ship full of Irish and Scottish sailors. At best, he was a common smuggler trying to evade the tariff. At worst, he was a traitor readying to arm the Jacobite rebels. In truth, he had no idea where his swords might end up, whose hand might grip the handle or whose flesh might feel the wound. He was no more than a craftsman, a lowly blade grinder. It wasn't his place to ask questions. His job was just to provide blades. Bleak thoughts crowded his mind. A smuggler might land in gaol but a traitor would lose his head, or worse. The wherry had gone. He must get off the ship with the rest of the swords so he didn't risk implicating Katrin and Liesl. If he could just get the blades into the water, they'd hopefully still be there when he returned for them another day.

He fumbled the first two bundles out of the porthole and held his breath as they landed with heavy splashes. The third bundle came apart in his hands, leaving oily paper, twine and straw everywhere. He grabbed the blades and poured them through the porthole. There were ferocious splashes, but quick, as if a shoal of metal fish had surfaced, leapt and plunged below the water again. He slid out of his jerkin and kicked off his boots, placing them at the bottom of the barrel before scooping the paper wrappings back into the barrel and replacing the lid. The last bundle contained hollow blades and he didn't want to risk losing them so he fastened the bundle to himself with his belt, squeezed out of the porthole and eased himself out and down into the water.

The weight of the blades took him straight down, as long and thin as a blade himself. He kicked and thrashed, lungs burning and head pounding as he wrestled with his belt. Once the hollow blades were free, they sank and he rose until he got his head above water, coughing and spluttering. The sea was so cold that it sucked the air from his lungs. He gasped and inhaled more water, flailing and kicking to stay afloat. He wouldn't last long in this frigid weather.

With shaking hands, he managed to hook an arm around a rope and clung to the side of the ship, panting and praying that he might go undetected. Would the wherry come back now that its pilot had the bulk of the blades? It had to come back or he'd die of cold and all they'd find in the morning would be his blue corpse, along with the sea-nettles, empty shells and seaweed. He had to get warm and he had to stay awake.

He turned his thoughts to home, to the log fire, his wife's soft arms, his daughter's ringing laughter, of sunlight on top of his head as he walked to and from work, of a bowl of cocoa in his hands, of flickering candles on the mantel, of hot soup over steaming pies, of the warm patch left on his chair after Griselda had slunk off it, of his mother's dry hands as she'd rubbed his in their farewell greeting. His skin shrank and pebbled, his hairs stood like razor wire and his teeth chattered. On and on his mind sought for heat. The forge, its charcoal heat blazing orange, the steel moving from cold iron through to cherry red, on to orange, yellow and finally white. He focused on that bright heat. Imagined bronze bubbling in a kiln pot. Molten metal pouring so bright it hurt the eye. He felt the heat radiate from the swords he beat. In his mind's eye, he beheld every source of warmth he'd ever experienced and moved towards the heart of the flame, the heat of the forge, the centre of the sun. He put himself in amongst the cinders, clutching glowing embers with his numb hands. He stretched out his toes on the fender, drawing the warmth. He dined on great slabs of boiled gammon, swallowing the hot, salty meat and washing it down with ladles of broth, scalding his gullet.

He clung to the side of the ship, shivering, until he heard the wherry returning. He'd have to stay out of sight until he could get on board. More than a few minutes more in this water would kill him. When the wherry drew near, he lowered himself into the water again, the ice-cold ripping the breath from him. As he began to flounder, the waterman haled him and leant out with a long hook. Hermann forced himself forwards, grabbed it and was hauled in over the edge of the boat. He lay flat on the bottom, coughing and trying to empty his lungs of water.

'You're mad, Mohll, adventuring at this time of year. Think yourself lucky you didn't set sail any sooner or the storm would have made matchwood of your vessel.' The waterman threw a tarpaulin over him. 'Where's the other swords? Under the sea? Never mind. Here come the customs men. Keep quiet. Let me do the talking.'

The sound of a boat rowing quickly worried him but Hermann didn't dare speak or raise his head. He felt the thump of the boat as it drew alongside. There were loud voices and he imagined the customs men with muskets trained on him. Death by lead. Death by drowning. Death by hanging. Which would be worst? He held his breath and chose the latter. Time in gaol might be time to think and time to get somebody to help him out. He thought of the swords lost in the sandbank. They wouldn't be lost for long. Once the tide changed, they'd be found. The Germans would fulfil their order and their families would eat this winter. The thin man spoke to the customs men for a while and there came the sound of coins clinking. Eventually, the customs boat moved away and the wherry moved off upstream.

When the boat stopped, the thin man whipped off the tarpaulin and Hermann saw they'd drawn alongside a small waterhouse. The little man ordered Hermann to follow him and the wherryman, so he clambered off the boat behind them. Inside, the waterman drew on a woollen garment that was too big for him and started poking the fire. Hermann had long since stopped shivering and backed away from the fire but the two men put their hot hands on him and stripped him before wrapping him in rough wool blankets. Such heat was an insult on top of the heat he already felt pulsing through him and he tried to throw off the blankets but they'd swaddled him like an infant and his arms were pinned better than with any metal cuffs. When he started to shiver again, they loosened the blankets and fed him hot beef tea, the vilest punishment the English could conceive.

~

When Hermann was no longer raving about fires and hot coals, the waterman gave him his clothes back, along with a pair of boots that were too big for him, then put him on a covered wagon. The driver was instructed to take Hermann to the coaching inn at Newcastle where he was to lie low. He fretted about the blades, the contract and the money the swordmakers had given to buy the blades. This was nothing short of a disaster. He'd made everything worse and would never hear the end of this from the men whose money he'd lost. It might be as well to wind up in gaol. He might be safer there. The waterman had promised him the local mussel draggers and coalmen would fish the blades out and he'd store them all till the next tide but was it wise to trust the word of a stranger?

Hermann lay in the wagon, warm and safe for now, praying that his family had returned safely to Shotley Bridge. Whatever was he thinking, taking them on such a dangerous venture? All for the sake of visiting Frau Gerner one more time. They should have stayed in England with his mother. He felt in his pocket for the juniper berries he'd picked but they were gone, no doubt lying at the bottom of the cold sea, along with the blades and his hopes.

WORM WARE

Morpeth Gaol, 1704

*T*here's no justice in the world for an honest God-fearing man, none at all. The day started well enough when I shoved the prisoners into the sessions. Ross's mother wept and wailed at the front. There were plenty of German folk there. Oligh waved his fist at me but it was water off a duck's back. Every man's brave till the key turns behind him. The Mole stared at his womenfolk. The fat's fallen from his wife and all her face-bones are showing, poor lass. Who'd have thought she could turn so frail in such a short time?

When Villiers finally marched in, he was enough to make a poor man's eyes ache. Weighted down he was with gems and rings. Fancier than the queen in his ridiculous garb.

The justice smoothed his great wig and considered the prisoners at length. When he turned to the Mole, the prisoner wouldn't meet the justice's eye and instead looked at a spot somewhere over his left shoulder. Villiers soon put him right, 'You may look over a justice's shoulder, Mr Mohll, but you cannot look over God's shoulder. Not when you're under oath.'

The Mole stared at his feet while the colonel made his mouth go. What a way he has of talking in his strangled Surrey tones. When he'd done, Villiers poked the clerk and held out his hand.

The clerk handed over a parcel of papers. Quite reluctant he was. Just as well for the Mole the clerk's not in charge of the trial or the Mole would be worm ware and no mistake.

The justice read the papers and rubbed his beak for a while before waving the letter at Sergeant Ross and beckoning him forwards. Turns out the letter was from none other than Dismal, writing on behalf of Queen Anne. Her Majesty was satisfied that Ross and the other redcoats were working on her service so there was nothing to warrant his further detention. Villiers released Ross there and then. Her Majesty's service! Dismal's wits must have deserted him. Ross might well be innocent but imagine Her Majesty thinking those Scots and Irish soldiers were in her pay when they were doubtless working for the enemy. Is she that hard up for arms and men that she employs Scots and Irish redcoats? Turncoats more like. No man's heart truly turns away from his chosen cause.

Ross's mother almost sang with joy and she swept her lad straight out of the sessions. Back to Marlborough's bloody war for him. He's not likely to find his way back to Morpeth again.

The Mole sat up straighter at this turn of events. The lovely Mistress Mole was pink in the face, but when I caught her smiling, she sharp clapped her hand over her treacherous mouth. There was a lot of German jabbering and a great to-do amongst the Mole's womenfolk. Villiers let it run awhile till he held up a hand for silence. Once more, he turned to Dismal's letter. This time, he stepped down from his bench to approach the Mole. What a shocking show for a justice to lower himself to a prisoner's level. This would never do.

Villiers held out the letter and let the Mole read it himself. It took a while as he read it twice before giving it back to the justice with a solemn nod. Villiers returned the letter to the clerk and took his leave.

A great grin split the prisoner's face and he stood up, raised his arms above his head and cheered as his womenfolk rushed to embrace him. None the wiser, I went over to the clerk. He showed me Dismal's letter. It said the Mole probably came over to follow his trade. Trade? Is that what they call it now? Not even a fine! At least the swords were to be confiscated as the queen planned to keep them for her own use. Hardly a surprise when she's as hard up for arms as she is for men to wield them. Dismal said Mohll wasn't guilty of treason or plotting. In the end, Her Majesty left it all to Villiers to decide whether there was any crime or not. There, Dismal ended his letter: I AM AND SO ON, NOTTINGHAM, with the great man's seal upon it.

So the queen left it all up to Colonel Villiers at the finish. She must trust his judgement. No surprise, since the Stuarts and the Villiers have been so thick all these years. I suppose she owes the man, after his mother killed herself nursing Her Majesty through the smallpox. Still, that was the end of that. The Mole's gone back to his warm hearth, a free man with a loving family. Just me to go back to the cold gaol, with only Roasting Jack for company.

THE EMPTY DRAWER

Shotley Bridge, 1704

*H*ermann returned from the forge with the handful of silver charms he'd just made. His mother was at the church keeping watch over the groom. Katrin had removed Liesl's new apron from the bottom drawer of the chest, but when she tried to shut the drawer again, it stuck on its runners. English workmanship again. He knelt to see what the problem was. Mother's red silk kerchief. Liesl certainly wouldn't be needing that, so he put it in his pocket and shut the empty drawer. Since arriving in England, this drawer had held all that Liesl would need for her wedding day and beyond in her new life as a wife and a mother. What would they put in there next?

Katrin sat at the window and began sewing the charms into the apron hem: a cloverleaf, a horseshoe, a Marian beetle, a nail, a penny, a pig and a toadstool. They should have been made from gold but Mother had insisted on selling it all to pay back the money lost on the swords. As it was, she and Katrin had both given up their silver cuffs so he could make these charms. Katrin kept stopping to wipe her eyes.

'Come, *Liebe*, our daughter will be happy and safe under her new roof. Her children will still be Germans. No need to worry about that.'

'Yes.' She sniffed and blew her nose on her pinny. 'But born on English soil.'

'Soil matters not,' he said. 'Blood is what matters and you can't wish Liesl was going back to Germany?'

'Of course not. At least not without us.' She raised her head, tears shining in her eyes. 'Oh, it's meant to be a happy day ... If only my mother were here for Liesl's wedding.'

'*Liebling*, your mother will pray at home.' Hermann eased himself down onto his knees, trying not to wince, and looked into her eyes. 'Our daughter will be happy and that will make your mother happy. Come, Liesl mustn't see her mother so sad.'

'You're right but it's hard for me to hide what's in my heart. I'll do my best, though.' She tied a knot in the thread and bit through the ends. 'There, I'm done. I'll take this upstairs to her. Now get up off your knees, Hermann. They're in a bad enough state without kneeling on the hard floor. Save them for church. When I think of what that dreadful Tipstaff man has done to you ...'

He took her face in his hands. 'Please don't think any more about that time,' he said. 'It's over now. I'm free and still in one piece.'

She nodded and swallowed before standing. 'I'll try not to think about it.' She took his hand and placed it on her lower belly. 'I'm glad you're still in one piece though, because there might be another child of German blood born before long.'

His heart thumped. 'You mean ...?'

'Yes,' she said. 'And one made on Solingen soil, which will make up for being born on English soil.'

Hermann wrapped his arms around his wife, pressed his face to her belly and closed his eyes. After so many years of trying, Liesl had been a blessing and he'd never dared hope for a second child. All those months and years of watching Katrin's hopes wax with the moon and then wane with it. Today was a new beginning for all of them.

When he stood, Katrin kissed him on the corner of his mouth, smiling up at him. 'We won't say anything yet, Hermann,' she said. 'Not today. It might be too much for Liesl. We'll wait a while.'

He laughed and rubbed her belly. 'But not too long or people will guess for themselves. Why didn't you tell me sooner? When I was in gaol?'

'Because I didn't want you to worry.' She smoothed his moustaches with her thumbs. 'You had enough to worry about, didn't you? Now, I must get this to Liesl.'

He knew what she was really saying. That she didn't want to raise his hopes only to dash them. She didn't want to have that terrible conversation, yet again. As he watched her go upstairs to their daughter one last time, he ran a hand along the bottom of the curtains where Katrin had tacked on a foot of green cloth. It had never matched and he wondered why she'd never changed them. He grinned. He needed something to do. His boots would need polishing. He'd do that.

⌒

Hermann's throat tightened at the sight of his daughter. What were they thinking, letting her go so soon? Liesl stood before them in her best frock, her new apron and a green bodice embroidered with deer, rabbits and bluebirds. She was as beautiful as a woodland princess. The greatest blessing of his life. How could his girl be leaving his keep to make her own home and family so soon? The speech he'd prepared fled his mind, so instead, he took his daughter in his arms and breathed her in one last time.

Griselda stalked in on stiff legs and barked once, causing Liesl to turn.

'Oh, Griselda, how I wish you could come with me but you

have to stay here.' She knelt and buried her face in the thin hound's grey fur. 'Good girl, Gris. Guard the house.'

The hound dabbed at a pink ear with her tongue. Maybe Liesl should keep the useless old creature but Griselda didn't have so many beats left in her heart. It wouldn't be the best start to his daughter's new life, having to bury her hound. Oligh's bitch had whelped again and there was a fat lump of a pup as dense and heavy as lead. Hermann had been promised her. She'd be named Galena and Liesl could take her once she'd been weaned and trained. Really, he should have done it years ago.

He watched his daughter, her hair still in two flaxen braids, which her mother was slowly winding round her head for the last time, as if in a dream. Katrin moved around their daughter, weaving cornflowers into the braids, sniffing occasionally, and Liesl kept turning her head.

'Mother? Are you sad?'

'No, *Liebchen*. I'm happy for you.' She turned Liesl round to face her. 'Oh, but I would be lying if I said I wasn't going to miss you.'

Tears shone in his daughter's eyes as she kissed her mother goodbye.

'I'll only be across the doors, Mother.'

Katrin blinked. For his wife, those few doors may as well be a few hundred miles because nothing could be the same again. It must have caused great sorrow to Frau Gerner when Hermann had taken her daughter to another country. Not once, but twice. There was nothing at all to prevent his son-in-law from doing the same. It caused such pain, having children only to give them away into the keeping of another. Still, it was the way of life, and there was a new child coming. Nothing could be done to stop the march of time.

He took Katrin's hands in his and bent to kiss her knuckles before she left for the church. She smiled up at him, little lines crinkling around her eyes.

Hermann led his daughter downstairs and turned to her. Would they lose the easiness they'd enjoyed all these years? Years that had flown too quickly and without his permission. Liesl was leaving her childhood behind and becoming a woman. He thought back to hushed words between mother and daughter about the mysterious movements, deep in the belly, that marked the two-score-years' long dance with the moon. And now this ritual to mark the end of her girlhood, the handing over of a girl from one man to another, as if she were a chattel, a precious one, but a chattel, nonetheless. This is how life was measured: births, baptisms, funerals, weddings. Today was a day to be glad.

He took his daughter's hand and stood back to survey her. 'You're so beautiful, Liesl, and you look exactly like your mother did on our wedding day. Go forwards in happiness and strength. Know that we love you, always.'

He brushed a stray cornflower back to its place and kissed her in the centre of her forehead. 'Come, let's not be late, girl.' He glanced at the old clock in the corner one last time. When he'd been in gaol, no one had wound it for fear of overwinding it, so it had stopped and they'd lost Solingen time forever. That might be no bad thing and the clock would still make a grand present to remind Liesl's children of where they'd come from.

'Time to go,' he said. 'A tardy bride isn't the best start to a marriage. Be always kind, honest and loving. I hope your husband shares those three qualities also.'

'Oh, Father.' Her eyes brimmed and her chin quivered.

'No need to speak, Liesl. I already know what lies in your heart.'

Hermann sighed at the sight of his daughter standing in the doorway for her last time as a maiden and the rough edges of his breath betrayed what was in his own heart. He should have let Katrin have her way with the lintel. When they had more gold, he'd see about one and make things up to her. Gruffly, he stuck out an elbow. Liesl slipped her hand through the crook of his arm and they set off on the short walk to the chapel.

Johnson, Blenkinsop and Wilson stood in the street to wish them well. Johnson had brought his wife, who was no doubt itching to see a German bride. Hermann raised his chin a little, pleased he'd spent extra time polishing his boots.

In the gloom of the chapel, Liesl glowed like a Christmas candle as Katrin's embroidery cast a shimmer of colour whenever their daughter moved. There, waiting near the altar, was the boy who would become a husband and therefore a man. Hermann sized him up and tried not to find him wanting. It was still hard to forgive him for not being the one to save Liesl on the day she went under the ice but that was a long time ago now. Pieter Schimmelbusch came from a long line of excellent bladesmiths and that would win through. Hermann caught Joseph's eye and the lad smiled at him. If his apprentice nursed feelings for Liesl that were anything other than friendly, he hid them well.

The groom gave his bride a ring that he'd fashioned from her grandmother's gift. A plain band with their initials and the date engraved inside. It was fine gold and he'd worked hard at perfecting the ring that would encircle his new wife's slender finger and so bind them together, through God, for life. A rough-edged sigh rose in Hermann's throat and he tried to keep it there, a stopper for the tears that would leach from him otherwise. It was a good day. Liesl had a good-enough husband and she'd be happy.

⁓

Hermann lay awake half the night, the worry-wolf gnawing at his guts. Liesl had gone to a home with a mere lad at the head of it. Would she now know what marriage was really all about? Would hers be a happy match?

When the sun came up, he was thick-headed and it was still

much too early to rise, even for him. By the sound of it, Katrin and his mother weren't yet up, so there'd be no food ready. Not that he could face eating but he could use a drink. What had made him bad would soon make him better. He began coughing and pushed himself out of bed but his head swam at the sudden movement and he clutched the bedpost for support. Curse these English walls and floors for being out of true and moving about. There was no way he was setting foot on the stairs. He lay back on the bed, sweating, his tongue a dry rock in the desert of his mouth. The pounding in his head would soon send him mad. English crops and rain were useless for schnapps. He'd never had an aching head like this at home.

When he was desperate to piss, he tried to stand again, stomach lurching and head swimming. Finally, he made it onto his feet long enough to stagger downstairs and outside. After relieving himself, he slid into the river, bending to cup water to his mouth before dipping his face into the running current. He might as well have put his head into the forge vice and tightened it. The pounding didn't abate and he clutched his head, pausing to vomit on the riverbank before standing up and creeping back into the house, where he wrapped himself in a rug and sat in the chair nearest the fire. Once he could face bending over again, he'd light it. He looked up to see Katrin in the doorway, hands on hips.

'Hermann. Look at the state of you. Between you and your mother, it's hard to say who's in the worst state. This can't go on. You'll kill yourself or someone else and your work will suffer even more than it already has.'

He coughed and spat in the cold hearth, earning a glare.

'Work? I might let the forge run cold today.'

'Oh, might you, indeed?'

He turned watery eyes to the unlit fire. 'Be my angel and light the fire. It's so cold.'

'And what if I let the household run cold for the day? How would that be?'

He tried to keep back the bile that was building. Let her win. Let her make the point. Don't rile her up or the suffering would only continue.

'Go to bed, Hermann. I can't bear the sight of you. But first, you must set Joseph to work. It's not fair for him to lose a day's pay because he has a guzzling woodpecker for a master. If anyone had an excuse for drunkenness last night, it was surely Joseph, who was sober enough to carry you to your bed.'

It was indeed Joseph, and not his new son-in-law, who had performed that small mercy. What was he thinking, letting Liesl marry young Schimmelbusch? Too late now, though. While Hermann had been in gaol, Oligh had got his way after all, as he always did in that quiet way of his, making sure his daughter married a German so all her children would be Germans.

'It's still early, *Liebling*. So first some more sleep and then I'll set Joseph to work.' He shambled upstairs to bed, Katrin's voice ringing in his ears.

'You'd better not even think of being sick up there.'

'Don't worry, *Igelchen*, I won't.' Ach, his little hedgehog would never change. He closed his eyes, smiled and slid under the quilt.

Queen's Evidence

Morpeth Gaol, 1706

*T*hree men fetched back from the sessions today. First, was an Ovingham molecatcher who pinched six fat fowl from his neighbour. Taking orders for Christmas, most likely. Him with five bairns and one on the way. Thirty folk put their names up for him and yet no clemency. Got sent to gaol till he can pay up. I suppose the justice had to make an example of him or there'd not be a goose this side of the border come Advent. Second was a crafty shifter from Hexham, who sold a butcher a carcass without its fur on. That's nearly a hanging offence for those Tynedale tykes. No doubt some spoilt miss is pining for a fat pup that went walkies and never came back. Third was a townie in for robbery. Fingers in too many pies and none of them his own. Full of himself, like all townies, but had gossip that made me shake my lugs. Tittle-tattle about Colonel Henry Villiers, justice at the Mole's trial. A keeper should never put himself in his prisoner's pocket but I had to know more.

Turns out Villiers himself has been up to no good! Fetching goods in under the table. Ably assisted by an Aberdonian, one Captain Gordon, on his regular convoy from Orkney. Quite a list of provisions, if the townie's to be believed: brandy, claret, white wine, pepper, doeskins and Scottish plaids. Mistress Villiers paid the local lads two bob apiece to fill her cellars. The townie's mate was one of those locals. When he found himself a pressed man aboard a naval ketch, he turned snitch to buy his freedom.

Imagine Villiers! High born but a lowly smuggler at heart, lining his pockets. Best news I've had all year! Mind, I cannot blame the man. It must be a constant hardship for the poor colonel struggling on his seventy pounds a year and him with a castle to keep. Still, there's no shame in smuggling and it's seen as downright honourable in some quarters. Plenty in these parts would clap him on the back for keeping back money destined for the queen's coffers. But tartans from Orkney? Not hard to work out where they were headed. To think, one of Queen Anne's own men working hand in glove with the Jacobites. By rights, she should have had his guts for garters but the townie reckoned Villiers got off with a hefty fine of five-hundred-odd pounds. A whole quarter of an hour it took to find him guilty.

Still, I had to hand it to my old friend, the Mole. That humble servant wasn't so humble after all. He did have friends in high places. Little wonder the Mole laughed so hard on the eve of his trial when he learnt who would be in charge of it. At least it explains why it took Villiers' men so long to find the ship's master. The whole lot of them must have been in on it: Soldart, his mariners, the brother in Rotterdam, the watermen from the Tyne and the redcoats – especially those two from Orkney's regiment. Now that can't be a coincidence. Even Sergeant Ross from Morpeth, though it breaks my heart to admit it. But Villiers? Him a noble, a colonel, a governor and a justice. It's beyond me, it really is.

The molecatcher snivelled next to me and I patted his shoulder. Gaol for him and his family left to starve. Villiers would pay his fine, or not, and nothing more would be said. It only goes to show, it's one rule for the quality and another for the rest of us. Aye, it only goes to show.

AFTERWORD

*W*hile *The Running Wolf* is based on years of research, I've used a degree of poetic licence. Hermann (Harmon) Mohll was a real person and he was imprisoned in Morpeth Gaol. The search for him began on 18 December 1703 and he was sent to the Northumberland Quarter Sessions on 21 January 1704, where he was bailed. The order to acquit him came from the Earl of Nottingham, secretary of state to Queen Anne, on 1 February 1704. Confirmation of Hermann's acquittal was provided on 5 February 1704.

Hermann Mohll was a blade grinder, rather than a swordmaker, but for the purposes of my story, I've made him a master of all trades (a rare beast, I know) and I've given him a crown and crossed swords for the family blademark because it's an emblem familiar in Shotley Bridge. There's no evidence that Hermann and his mother liked to drink and the people in my book are ultimately creatures of my imagination. (That said, it's worth reading Augustus Bozzi Granville's *The Spas of England: The North* (London: Henry Colburn, 1841), p. 292 as Granville alleges that 'drinking, evil ways and lack of religion' led to the swordmakers' demise.) Archive documents show that Hermann sailed back to England in the company of his two sons and either one or two women, depending on whose deposition you read. For the sake of my story, I've dispensed with

Hermann's real family and created the fictional Anna, Katrin and Liesl Mohll and Grandmother Gerner. It seems Hermann was rather better with money than I've shown here as he was one of the few swordmakers who didn't ask William Cotesworth for a loan.

While Engel Schimmelbusch did die shortly after arriving in England, I've taken liberties with him and Pieter is my own creation. There is nothing to say that Adam Oligh and his sons were pious, that Tiergarten was hysterical or that Hermann's mother came from Magdeburg. There's certainly nothing to suggest that the real Frau Mohll and Herr Oligh were up to no good.

I've also massaged several dates in the interests of serving the story, which I wanted to end shortly after Hermann's release from prison. Thanks to Henry Wupper, Thomas Carnforth and Peter Renau providing sureties, Mohll was granted bail a couple of weeks prior to his acquittal, but because it's the author's job to make characters' lives difficult, I decided to keep him in the not-so-tender care of Robert Tipstaff a while longer. The unreliable gaoler is entirely my own invention but inspired by historic complaints of maltreatment at Morpeth Gaol.

While this novel ends at the turn of the eighteenth century, I've borrowed material from the future, such as the problem with Den Hayford, the steel supplier trying to take over the sword mills, and also the Bensons, to illustrate how the sword mills were struggling. If you visit the Tyne & Wear Archives to read the Bensons' complaints, you'll notice they weren't addressed to Hermann but to William Cotesworth; they weren't complaining about the Solingen men's workmanship but about other, shoddier workers who weren't German. The correspondence contained such lovely detail that I couldn't resist weaving it into the story.

I think I've owned up to all of my writerly sleights of hand here but if you prefer your facts unvarnished by my imagination, please visit my website, helensteadman.com, where you'll find lots of factual articles about the swordmakers and associated people. During my archive research, I discovered a cache of documents that have not so far been mentioned in any of the existing literature about the swordmakers. My discovery of these documents means I'm able to shed some light on some unanswered questions about Hermann Mohll. On my website, you'll find details of these findings.

I've also taken liberties with Ralph Maddison. There are no records to show that there was any trouble between him and the swordmakers, but since he was probably their nearest neighbour, their paths must have crossed. Of course, it wasn't the swordmakers who captured him, but a troop of soldiers, who finally tracked him down in Muggleswick. For a more truthful rendering of Maddison and his ways, you might like to read *The Monthly Chronicle of North-Country Lore and Legend*, (Newcastle-upon-Tyne, Walter Scott, 1887) pp. 70–71, which is filled with fascinating tales. It's also worth reading the depositions from York Castle, which mention his 'debauchery'.

Finally, on the subject of dates, to avoid confusion and untidy chapter subheadings, I decided against using old style wherein January, February and most of March 1704 would be recorded as either 1703 or 1703/4, because at that time, the new legal year began at Lady Day on 25 March. Also worth noting is that by 1700, while most European countries (including Germany and the Netherlands) were using the Gregorian calendar, England was still using the Julian calendar, so it was several days behind the rest of the continent. To avoid confusion, I've stuck to the Julian calendar for both England and Germany.

ENGLISH TRANSLATIONS

of German words used

Auf wiedersehen: Until we meet again

Christstollen: Christ stollen (fruit bread with nuts and spices)

Danke: Thank you

Geweihe: Antlers

Glühwein: Mulled wine

Heimweh: Homesickness

Hexe: Witch

Hündchen: Puppy

Igelchen: Little hedgehog

Kalenderschwert: Calendar sword

Kerzenauktion: Candle auction

Leberknödel: Liver dumplings

Liebchen: Sweetheart

Liebe: Love

Liebling: Darling

Pfefferkuchen: Gingerbread

Sauerbrauten: Marinated roast meat dish

Schwan: Swan

Verdammt: Damn it

About the Author

Helen Steadman's bestselling first novel, *Widdershins* and its sequel, *Sunwise* were inspired by the Newcastle witch trials. Helen recently completed a PhD in English at the University of Aberdeen and is now working on her fourth novel.

By the same author

Widdershins
Sunwise